P

"In this highly imaginative and compelling novel Martina Devlin has shown us an eerily plausible future. Reader beware — Big Sister is watching you"
— Christine Dwyer Hickey, author

"An extraordinary novel. At various stages I was thinking of apartheid, gender politics, sexual politics, 1916 and the foundation of the Irish state, slavery, body dysmorphia, how power corrupts, environmental conservatism, the Magdalene laundries, religious cults inter alia. It is a very clever and brave book on such a contentious subject" — Liza Nugent, author

"An amazing, thought-provoking page-turner — I found myself captivated by the characters and the strange lives they led"
— Marita Conlon-McKenna, author

"I was gripped, couldn't put it down and was bereft at the end. Shades of Ursula Le Guin and Philip K. Dick — as well, of course, as the masterly Margaret Atwood" — Mia Gallagher, author

"Utterly imaginative and compelling" — Justine McCarthy, journalist

"This is a *Brave New World* for the modern day that cleverly explores gender politics, political extremism and how we control women's bodies. A book for our times by a smart and chic writer — Edel Coffey, journalist

"Devlin pokes fun at the foibles of her own sex" — *Irish Mail on Sunday*

"A very human story of love, friendship, loss and desire" — *Irish Examiner*

Praise for *The House Where It Happened*

"An immensely skilled storyteller — I was utterly gripped by this book's power. Its sulphurous shadows and air of suppressed menace remind you that the author of *Wuthering Heights* had Ulster blood, like Devlin"
— Joseph O'Connor, author

"Vivid and convincing, layered with authentic detail and lit by striking turns of phrase. Martina Devlin has given us scenes we want to look away from but can't, a whiff of the past that lifts from the page and stays with you, once the story's told" — Lia Mills, author

"An astonishing achievement … a wealth of scholarship and research"
– Nell McCafferty

"Gorgeously atmospheric and gripping … meticulously researched"
– Claudia Carroll, author

"A novel that grips onto you tightly from the outset
– Claire Savage, Culture Northern Ireland

"A memorable and spirited narrator" – *Irish Independent*

TRUTH & DARE
Short Stories about Women Who Shaped Ireland

MARTINA DEVLIN

POOLBEG

Published 2018
by Poolbeg Press Ltd
123 Grange Hill, Baldoyle
Dublin 13, Ireland
E-mail: poolbeg@poolbeg.com
www.poolbeg.com

1

A catalogue record for this book is available from the British Library.

ISBN 978-178-199-813-7

Printed and bound by CPI Group (UK) Ltd, Croydon, CR0 4YY
Cover design by Derry Dillon
Cover image adapted from an original Gladys Maccabe painting

ABOUT THE AUTHOR

Omagh-born Martina Devlin is an author and journalist. She has won a V.S. Pritchett Prize, a Hennessy Literary Award and was shortlisted three times for the Irish Book Awards. Newspaper awards include being named Columnist of the Year for her weekly column with the *Irish Independent*. More information is available on her website *www.martinadevlin.com*. She also tweets @devlinmartina.

Also by Martina Devlin

About Sisterland

The House Where It Happened

Banksters (co-authored with David Murphy)

Ship of Dreams

The Hollow Heart

Temptation

Venus Reborn

Be Careful What You Wish For

Three Wise Men

The cover image shows a painting by Gladys Maccabe (1918-2018), born in Randalstown, County Antrim. She was a highly regarded artist who was also pro-active on behalf of other women, and in 1957 formed the Ulster Society of Women Artists to help showcase their work.

Her paintings are held in the Ulster Museum, the Royal Ulster Academy, the Arts Council of Ireland Collection and London's Imperial War Museum, but they also have pride of place on the walls of many people's homes. She received numerous awards including the World Culture Prize and an MBE for services to the arts from Queen Elizabeth II.

In addition, Gladys Maccabe worked as a fashion and arts correspondent for newspapers and television.

I am grateful to her son Christopher Maccabe for permission to use her striking artwork, *Lady with Dark Hair* — Gladys does the *Truth & Dare* company proud.

*For my friend Sarah Webb who's been
urging me to write a short story collection for years*

CONTENTS

INTRODUCTION

The stories which follow are about women, each of whom was true to her cause and dared to pursue it. Clever, steadfast and ambitious, they rejected the limitations of manmade rules designed for men's benefit. Instead, they asked an incendiary question for the times they lived in: why shouldn't we shape our own destiny?

They were trailblazers, these women – they left their footprints on Irish life. But while some are remembered, more are forgotten. Or if not quite forgotten, then reduced to two-dimensional historical figures.

For this collection, I set out to retrieve women who were submerged – overlooked, undervalued – and by placing them in context write them back into history. Each one pushed against boundaries and broke new ground. While they didn't always succeed in their aims, they never shirked from decisive action. And they took it without asking anyone for permission first.

Opposition to their activities ranged from mockery to violence, while often they met with family disapproval in addition to the might of the law ranged against them. But they persevered. They supported one another. They found ways to circumvent obstacles. Above all, they believed wholeheartedly in something they knew they might not live long enough to see happen.

When I began thinking about them, wondering how to tell

their stories, I had a choice to make. Should the collection take the form of fiction or biography? I decided on fiction because of the uncanny hold which stories have over us. Fiction is laced with enchantment. It hums with energy. It has the power to transport readers – to let us inhabit someone else's life. Stories connect us with one another on a more intimate level than history or biography allow, creating space for magic to happen – the imaginative leap.

Consequently, while the women I write about here actually lived, certain events, conversations and a number of the characters they interact with are invented. That said, truth occasionally proved to be stranger than fiction, such as the central element of the Maud Gonne story. Some things you just couldn't make up.

None of these stories represents the sum total of the woman concerned. After all, each of them led fascinating and productive lives, whereas a short story can do no more than filter light towards some element or other which caught my attention.

The women you are about to meet (or become reacquainted with) operated at a time when the notion of female autonomy was ridiculed by the majority of people, other women included. Why should a woman even care about earning her living when a husband, father or brother had a duty to look after her? Why would any decent woman seek to function outside the domestic sphere? Many people were mystified by the notion that self-respect and self-determination might be factors.

The women between these pages share some areas of kinship. They were Irish by birth, upbringing, or because they opted to make Ireland their focus. All mounted a challenge to the orthodoxy of traditional female roles. But their backgrounds, influences and political convictions were diverse. A number of them championed nationalism, others supported Ireland's union with Britain. Some lobbied for the vote, others for a political function, education rights, or to be treated as men's equals in the labour force.

A common denominator among the ones born into a comfortable lifestyle was their refusal to accept the restrictions of ornamental status. Women from poorer socio-economic backgrounds, by comparison, had no choice but to join the workplace, doing so with fewer opportunities and at lower pay rates than men. Some of the women who acted as persuaders for change were conscious of the need to speak out, not just in their own interests, but on behalf of their harder-pressed working sisters.

Mary Ann McCracken is where we begin. A social reformer, she figured among women who joined the anti-slavery movement, that campaign opening their eyes to their own lack of freedom. Later, centenary celebrations to mark the 1798 rebellion, many of them organised by women, were another catalyst.

And they were inspired by one another. These highly politicised women were conscious of their forerunners and read their writings – for example, members of the women's suffrage movement were stirred by the vision, commitment and organisational skills of activists in the Ladies' Land League.

A number of them straddle the labour, suffrage and nationalist movements, while others concentrated on one cause alone. Some decided they were feminists first and foremost. Others gave their principal loyalty to nationalism because it appeared to offer equality: if a new state was founded, they presumed the rulebook excluding women would be torn up. Post-independence, however, their male colleagues marched ahead and left them behind. The new Irish state proved to be conservative, paternalistic and controlling, as expressed by the 1937 Constitution which tried to contain women in the home.

What can be learned from the legacy of these pioneering women who became thinkers, writers, educators, lobbyists and politicians – when they could get elected, which didn't happen often? That any group with power does not surrender it lightly. But by collaborating, being persistent and inventive, and having faith in their capacity to effect change, women could chip away at opposition to equality.

A century ago, a limited group of Irishwomen won the right to vote; four years later, in 1922, they finally had their due with the franchise on equal terms with men. Battles remained to be fought, however, and are outstanding still – a lot done, more to do.

As I worked on this collection, it struck me how many of the women were either single or widowed. That situation seemed to offer them a certain freedom. I also noticed the tendency for political activists to be marginalised, especially if they were radical progressives. Only after the stories were finished did I become conscious of how frequently spectral elements flitted through them, reflecting my sense that vibrant women were reduced to shadow figures during their lifetimes. Marginalised, their voices ignored, their achievements minimised, often they ended up as living ghosts.

Don't be deceived. These women were sticks of dynamite – the repercussions from their actions reverberate still. They are my heroes.

Martina Devlin, Dublin, Autumn 2018

MARY ANN McCRACKEN

Born Belfast, 1770; died Belfast, 1886

Social reformer, abolitionist and businesswoman

Mary Ann McCracken was born into a notable Ulster-Scots entrepreneurial family of McCrackens on her father's side, and on her mother's side the Joys were an equally industrious family of French Huguenot decent, who founded the *Belfast News Letter*.

Mary could be described as a proto-feminist, was in agreement with Mary Wollstonecraft's *Vindication of the Rights of Women*, and in her letters argues for equality between the sexes.

She and her sister Margaret ran a successful muslin manufacturing business in Belfast which respected the rights of workers. She believed passionately in social justice and human dignity, arguing that people ought to be given the tools to improve their condition. During downturns, the sisters absorbed losses themselves rather than dismiss workers.

She was involved in early campaigns to advance women's suffrage, as well as to reform the prison system, ban the employment of children as chimney sweeps and revive traditional music. She immersed herself in organisations to alleviate poverty in Belfast, including a school for orphans. Even in her eighty-ninth year she was to be seen at the docks, handing out anti-slavery leaflets to emigrants boarding US-bound ships.

Mary followed political events closely and became involved in the Society of United Irishmen through her brother, Henry Joy McCracken. After its unsuccessful rebellion in 1798, which led to his capture and court martial, she walked with her brother to the scaffold.

Free as a Bird

Belfast

1778

When you peep through a keyhole you see things you ought not to witness. This I knew. But my love for Harry drove me to it. I put my eye to the door, beyond which a doctor and an apothecary were working on my brother, trying to revive him. And I cried aloud at what I saw.

They were pounding on your chest with all their might, Harry, the pair of them scarlet in the face.

They had your shirt open, you lying on the dining table. Dr McDonnell was leaning all his weight on you, pushing with the heels of his hands above your heart — making your body jerk like a puppet. Half a dozen times he'd deliver his blows to your chest, then he'd pause. While he rested, Mr McCluney massaged your flesh, chafing as though to rub you out. And back would go Dr McDonnell, hammering away at you.

I knew they were trying to start your heart pumping again. I knew they had to be vigorous. I knew they were doing it because I sent for them, entreating them to use their skills on you. Even so, it was more than flesh and blood could thole to see you shrunk to a haunch of meat on a table.

I shouldn't have been keeking. Better to be on my knees praying for their success. *Heavenly Father, have mercy. Spare my brother.* But the prayers jammed in my throat, refusing to pass to my tongue. Instead, I put my faith in medical men. Is that a sin? So be it.

Hope kept me from throwing open the door and demanding they let you be. Hope that your life wasn't extinguished when the hangman cut you down. Hope that you had lost consciousness on the end of the rope and were teetering in a limbo land between one state and the other.

I wanted Harry to be something you see from time to time here in Belfast, the half-hanged man. It's a punishment devised by the Redcoats. They've a range of them. The pitch cap, the lash, half-hangings. That's when they string up men – aye, and women, forbye – but cut them down before death claims them. Information is demanded, and if it isn't forthcoming, they swing them back up again. You always know a half-hanged man from his crooked neck, or the kiss of hemp on his throat.

Harry was marked by the rope. It burned its weave into him. I saw it across his Adam's apple when he was carried into the house. His skin was grey, his limbs flopped. But his neck hadn't snapped, praise the Lord. That's a point of no return.

I bribed the hangman to go easy on him. To push Harry off the platform gently, so his neck wouldn't break. Not to leave him dangle for long but to cut down his body in time to give him a chance of regaining consciousness. You hear tell of folk being resuscitated that way. Of a hanged man's friends managing to start his pulse beating again.

I gathered together what money I could beg or borrow to carry with me to his prison cell. Harry had been condemned to a felon's death and I thought to use the bright guineas to change the outcome, or failing that, to buy him kinder treatment before the sentence was carried out. But the order arrived while I stood at the cell door waiting to go in – I heard it read out with my own ears. He was to hang on the self-same day the verdict was delivered, before the sun set.

Harry was stoical – I wonder did he welcome death? Did he hope he might achieve something by dying that he couldn't by living? As for me, my mind raced – I couldn't indulge in tears. While there was life there was hope.

I had a scheme in train, before ever he stood trial, and coached our mother to play her part. She went to General Nugent, intending to kneel at his boots and petition for Harry's life. Let her boy be imprisoned or transported. Only pardon him the noose.

The general would not see her. Henry Joy McCracken had led the Northern army against the Crown. He must pay the penalty.

I had my mother primed for his refusal. She sent in another message by the captain who barred her from the commander's presence. Would the general, in his compassion for a mother's grief, stay the fall of the axe after her son was hanged? Would he spare Harry from being spiked?

Other men who turned out in Ninety-Eight had their heads struck off and posted onto spikes – there to feed the birds, moulder, and serve as a deterrent. Ireland was in the grip of a summer heatwave, and Belfast was black with flies from spiked heads during those months clotted with dread and death. The city authorities were obliged to issue a warning against eating uncooked fruit, because insects gorged on human flesh had surely crawled over it.

Even military leaders accustomed to slaughter can be moved to compassion by a grey-haired woman whose haunted face reminds them they, too, are mothers' sons. The general excused Harry the axe.

"No decapitation. Because he is a gentleman, despite being a rebel," said the captain.

That was leg one of my plan, and the most important

ingredient, for without a head there could be no resurrection on this side of the grave. Now, I put the second stage into effect. While Harry made his peace with God, I left prayers to others. For myself, I was plotting to turn him into another Lazarus.

In a frenzy of activity, I found a friendly minister at the prison, and persuaded him to take my purse and use it to strike a bargain with the hangman. Next, I sent a message to Dr James McDonnell to make his way to our house in Rosemary Lane with his surgical tools, there to move heaven and earth to save Harry. Finally, I arranged for two men with a horse and cart to wait near the gibbet and convey my brother to us without delay. Fortunately, our house was no great distance from the gallows. I understood there was a short window of time when the surgeon and his assistant might have some chance of success.

My plan was a good one, but it depended on too many elements of chance. The first setback was Dr McDonnell's refusal to answer my call. He had been a friend of my brother's, an intimate of our family circle. But in our hour of need he turned his back on us. I know I shouldn't judge him harshly – maybe dread or disapproval had him by the throat. He gave no reason, and when I met him later I could not bring myself to ask, for fear of railing at him right there on the street.

In fairness, he sent his brother in his place. Or maybes he volunteered. I never had the right of it. Anyhow, a rap sounded on the back door and Bessie, our cook, answered it to Dr Alexander McDonnell. Beside him was our apothecary, Mr McCluney, a leather satchel bulging with stoppered bottles tucked under his oxter. No sooner was the door opened a chink than the two of them ducked inside out of sight, in a lather for fear they'd be spotted. I mean no disrespect, but I was disappointed when Dr Alexander turned up. He is a proficient surgeon and decency persuaded him to attend in lieu of his brother. But Dr James was the one who had made a study of resuscitating drowned men, with notable success. If drowned men, why not hanged men?

Still, I dared to have faith.

"My brother has told me what to do, Miss McCracken," he said.

I clung to that, the whiles I crouched on the floor outside the dining room, my back to the wall, waiting for a miracle. The house itself held its breath while the medical men toiled over Harry.

"For pity's sake, Alex! Go 'asy! There's sodjers outside!"

A party of dragoons was trotting along our street, exciting Mr McCluney's anxiety.

I put my ear to the door and heard the men's ragged breathing. If our house was raided the military would query their presence. But the hooves kept knocking out a steady rhythm and after an interval Dr McDonnell resumed work.

Plangent music floated along the hallway. In my confused state, it felt as if heaven itself was an interested bystander in our labours. By and by, I realised harp strings were being plucked, not by celestial hosts but by Atty Bunting, playing Irish melodies in our drawing room to offer such comfort as his hearers might draw from it. My foster brother was born with a genius for music. His fingers said what his voice could not.

I closed my eyes and drifted with the notes, the nausea in my stomach allayed. All at once, the door opened, jolting me to my feet. Dr McDonnell sagged against the doorframe, visibly exhausted. I could not see past him to the table – Mr McCluney was blocking my view. Nor could I read the doctor's face. Frantic, I forgot myself so far as to lay my hands on Dr McDonnell's arm and tug at his sleeve.

"Did you save him?"

1788

Caged songbirds were my indulgence – I bought them and set them free. It was a luxury I anticipated each Saturday morning. As soon as I had breakfasted, I tied on my bonnet and hastened to the Market Square, where the boys who trap the birds for sale awaited customers.

"Here comes the wee McCracken one, with her crackpot ideas about birds," they whispered behind their hands.

I knew right well they sniggered at my approach.

"Let the birds be," I pleaded. "Leave them singing from joy on the trees, with their songs bubbling out of them. Don't sell them to folk who'll keep them behind bars, coaxing them to make music for their selfish amusement."

The boys shrugged about needing to eat, and would I prefer them to boil up the birds for a pie? The songbirds get used to the cage, they said.

I could not believe they ever became reconciled to bars, these feathered creatures born with the ability to soar through the heavens, as the clouds did. And, so, on Saturdays I bolted my food, usually incurring a reprimand from my mother for unladylike behaviour.

When my father was at home, he would take my part. "Loving birds is the closest we get to heaven on earth," he told Mother, and she'd nod permission for me to leave the table.

I'd pelt from our house, every coin I was able to scrape up clinking in my reticule. Economies practised, gifts sacrificed, small sums earned by my own endeavours – nothing gave me more pleasure than to hoard it all, funnelling it into my songbird fund. Not even a letter from my beloved brother Harry when he was absent on business could compare with the rush of joy at having the power to open a cage.

I knew I was a nondescript person. I took after my mother, a woman with admirable qualities but nothing commanding in her presence. Being plain has its advantages: I could slip easily through crowds without attracting a second glance, whereas folk stared at Harry. He had charm to match his looks, too. Still, the bird boys knew me and kept watch for me. They were guaranteed my custom.

Sing a song of sixpence a pocket full of rye
Four and twenty blackbirds baked in a pie

When the pie was opened the birds began to sing
Wasn't that a dainty dish to set before the King?

One Christmas, when I was nine and Harry twelve, I was given a storybook containing that rhyme. To everyone's surprise, it caused my eyes to swim with tears at the cruelty of a world where birds were baked into pies.

"Don't cry, Mary," said Harry. "The birds weren't cooked. Didn't they sing for the King?"

"How?" I hiccoughed.

And, improbably, my brother explained pie construction in the Middle Ages to me – the crust baked separately, attached with toothpicks to a pie dish in which live birds were placed immediately before being served. At the feast, when the lid was removed, the birds would fly out in a welter of wings, and the courtiers would applaud. Live frogs, dogs and rabbits were also 'baked' into cakes as novelties. Harry was highly entertained by the notion. But I couldn't laugh, not even when he pulled faces to amuse me.

"Birds sing best from a tree branch," I protested.

"The place doesn't change the sound of the music. A song from a cage is just as sweet to the ear."

"Ach, don't say that, Harry. They share their songs freely, from simple joy. Why do we need to own their music?"

"Aye." He looked thoughtful. "You have the right of it. Birds make no distinction between paupers and kings. We can learn from them."

It was then I thought of buying the birds' liberty from the urchins who sell them. My brother John used to tease me that it was the same few birds freed at my hands over and over again.

"Song birds, lovely song birds," cried those boisterous boys, Barney, Ned and Charlie, holding up their feathered wares.

I was a figure of fun to them. No matter. I never looked to follow the path well-trodden.

The sight of the birds spreading their wings and taking flight always enchanted me. I shared their ecstasy in that moment of release when they realised the bars were lifted. How could new trimmings for my bonnet, or coloured gloves to match a sash, compete? Yet my pleasure was mixed with pain. Unfortunately, I could only liberate some of them. And so I must choose, for which I had to harden my heart, because there were always birds left behind. How to decide which should go free and which must remain prisoner?

Fortunately, I have always been able to do complicated sums in my head, and I hit on the idea of negotiating discounts for multiple purchases. The bird boys complained I made a mockery of the old saying about a bird in the hand. "A bird in your hand is only worth one and a half in the bush, Miss McCracken," they carped. But Barney, Ned, Charlie and the others remained willing to trade. I was their best customer. Our deal-making stood me in good stead in later life when I went into partnership with my sister.

Once, after buying a cage with two starlings inside, I opened it immediately, in the bustle of the marketplace. Their sudden liberty confused them. Out they hopped, in that skippity way of theirs, but stayed near-hand, futtering at their feathers. I can't claim to have seen uncertainty in their shiny droplets of eyes because I can never read any emotion in a bird's face. Only on the wing does this most glorious of God's creatures express its feeling. But I dare say they were disorientated.

I waited for that moment of dawning. If they dallied, I'd clap my hands to startle them into flight. Except a stray cat pounced and skited off with one. And I realised how self-indulgent it was to free birds there. I wanted people to see what I did in the hopes of inspiring by example. Such a step lacked humility.

After that, I always carried the cage home to Rosemary Lane, locked my cats Faith and Hope in the house, and set the birds onto a low branch of the apple tree in our garden. Every tree is familiar to birds, I think. Once they feel the bark beneath their claws they relax. Their wings unfurl like twin fans and with a few flaps they rise up almost vertically.

Often, I saw the cats' faces pressed to the window the whiles I performed my wee ceremony of setting the birds free. Faith and Hope looked intent. Not reproachful, as you might imagine. But their ears were pricked up, eyes gleaming. When I went indoors, they sniffed my fingers, excited by the scent of bird flesh.

By way of compensation, I'd go to the kitchen and beg some cream from Bessie. After all, it was only their natures that made them want to eat birds – even well-fed cats such as mine. They juked down to lap at the cream, but I knew it was meat they craved. I did not seek to deprive them of it. But they could not eat another creature alive, biting down on its still beating heart – that, I would not allow.

1792

"One day, our Mary Ann will give over eating meat altogether," my father remarked, as he carved the chicken and I asked for only a sliver of white meat.

My brothers laughed at such a notion, shovelling meat into their mouths. I had four brothers and a sister, plus Edward Bunting, our foster-brother and the youngest among us, whose passion was harp music. We called him Atty for a pet name. He never said much – his head was in the clouds – but he never forgot to eat a good dinner.

My mother fretted over my appetite, urging me to try another pick of meat for strength. I was the runt of her litter, although older than both John and Atty. She was convinced my diet was to blame for my size.

"Have a leg for a change," she said. "The brown meat has more goodness in it. Look at you, pushing round that wee bit on your plate, sure it's not even the length of your middle finger. John, give the child a leg."

My father skewered it. But when my eyes implored him he took pity on me, dropping it onto Frank's plate, while my mother tutted about his being too soft with me.

It was a charade the family played, baiting me a little, as brothers and sisters do. However, they were not cruel. They knew better than to offer me a wing. Above all, I loathed the sight of wings on the platter. Those God-given instruments with which birds ascend, circle and plummet should never be reduced to meat.

My brother John was the only one vexed about my disinclination to eat meat and drew attention to my stubbornness at every opportunity. "If it's not meat, it's sugar she's refusing, on account of the slave trade," he complained. "I don't see why we should have Miss High and Mighty's principles forced down our throats at table."

We rubbed each other up the wrong way, John and myself. I dare say its origins lay in his boyish resentment at my running after Harry, who was nearly three years my senior, instead of being playmates with him. John and I were nearer in age and it would have been natural for us to be close. But my heartstrings were entwined with Harry's.

Sometimes, Harry squeezed my hand under the table and left his meat untasted, in solidarity. An inch short of six feet and handsome as a storybook hero, he had a gift for mimicry, so that laughter followed him wherever he went. Like me, Harry felt keenly the world's injustice, and believed in liberty for all God's creatures.

"Freedom is a right. It isn't something that should be granted as a gift, or withheld on a whim," he said. "No man deserves that."

"No man or woman," I put in.

"My wee conscience — Mary. You keep me straight."

I liked it best when I could sit watching Harry when he worked at mechanical contrivances. He had a talent for machinery — there was nothing he couldn't fix or turn to another use — and even when he was a man he'd make time to contrive ingenious toys for the bairns of the neighbourhood. While he worked, I'd sit watching him, maybe handing him a spanner or strip of rag as the need arose. We talked about the sun, moon and stars while he tinkered with pulleys and chains. He never paid any heed to John, who tried to mock him for spending time with me.

"What are the two of you blabbing about?" John would demand, lip curled. "A pair of blatherskites, you are. I wonder at you, Harry, bothering with a silly wee girl."

As vexing as a smoky lamp, was John.

Harry would let on not to hear him. "Mary, have you any notion where I left thon wooden sparrow? The one that hops along when you wind its key? I've an idea for how to maybes make it fly."

And John would grind his teeth the-gether and stomp off.

In between making mechanical birds, Harry gave me money to free living ones. He wouldn't walk with me to the market to buy them – some busybody would report it back to his friends in the Muddlers' Club, and he'd never hear the end of it. How and ever, maybe because he was preoccupied by thoughts about liberty, my brother liked to hear about the cause being extended to our feathered friends. Sometimes I wondered at him for spending so much time in Peggy Barclay's Tavern in Sugarhouse Entry, where the club met, drinking and plotting, instead of attending to the family business. But dreams must be woven somewhere.

When Mother chided him about keeping low company, he'd tickle her under the chin. "When Adam delved and Eve span who was then the gentleman?" That was his answer. Harry gave no attention to his affairs. He was always riding here, there and everywhere on United Irishmen matters, neglecting his calico printing business. Naturally, it failed. Naturally, we forgave him.

1796

"Mary, I have a favour to ask. Something requiring pluck, which I know you have in barrel-loads."

"You want me to sail to France to petition the revolutionary generals for help. Or hide one of your comrades on the run, with a warrant out for his arrest."

Harry laughed. "Nothing so exciting. Though I can see you snap your fingers at danger. What a fearless wee thing you are!"

"Fearless? When I'm stuck among the teacups?"

"I know you better than you know yourself. Inside Mary Ann McCracken beats the heart of a lion."

I tilted my head back to look Harry in the eye. "Thon must be a right big favour."

"I need you to find a safe hiding place for a coat I have a mind to wear soon."

"You're talking in riddles, Harry. Why conceal a coat?"

"Ah, but this is a seditious coat. A coat of green. Still, it's an elegant item of clothing and cost me dear – I'd not like to lose it. It's nearly as handsome as the one Lord Edward Fitzgerald intends to wear at the head of the army in Dublin. But not quite so fine, because I'm only the son of a ship's captain and his father was a duke. So, Mary-Mary-Never-Contrary, could you slip my rebel's coat in among your personal garments – somewhere private where the soldiers won't look if they take it into their heads to search the house?"

And that was the moment when I knew my brother intended to march into battle with a rebel army.

From then on, I watched and listened. Soon after, I stopped buying caged songbirds – instead, squirrelling away money for other purposes.

I confess, I tried on his magnificent green plumage before stowing it away in my chest. It swamped me, like a wee lassie playing dress-up, yet I found myself preening all the same. Its stiff folds made me feel martial. Wearing it, I grasped why men deck themselves out in such finery – looking warlike makes them feel it, I dare say. After I took it off, and folded it away beneath nightdresses and the like, I spied my commonplace book. When I was younger, I wrote in it daily or glued in items cut out from journals. Curious, I studied its pages for a glimpse of the girl I once was.

Mary Ann McCracken's Book of Resolutions
I: be useful in all that I do
II: never think I am only one and cannot make a difference – change comes from ones and twos
III: eat no sugar or confectionary while the slave

trade continues

IV: practise frugality, the better to spend my money wisely on the needy

V: labour to relieve the distress of my fellow Irish people

VI: dress modestly, avoiding vanity and luxury

VII: wear only clothes manufactured in Ireland

VIII: educate the children of the labouring classes

IX: educate myself so that I can think independently

X: remember my Presbyterian faith is a chart to save me from the rocks

It was my set of rules for living. They have stood the test of time. When I was growing up, my ambition was not to be a useless drone in life. My sister Margaret felt the same. We talked it over and determined to be industrious. That's why we set up a muslin business. It kept us occupied and provided work for folk in sore need of income. Commerce was in our blood, I suppose. As a ship's captain, Father was paid to undertake voyages but did some private trading on his own account, while before her marriage our mother had a milliner's and fancy-goods shop beside Pottinger's Entry. Both of them encouraged us to be enterprising.

After taking care of his fancy coat, I showed my rules to Harry. "Margaret says if everyone in the kingdom would only work hard and be productive, Ireland would be sure to thrive. It would generate a happy change in Irish affairs."

"Margaret doesn't know what she's talking about. Virtue won't save our country. Kinder laws must be put in place – there'll be no deliverance from poverty and misery without them."

"Harry, I know you're minded to make things fairer for ordinary folk. It's greatly to your credit. But there are other ways to do it. Couldn't you use your skills with machinery? Imagine if you could devise a contraption to do Bessie's work for her – to sweep floors and scrub the laundry. Or one that helped the women embroidering our muslins to produce more work. That way, they'd receive higher wages and maybe have some leisure time, forbye. They could use those free days to educate themselves. As it is, they're too fatigued to study reading and writing. You could do something for God's helpless creatures, too. Suppose you invented a machine to take letters about so the mail-coach horses aren't flogged to keep to the schedules? Rebellion's not the only path to progress."

"Improvements take time, Mary. Strike fast and strike hard. A republic along French lines, with assets shared out – not grabbed and held by a ruling class. That's the way to effect change."

"But what if the rebellion fails? Your life will be forfeit!"

"My life doesn't matter."

"It matters to me!"

"I'm glad to hear it, kitten." He deposited a kiss on my nose.

Soon after, he was imprisoned in Dublin, along with a great many members of the Muddlers' Club. Harry was different after his release. More solitary. Margaret said being locked up for fourteen months clipped his wings. For my part, I saw prison had stolen away our brother's playfulness, but it was plain that something had put down roots in its place. His cause consumed him.

1798

Tomorrow we march on Antrim – drive the garrison of Randalstown before you, and haste to form a junction with the commander-in-chief.

   Henry J. McCracken

   The First Year of Liberty, 6th June 1798

As he wrote the order, I watched Harry use the French fashion to date the proclamation for the United Irishmen of the North. The First Year of Liberty? Pray God he was right. His jacket and feathered hat were ready for him to wear at the head of his troops the following morning. What a bird of paradise he'd be! But what a target, too. I pushed away the thought. Leaders must be visible.

That last night we had him at home with us, Harry's head was on fire about the battle he said must take place in Antrim. He and Father talked over the location's strategic importance and speculated about the number of men who'd answer his call. Meanwhile, Mother and Margaret went backwards and forwards to the kitchen, helping Bessie to prepare supper and food for him to carry away in a leather satchel. As for me, I parked myself beside Harry and never budged. Frank and William were to join him on the road the next day but were spending the night before the battle with their wives and childer, as was only right and proper. Our other brother John was no United man, but a King's man, and knew nothing of what was planned though I dare say he had his suspicions.

After Margaret, Mother and Father went to bed, Harry and I lingered in the parlour. We fell to talking about Greek histories which, in less uncertain times, we had read together.

"I should set off with some hefty volume from Tom Russell's library strapped to my chest," joked Harry. "Something by Homer or Virgil, so dense with words no musket ball can penetrate its cowhide."

My heart quailed at the prospect of metal piercing his beloved flesh. "You always said you understood why Achilles had no desire to grow grey, dozing by the fire."

"I'm thirty years of age. I don't want to reach seventy and find myself riddled with regrets when I look back over my life – wishing I'd seized the moment. But that's not why I've summoned the men, Mary. We must march because it's now or never. Some say we should have risen in the spring. Or last year. Or the year before. We've futtered about, waiting for the French. Perhaps the right time has passed already. There's only one way to find out."

"Harry, let me carry a pike by your side!"

"Wee Mary, you couldn't lift a pike let alone march with one. Sure you're no broader than a man's arm. But if the men of Ulster have half as much heart as you, we'll win the day."

It amused him betimes to talk to me as if I was a bairn, although I was a month off my twenty-eighth birthday. I was also a Christian. I could not, in conscience, fire a musket or shoulder a pike. All life was sacred to me. But I was a McCracken, too, and resented the cruelties visited on the people. Truly, they were driven to rebel. Even so, to fight without prospect of success was to bare your neck to the butcher's knife.

"What are your chances, Harry? Truly?"

"It depends on how many of the boys turn out. It depends on the element of surprise. It depends on whether we can lay our hands on more weapons. It depends on where the luck falls."

"How can you be so calm talking about possible death? It gives me the shivers. To look at you, you'd imagine you were planning an outing to the Giant's Causeway with Atty Bunting and Tom Russell."

"Mary, it's a relief to know my fate is decided one way or the other. Now, all I have to do is be true to the vows I took. By example – that's how we can give hope to our people. God knows, they need it. By this time tomorrow night we'll be victorious – an Irish Republic declared. Or I'll be dead."

Despite those fighting words, there was tension in his jawline. The night before any battle is a long one. And yet not long enough. I thought about telling him that with a small spark he could light a great fire to warm the entire kingdom. I knew it would cheer him up. But I could not say it with conviction. In truth, I no longer knew what I did and didn't believe about causes. I believed in my brother. Let that be enough.

I stroked the coat of green hanging over a chair back. "Achilles was keen to cut a fine figure on his way to battle, too. Do you remember the pains he took, with his polishing and titivating?"

Harry laughed. "Are you calling me conceited?"

By and by, I left him and lay on top of my bed for a few hours, fully clothed, on that hot June night when the sky was so light we scarcely needed to light candles. My heart was brimming over with the wish to be a man and able to shape events like my brothers, instead of hunkering down to pick up the pieces afterwards. It's harder to wait than to do. I didn't dare drift off to sleep, suspecting Harry might slip away at screek o' day without giving me a chance to say goodbye. I rose with the dawn, conscious it might be the last time I saw him alive.

Neither of us said this, of course, but it was in both of our minds. Harry refused breakfast, apart from a tankard of water. His face was clear in the morning light. The previous night, it had been grave in repose. Now he was full of purpose and impatience to be on his way, sure-fingered as he buckled on his sword and buttoned up the fancy jacket.

I stood on the front doorstep and watched him clatter off on his dappled grey horse. A sash window lifted upstairs, and Mother and Father appeared. They had said their farewells before going to bed but, like me, were loath to lose a last glimpse of him. They dared not call out for fear of drawing attention – Harry's warlike appearance could trigger his arrest. In silence, they leaned out to wave their handkerchiefs, while I blew kisses below them.

Harry paused at the corner and doffed his black hat with its white, curling feather. And we three McCrackens left behind felt some measure of ease. We looked up the street and saw him, and he looked back and saw us.

"God turn aside a hard fate," said Bessie, when we heard Harry was taken.

It's an expression they use, the Catholics. But Harry and I had read in the Greek myths about fates being woven – unpicking the threads is no easy task. All the same, I thought I could break my brother's hard fate. That's my nature. Ever since I was a small girl, I've been on a crusade to improve life for folk. Animals, too. John says I have delusions about saving the world. Maybe so. But, every once in a while, it's possible to make a difference. Success doesn't come often but I keep trying.

After the Battle of Antrim, when the United Irishmen were

routed, Harry went on the run. While he hid himself away in a cave on Cave Hill, high above the city, I set about planning to spirit him away. No beehive could have been more active than my mind, making arrangements for him to start a new life in America. In time, I'd have joined him in that vast land which has soaked up so many of our people – the informer and the informed-on alike. Are they all washed clean there, as though dipped in the River Jordan?

He almost reached the vessel that would have taken him to safety, travelling as a ship's carpenter. But Harry hadn't the set of a carpenter – that's what caught him. He walked upright like a free man. A mile or so outside Carrickfergus, some yeomen recognised him and he was taken. My brother was tried for treason and rebellion. He told his accusers he was proud to be a rebel and owned that he was commander-in-chief of the Northern army. But he pleaded not guilty to treason. "I am no traitor but a patriot," said Harry.

My father and I were present at his court martial in the Exchange. At one stage, we saw the Crown attorney speak privately with Harry. Later, we learned he was offering banishment if Harry would supply information about his comrades. He refused, knowing the death sentence was inevitable. The officer approached my father to intervene, because a parent's pleas can succeed where bribery fails, but Father put on his ship's captain voice. He spoke out loud and clear for all to hear. "I trust Henry Joy McCracken to act in accordance with his own conscience," he said.

Immediately after the verdict, Father went home to break the news to our family circle, while I followed Harry to the Artillery Barracks where he was being held. My hope was to make myself useful.

Major Fox arrived at the same time as me and I was told to wait my turn. "The King's business takes priority." He clicked his boot heels with a false show of courtesy. In he went, leaving the cell door ajar, soldiers loitering outside, but I heard the conversation between my brother and the major.

"McCracken, you must prepare to meet your Maker. General Nugent's orders. You'll be given a little time to pray with the minister of your choice. But before nightfall the sentence of the court will be carried out."

My hands flew to cover my mouth.

But Harry sounded as collected as he was during the trial. "I'm in your hands, sir. Today, tomorrow, next week — it's a matter of indifference to me, I assure you."

"It's not too late to strike a bargain."

Harry remained pleasant. You'd have thought he was turning down the offer of a slice of cake. "Major, don't insult me."

Changing the subject, he asked for a few minutes with the Reverend Sinclaire Kelburn, and a pair of soldiers were sent to fetch him. Mr Kelburn was minister at the Rosemary Street church where we McCrackens worshipped. As it happened, Doctor Steele Dickson from Portaferry Presbyterian Church was also confined to the barracks because he was a United Irishman, and Harry said he'd like to pray with him in the meantime.

When Major Fox withdrew, Harry asked me to write and tell his comrade Tom Russell how he died. The surviving United men were in his thoughts.

"Do you hope for another attempt?" I whispered.

He gazed into middle distance and gave me no answer. Another name preoccupied him, I suspected — he tried to utter it but reconsidered, shaking his head.

"Only tell me the service and I'll perform it," I promised.

"It's a private matter, Mary. Dr Dickson will take care of it for me."

Loathe to trouble him during the brief time remaining, I swallowed my hurt. After Dr Dickson read a Bible passage to him, I stepped aside, giving them an opportunity for private conversation.

Time was ticking by. Mr Kelburn arrived, all of a-swither at the turn of events and inclined to wring his hands but managed a breathy prayer about trusting to Providence to deliver good from evil. Afterwards, he suggested escorting me home. I knew it was essential for me to strike a firm but calm note: if they scented what men are pleased to call feminine extravagance I should be hustled away. I would not raise my voice. I would not become flustered. I would not refer to my emotions.

"Where my brother goes, I go." Taking Harry's arm, I held tight.

Bright-eyed, Harry gazed down at me. Words were unnecessary between us.

At that, a bell pealed five o'clock. Major Fox returned and ordered Harry to the place of execution. We set out on foot and, if my brother felt fear, he never once showed it. Still, I knew he was glad of my company.

Sometimes, people ask me how I did it. How I walked, to a drumbeat, with a condemned man as far as the scaffold. How is it you didn't swoon away from the horror, they say? The men lean forward to study me as if I were a specimen pinned within a glass case. The women give a wee shudder – a quiver close to delight, I suspect, from the way their eyes dance.

The truth is, there was nobody else from his family to walk with him. Father had used up all his strength to attend the trial. Frank and William were in hiding, at risk of being taken and tried. Our third brother, John, was ashamed of Harry because a court had pronounced him traitor, while Mother and Margaret weren't fit for the ordeal. That left only me to share his journey. How could I fail my favourite brother?

Besides, if infinity was where he was destined – and I hoped to delay it, with Dr McDonnell's help – I wanted the face of someone who loved Harry to be the last image he saw from the gibbet. Not the hangman knotting the noose at his neck. Nor the minister praying with him. Nor the soldiers guarding him. Nor the crowd jostling below, excited by the sight of a fellow human condemned to a felon's death. My face would shine up at him, speaking all the words I knew I would be too choked to say.

Horrible though the prospect was, I intended being with Harry right to the end. I did not want his final minutes, if so they proved to be, burdened with folk mocking him. A contemptible and botched rebellion, they were calling it. For my part, he should know that what he did was neither a vain nor vainglorious exercise.

Losing is not the same as failing.

So that's how I was able to go through with it. That's where the strength came from when Major Fox landed back in the cell.

"It's time." He indicated the door.

My brother walked through it without a protest, me clinging to his arm. In the yard, I lowered the veil on my bonnet to shield my face from the public gaze. Orders were barked, we were surrounded by a cordon of soldiers, and a drummer boy began to beat a tattoo. Our party moved away.

It was a long walk and yet a short walk.

We didn't speak, Harry and me. It seemed as if he had entered a state of heightened reality, and I had no desire to separate him from it. But he stretched his right arm across his body to settle my hand into the crook of his left elbow, and kept his hand there, on top of mine. He looked straight ahead – concerned, I dare say, about betraying any comrades who might be standing along Ann Street or Corn Market to watch for him. In those jittery times, a show of recognition, however fleeting, was all it might take to condemn a man.

How intensely alive he felt beside me! I was convinced I could hear the light puff of breath exiting his nostrils, the tingle against his skin as the late afternoon sun touched it. In hindsight, it maybe sounds odd, considering the circumstances, but I felt a spill of absolute pleasure when I noticed his shadow and mine form one outline crossing the warm stones.

The air was skittish, as if the weather was about to break. The people, by contrast, were silent when our procession passed. Dragoons led the way. Hooves struck the cobblestones, harnesses jingled, saddles creaked. But human voices were not woven into that medley of sounds.

Just once, I let out a cry of protest. We passed a phalanx of soldiers on horseback, forming a barrier between us and the crowd. Casually, as though lifting a dropped handkerchief, one of them leaned forward in the saddle and plucked away my veil.

Agitated for the first time, Harry made to follow the scrap of material but another man in the King's scarlet uniform snatched it from his fellow with an oath and handed it back to me. It was ripped. I stuffed it into a pocket.

"It's not worth bothering about, Harry," I said, and we continued walking.

The loss of that protective cloth left me feeling as though each and every one of my thoughts was visible to that horde of onlookers. But I remained dry-eyed. Time enough for tears.

When we reached the place of execution, at the junction of Corn Market and High Street, I couldn't help giving a start. The gallows was raised by the old Market House, on land gifted to Belfast by our great-great-grandfather, George Martin. Oftentimes, Father pointed it out to us.

The throng was dense here. People leaned from windows, and those on the ground pressed up against one another. Still, it lacked the carnival atmosphere which characterises hangings, or so I have heard. This was a sombre gathering.

An argument between birds, jostling and hovering over the Market House, caused me to look up towards a cloudless blue sky. The swarm was feasting on human fruit – spiked heads. Though their eyes were gone, I recognised them. The one nearest to us was James Dickey, an attorney, while beside him was the printer John Storey. Both men fought at Antrim with my brother. Further along were Hugh Grimes and Henry Byres, leaders at Ballynahinch. After several weeks on that sacrificial perch, the flesh was peeling in strips from their heads, flashes of bone exposed.

I was nearly afraid to look at Harry, but his expression was serene. He dipped his head in their direction, acknowledging comrades with a bow. I suppose I should have felt a sense of betrayal at the birds for dining on human flesh. But they were being true to their nature, as Harry was to his.

Now, I studied the apparatus by which he would be despatched. A set of wooden steps led to a platform from which the gibbet reared up. Considered dispassionately, it was composed of clean, straight lines. But menace warped the device. To my mind, it is impossible for anyone with an ounce of compassion in them to see a gallows, empty or occupied, without shuddering.

I had never been a spectator at a hanging. But for Harry's dear sake — to bear witness to his bravery — I was resolved to observe everything. Here were dragoons, several rows deep, controlling their horses hard-by the scaffold. There was the hangman, hooded from the public gaze as Harry was not. Surely a condemned man deserved that scrap of privacy at least as much as his executioner? I stared at the outline of his face beneath the hood — the curve of forehead, the point of a nose. How to tell if a man was honest or base? The executioner had accepted the purse I sent ahead to him. But I had no way of knowing whether he would honour the debt — or pocket the money and refuse to complete the transaction.

Looking away, towards those who were collected near the steps, I saw the glint of buttons on uniforms. My eyes swept the area. Uniforms everywhere. Perhaps the authorities feared a rescue attempt. Behind the soldiers, the people were crowded forward. Faces were a blur. I could not detect any friends. No doubt there were some.

I felt myself caught in that state of tension which precedes a thunderstorm. Harry, however, was an island of stillness amid the hubbub of activity. He must have sensed my unease because his fingers stroked my hand. Be strong, they said.

I wanted to have some conversation with him which I could unspool later for consolation. But I could think of nothing to say. I didn't dare to unsettle him before his ordeal by revealing my plan. Nor could I tell him others would be inspired by his sacrifice, that another rebellion would succeed where his had failed. I could utter none of it with conviction. Maybes I ought to have promised that we'd meet again in the Kingdom of God. Or I might have said, "Harry, I'll live my life for both of us." That would have had the ring of truth.

Emotion would not allow me to open my mouth, however. I remained silent, kept my hand on his arm, and continued beside him towards the scaffold. It was the best I could manage.

At the foot of the steps, they stopped me.

"No further," said a cavalry officer, leaning down from his horse. "No ladies on the platform. General Nugent's orders."

"Then I'll wait here."

"Best not, miss. This is no place for you."

Thoughts flashed through my mind. I could attach myself like a limpet to Harry's side, forcing the soldiers to tear me from him finger by finger. I could wail like those banshees Bessie talked about on stormy nights. But a glimpse at Harry told me his composure was draining away. I realised it in the hunch of his shoulders, the glaze icing across his eyes. My resistance would trouble him further.

I slid my arms about his waist and pressed my head against his shirt front. The rhythm of his heartbeat drummed against my cheek. His arms folded me into him, chin bristles prickling my forehead.

"At least we flew, Mary. The United men and me. For one day, we spread our wings. That's something."

I looked up at him and saw he had raised his head. His eyes were searching the sky.

"That's enough," said the officer.

Twice, Harry kissed me, begging me to let go now. I clung on, telling him I could bear anything but leaving him. He kissed me a third time and unhooked my arms. At that, I knew I must oppose his wishes no longer. A look passed between my brother and me.

Just do this for me, Mary, said Harry's.

You don't leave me much choice, said mine.

A shrug, a smile.

I wonder what it cost him, that smile? I couldn't return it. No, I couldn't manage that. But I could nod.

"My sister needs to be escorted to safety," he told the officer, in the same breath signalling to a minister whom he recognised.

Then, light as a feather, he mounted to the platform.

For my part, with many backward glances, I allowed myself to be led down the street by Mr Boyd. Each time I looked over my shoulder, Harry was watching me. At the corner, I stopped. Now, my brother stood facing the onlookers while the hangman tied his hands behind his back. That done, Harry stepped forward to address the crowd.

I saw no more – Mr Boyd, mouthing something that went over my head, steered me away. Prodded and dragged me, in truth. What I heard next was the clang of hooves. Major Fox had given a signal and the dragoons were using their animals to drown out my brother's final words. A drumroll rumbled, ending abruptly as Harry was pushed into thin air on the end of a rope.

There and then, I knelt in the city dirt, lowered my head and prayed for my brother. Not for a quick death, as others might, but that he would struggle and linger. Then I wiped the moisture from my face with my sleeve, for want of a handkerchief, stood up and straightened my back. I had work to do.

A scheme to cheat death.

"Did you save him?" I demanded of Dr McDonnell.

He was slow to respond. Reading nothing from his face, I craned past him into the dining room, to where my brother lay.

Dr McDonnell cleared his throat. "Once, we thought we had managed to start the heart beating again. But it was a false alarm. Our concentration was interrupted at a crucial point. A detachment of soldiers passed beneath the window and we had to stop working. When we renewed our efforts, I regret to say the favourable symptoms had gone. Your brother is with God now."

He stepped to one side and I could see Harry. He was spread

out on the table, his head lolling away from the door. Mr McCluney was straightening his limbs. The transport of emotion which had sustained me drained away. Even so, I am not one of those women who weep easily. Tears are no substitute for facing life head on. Numb, I pushed past the doctor, batted aside the apothecary, and climbed onto the table beside Harry.

They lifted their bags with their useless phials, their inadequate surgical instruments, and backed away from me.

There was a dribble of brandy on Harry's chin and his lips were shiny with it. The doctors must have tried to restore him with spirits. I wiped it off, his skin cold beneath my fingers.

I registered the door shutting as they left me alone with him. But the sound appeared to travel from a great distance. One by one, I did up the buttons on his shirt. I had sewn it for him with my own needle. I recognised by the buttons that it was one of mine and not Mother's. It was stained now – marked with the day's events, as we all were – and would have to be changed. Still, it should not be left to gape open.

I took Harry's head on my lap, rested my forehead against his, and twined my fingers among his fair curls with their golden flecks. My sister Margaret and I are obliged to take the curling tongs to our hair if we want waves, but it happened naturally for Harry. Much came easily to him. My brother was a man who could sail an ocean, write a sonnet, invent a mechanical marvel, converse with prince or ploughboy, dance a jig and lead an army. But he could not sidestep death.

My heartbeat slowed, in sympathy with his stopped pulse. A wail travelled from another end of the house, joined by others, rising and falling in unison – the news was spreading. Atty Bunting left off playing the harp.

Maybe I loved Harry too much. His death hollowed me. But wisdom can play no part in loving. If we tried to love wisely, we would parcel it out in measly bites and kill the love through lack of nourishment.

His eyes were closed. Who had performed that service for him? I wished it was me. I touched his lids, with my fingertips first, followed by my lips.

Footsteps approached. A man's. Father's, I supposed. My time alone with Harry was all but gone already. Others had a right to mourn beside him. And General Nugent's orders were to bury him before nightfall.

Oddly enough, the walk from the barracks to the gallows was not the hardest journey I ever undertook. After all, I had my plan. Harry's arm was in mine. He walked beside me, the breath of life in his lungs. Later the same day, I had a second journey to make on my brother's behalf – that one was more difficult. Like before, I was on foot. But this time I stepped out alone, following behind Harry in his coffin.

It was evening time now, July the seventeenth. The doctor was gone, as was the apothecary. You could tell they were anxious to leave our house. Any officer could hammer on the door and demand a head count of the occupants. How to explain their presence? At least Mr McCluney had sedated Mother before he left – she had collapsed after viewing Harry's remains. As for Father, he was speechless with grief and barely conscious of what was happening around him. Margaret sent a message to John that his help was needed in the house, after which my sister and I washed Harry and changed his soiled clothes for clean ones. We didn't speak as we worked. It was a job that took all our powers of concentration.

Meantime, John organised a hastily constructed coffin, a few planks nailed together. He knocked on the dining-room door, whispering to Margaret that it was time for Harry to be placed in it. So soon, I thought?

Silently, I went upstairs to tidy myself, ready to accompany my brother once again. Margaret fluttered about, trying to dissuade me.

"It's not seemly for a woman to follow a coffin, Mary."

"It's even less seemly for Harry to make his final journey alone," I snapped. "Lend me a veil, mine was torn by a soldier."

The whiles I splashed water on my face, she went to fetch it. But Margaret hadn't given up hopes of keeping me indoors. When we two went downstairs, she beckoned John over to us. He was standing among a knot of neighbours, talking quietly with them.

"John, won't you go to Harry's funeral?"

He turned puce. "Do you want to ruin this family entirely? We're under enough suspicion as it is."

Out of the corner of my eye, I watched my sister knead her fingers together. I was curious to see if she'd persist. When all's said and done, she loved Harry, too.

Margaret spoke with a sudden flame, "Aye, but there's no one to follow his coffin. That's not decent, John. Sure, you know it's not. You see, if you went, there'd be no need for Mary to walk behind it. Folk'll be scandalised at her, so they will."

He chewed his lip. "I can't risk it. I've a wife and childer to consider. What good am I to them in prison? Maybes the sodjers won't pay any heed to a wee slip of a lassie."

I left the room, convinced I'd explode if I had to listen to that smokescreen of words. William and Frank, both expecting to be seized as United men if they showed their faces, would have done right by Harry. But only John, the brother loyal to the King, was to hand.

I dropped Margaret's veil over my face and left by the front door. A horse and cart were waiting to transport Harry. The driver was a stranger to us, taking a chance for money. I wondered if it was the same cart used to carry him home from the gallows, wrapped in sacking. All at once, I became conscious of being the focus of attention: faces at every window on the houses along Rosemary Lane were watching me. Under the veil, my cheeks glowed.

The front door opened, and four men appeared with a burden on their shoulders. John's face was tense with concentration. He and three neighbours, who worshipped at the same church as us, were bearing Harry's coffin to the cart. Our fellow Presbyterians had to dig into their reserves of courage to do even that much. How and ever, none were willing to follow his remains. Some folk left their houses and stood on the street, dipping their heads out of respect. At funerals, it is the custom for men who know the deceased to fall in behind the family, but this evening they stayed put.

In all honesty, I couldn't blame them. The world was in a state of wickedness. Belfast was flooded with soldiers and riddled with informers – the city stones seemed to quake with fear. The military recognised guilt purely by association. Floggings, hangings and pitch-cappings were routine – they said it would make Ireland loyal. If you ask me, loyalty can only be given, not demanded. It is driven by affection rather than fear.

While they were loading the coffin, Margaret pattered out in her slippers, holding a nosegay of Sweet William and baby's breath. "There's not much else in the garden – it's the heat," she panted. A green ribbon was wound about the stems, calling to mind his coat on the day he rode off. She climbed up beside the driver, leaned round, and placed her flowers on the coffin.

"Miss Mary, you forgot your gloves. Master Harry would want you to look your best." It was Bessie, who had run around from the back of the house. She walked over to the coffin and stroked her hand across the wood. A caress, I suppose you'd call it. She'd known Harry most of his life.

Margaret stepped down and joined her on the roadside. At once, the driver cracked his whip, and the cart trundled off, me pacing behind. In truth, it was lonely, being the only living soul to follow Harry. But I held my head high, just as Harry had done.

By now, it was growing dark, and my foot caught on a cobblestone. I stumbled, and would have tripped, but for a neighbour who stepped forward to catch me. In his decency, he walked along with me, and I remember him daily in my prayers for that act of kindness.

"Mary, wait!"

Before we reached our destination, John overtook us, panting from the exertion, and did his duty by his shared blood with Harry after all. Margaret, or his conscience, or maybe Father had coaxed him to it. Despite the antagonism between us, I was glad to see him. The neighbour fell back, allowing John to take his place beside me.

And so we laid Henry Joy McCracken to rest in the Parish Burying Ground, where he would wait among the godly for resurrection. I should have liked to bury him in his fine feathers: that seditious coat of green, with the plumed hat on his head. But the hat was lost in the field at Antrim – stained with mud, no doubt, and maybe blood forbye. As for the coat, it was left behind in Cave Hill.

Still, this time I watched at journey's end, as I was not able to do by the gallows. I stood while the box containing my brother's body was placed in a hole, the cavity covered with earth. I listened to Mr Kelburn's prayers, spoke the responses, and when he was done I laid Margaret's posy on Harry's grave.

"*These are the times that try men's souls*," Harry wrote to me, in the days following the United Irishmen's defeat. Little he knew. It's women's souls that are put to the test by the long years of remembering.

Before Mr Kelburn left us at the grave, he used the selfsame words Dr McDonnell said to me. "Your brother is with God now." It's something to say to folk when they're grieving and meant kindly. Except that wasn't where I saw my Harry. When I picture him, it's soaring high above us all, caged no longer.

Since Harry's hanging, I have grown impatient, no longer content to labour in the background. To be someone who unpicks mistakes made by others. Don't misunderstand me – I have no desire for the front row, or to be noticed. I'd sooner move a boulder the size of a house than speak in public. But I am resolved to do what I can.

It can be tedious dealing with the United men who didn't flee overseas or end up on the end of a rope. Granted, the ones who are out of jail and organising again have impressive ideas. But sometimes they let themselves down.

"What a big sentence from such a tiny mouth," they say.

Or, "I'll have to put you in my pocket and keep you out of harm's way."

That's when they pay attention to me at all. Mostly, they don't. I know I have no knack for those feminine wiles which draw men to women. I don't simper and pretend to be helpless, giving them an opportunity to save me from misfortune. I use no smelling salts to suggest frailty. It is fashionable for women to speak of their nerves but mine cause me no agitation.

Outwardly, I am compliant but inwardly I churn. My thoughts are my own and they run tumultuous through the channels of my mind. Our people are Dissenters. Neither the McCrackens nor my mother's people, the Joys, take instruction from on high readily – we make up our own minds. Like Harry, I am a rebel. Rebellion passes along the generations, as an aptitude for figures or a long chin is handed down. It reached me, too. But I don't burn to raise armies and conquer citadels. No, I seethe to change the ways of the world – to force a space in it for women. That's a stony path to travel and no mistake.

Be that as it may, I never set out on a journey, whether short or long, but I feel the warmth of my brother's hand and hear the echo of his footsteps beside mine.

After Harry's death, Mary discovered he had an illegitimate daughter, Maria Boal, aged four, whose mother was a Cave Hill gamekeeper's daughter. Before he died, Harry confided in Steele Dickson and the minister told Mary. Against her brother John's wishes, Mary made arrangements to take the girl into the McCracken family. After a lengthy and productive life, Mary Ann McCracken died with her devoted niece Maria by her side.

NANO NAGLE

Born Ballygriffin near Mallow, County Cork 1718; died Cork City 1784

Educator, founder of a religious congregation

Nano Nagle was a pioneer both of female education and schools for impoverished people. Her achievements took place during the Penal Laws when Catholics and Presbyterians in Ireland were stripped of a number of rights. Prohibitions included being forbidden to establish schools or send children abroad for an education according to their own faith. The Nagles retained much of their wealth and had a substantial rent roll because an uncle of Nano's converted to Anglicanism – possibly to hold property on the family's behalf.

Despite the ban, Nano was educated in either France or Belgium. When she returned to Ireland she was troubled by the ignorance and poverty in her homeland. She entered a French convent but left it to embark on her life's work. Around 1754, she set up a free school in Cork for girls from poor families, which grew into a network of schools. She hired teachers but taught religious instruction herself as well as running the schools. When an uncle left her a substantial legacy, she devoted it to building up a more substantial group of schools, as well as a number of centres dedicated to the needy.

In 1771, hoping to put her work on a structural basis, she introduced the Ursuline Sisters to Ireland and built a convent for them in Cork. In 1775, she founded her own religious order which became the Sisters of the Presentation of the Blessed Virgin Mary (known as the Presentation Sisters). She received the religious habit in 1776 and was professed the following year.

In 2000 she was named Irish Woman of the Millennium by public vote. In 2013 she was declared the Venerable Nano Nagle.

Nano's Ark

On her first day in the secret-school, Nano told the Master she knew how to write already because Mama had taught her.

"Show me." He gave her a slate and stick of chalk.

She drew N. "N is for both my names, Nano and Nagle."

The Master nodded.

Then she traced H. "It's for Honora," she said. "My real name."

"That's a big name for a little lady."

"Everyone calls me Nano. You can, if you like."

Every morning, Nano skipped into her secret-school. Some of the class called it the hedge school – *scoil scairte* – although lessons were held indoors, not outside, in a barn on the Nagles' land. Every evening, Dada asked her what she had learned, and she told him about faraway countries over the sea – Italy, Spain and France, whose capital cities she had to sing out when the Master pointed to her.

"Ah, France," said Dada. "You'll go there one day."

Dada knew about those places because sometimes he travelled to France, taking care of Nagle family business there, she was told. To Nano, 'one day' was as distant as the countries on Master O'Shea's map.

The Master had a habit of holding his hands chest-high, the way a dog sitting up rested its paws. Nano watched to see if he would poke out a pink tongue and pant, but he never did. All the same, he was worth paying attention to because he told stories. One of her favourites was about Manannán MacLir, the sea god, who was able to read the weather, and sang as he raced along in his boat called *Wave-Sweeper* that needed no sails to go like the wind. He had a powerful sword, *The Answerer*, a cloak of invisibility and a goblet of truth. Nano repeated the Master's stories to Dada, who said a cloak of invisibility would be a useful possession.

She had a friend at the secret-school: Ita McAuliffe, the blacksmith's daughter. She was two months older than Nano, with curly hair. Ita was better than her at spelling and writing.

"Ita has a gift for learning," the Master told the class, and a pink tide crept across Ita's cheeks.

Nano felt a pang. That evening, she complained to Mama. "The Master never says I'm best at anything."

Mama flicked a look at her over the head of the baby boy she was bathing. "What do you think you're best at, Nano?"

Nano couldn't say counting because Cáit was able to add, subtract, multiply and divide any sum quicker than blinking. Nor Latin because Thady was a match for the Master, nearly. Nor history because Philip was top of the class at that. There was nobody to match Nano for whipping a spinning top, and keeping it whirling, but that could be because nobody else at the secret-school had one. Some had whistles, and some a hand-carved figure, but there was nothing to compare with her red-and-blue spinning top.

"I'm not best at anything, Mama."

Mama lifted baby Joseph out of the water and began to pat him dry. "Then why should Master O'Shea tell a lie? Lies hurt God's ears. Work hard, and you'll find something you have a gift for."

Some of the pupils were aged five or six, like her and Ita, while others were seventeen or eighteen and helped the Master with the lessons. There were only a few books to share, tattered from use. Dada wrote off for more books for the secret-school and they arrived on one of the Nagles' ships.

Dada it was who named the mountains she saw every day, misty blue in the distance.

He lifted her onto his shoulders for a clear view. "Those are the Nagle Mountains, Nano."

At first she thought he might be teasing her, but he insisted it was true.

And, so, it became normal to her that her family shared its name with the mountains — she imagined it was commonplace, although if she had stopped to consider she would have realised there weren't enough mountains to go round.

In wintertime, it could be cold in the secret-school, even with the cattle inside. Sometimes they mooed during lessons. The Master would pretend they were joining in, offering answers or asking questions of their own, which made the children laugh — even though the joke was always the same. He couldn't light a fire because of the risk the barn might burn down but everyone knew to burrow down into the straw for warmth. Mama sent Nano to school bundled up in layers, which made her feel as awkward as a waddling goose. Still, she preferred too many clothes and the straw's prickles to a peat fire. She had been in the cabins where most of her classmates lived and all of them were smoky. Unlike her house, there were no brick chimneys, so you went home with stinging eyes and a throat scraped raw from coughing.

On her eighth birthday, Nano's parents produced a present so magical that Nano almost forgot to breathe. It was a wooden

Noah's Ark. When you opened the roof, Noah and Mrs Noah were sitting inside surrounded by animals – two of everything. The Noahs were the largest, next biggest were the giraffes because of their long necks, followed by the elephants. One after another, she took them out in pairs: lions, horses, pigs, sheep, goats and so on.

When Mama said it was time for school, Nano begged to take the ark with her to show the others. Not to be boastful, she said, but to share. Mama and Dada whispered together before agreeing. Dada's manservant Denis carried it there for her. The Master asked him to set the ark on a high place, beneath which everybody could gather and marvel. After Denis left, the Master lifted out the animals, even though that was Nano's job, and lined them up.

Nobody was to touch anything because it might get damaged but they could all look. "A cat may look at a king." The Master wore an odd smile such as adults had sometimes for no particular reason.

He picked up one of the doves, despite nobody being meant to handle the figures, and held it while he told them the last part of the Bible story about the Flood: how Noah knew the water was dropping away thanks to this little bird. The first time he sent it out, the dove could find nowhere to land and returned to the ark. Seven days later, Noah sent it out again, and it flew back with a freshly picked olive leaf in its beak. After another seven days, he tried once more, and this time the bird stayed away so Noah knew it was safe to leave the boat's shelter.

At bedtime, when Nano chattered about how everyone at school had enjoyed the ark, Mama said, "Maybe that's what you're best at, *a stór*. Sharing your treasures."

That August, Ita couldn't go to school because she had to help on the land. Nano thought it might be fun to work in the fields, but when she saw Ita in the village her friend's hands were swollen with cuts and she was too tired to play hide and seek.

At the end of the summer, instead of returning to the secret-school, Nano heard she was going to a place called a convent in

France. However, she mustn't breathe a word because she would have to be sneaked over, in a merchant ship that traded between Ireland and the Continent. Dada would go with her to keep her safe. How long the journey might take depended on the winds. Nano considered telling Mama they should call on Manannán MacLir for help with filling the ship's sails with wind but decided against it – Mama pressed her lips together at any mention of what the Master called the old gods.

Nano presumed Ita and the others were going to school in France, too. Forgetting it was a secret – she always struggled to keep them – she mentioned it to her friend. Ita's face took on a fierce expression, as if she no longer liked her.

"No, Nano. You're the only one."

"But why?"

Ita looked down. A clump of pebbles lay underfoot. She kicked at them before walking away.

Nano felt stupid. After all, she would be nine soon; she understood her family had a big house and owned land when others didn't.

Before leaving Ballygriffin, Nano went to say goodbye to Ita. She wasn't in the blacksmith's forge and Mr McAuliffe didn't know where she might be. Striped with sweat, hammering sparks from iron, he could not spare the time to talk with her. She tried the riverbank, but there was no sign of her there, nor was she under the bridge. Finally, she went to the barn because Ita sometimes stayed on after school to read. There wasn't much peace in their cabin beside the forge.

The Master was alone with important-looking papers spread out in front of him. Nano had overheard her father say O'Shea made extra income on the side by translating leases and other documents into English for those with only the Irish. The Master said he hadn't laid eyes on Ita but he'd pass on a message.

"Tell her I'm sailing from Cork in a ship called *The Grey Lady*."

The Master tapped the side of his nose. "Say no more. But

remember this when you set off. On the ocean's open highways, we Irish were busy in trade but busier still in learning – shared freely throughout Europe by the monks. They travelled to Brittany, and from there journeyed east over northern France, beyond the Rhine to the North Sea and the Baltic. And wherever they went, they left it richer than they found it."

"Why did they share their learning freely? For the same reason you teach?"

"I teach to put bread in my belly. But the monks passed on their learning for a higher purpose. It was an expression of their love for Christ. 'We have wisdom to offer,' they called out in the marketplaces, in the days of Charles the Great, and schools were opened using Irish teachers and Irish manuscripts."

"Did women share their wisdom, as well?"

"If they did, we don't know about it," said the Master. Nano frowned. "I'm sure there were women with stores of knowledge. But women tend to have their hands full raising children. Ask your good lady mother."

Nano took a last look at the secret-school while the Master returned to his work.

Just before she left, he hunkered in front of her, eyes blazing. "Never forget when you go over the water, Nano, that you come from an ancient civilisation."

The Grey Lady was berthed along the Cork quays, a place of noise and bustle which simultaneously petrified and fascinated Nano. The ship had three masts, a forest of square sails on each. Twisting her neck, she half-expected to see clouds clinging to them. Dada was busy with a man who stopped counting wooden crates to talk to him. Nano picked up that the chests contained Irish wool bound for France, where it would be turned into clothing. Dada kept his hand clamped on her shoulder while he chatted with the man and she was glad of its weight.

They spent the night in a lodging house where the cries of the quays floated in to them. By candlelight, Dada said Nano was to be carried onto the ship inside one of those chests stuffed with wool. It was ready in the yard outside. Patient at her questions, Dada explained again that she had to be smuggled on board because a Catholic education was forbidden in Ireland – the new King of England, George II, banned it, as his father before him had done, and the king before them.

"But learning is worth any risk, pigeon. We can't let you grow up with a head full of nothing."

At dawn, Dada woke her and they ate breakfast together, just the two of them. She had never had breakfast with just her and Dada. Afterwards, he kissed her and said he was depending on her to be a brave girl. In the yard, he showed her how the lid was only resting on top of her container – it lifted away as simply as the Noah's Ark roof.

"It's a secret place in there, like my secret-school," said Nano.

"That's exactly right. But we'll have to nail down this roof in case it slips off. We can't let that happen."

Dada checked to see if anybody was watching. When the coast was clear, he picked her up and set her inside. Heart pounding, she crouched in the tickly wool. This didn't feel like the games of hide and seek she and Ita used to play.

"Now for the nails to help keep my pigeon safe," said Dada, and he banged them in himself.

She didn't like the hammer blows but felt comforted by the grey-blue slice of sky she could glimpse through a crack in the lid. Now, she heard boots tramping, followed by voices. The crate tilted, she slid back, and felt herself swung through the air.

"Careful there!" Dada called out.

Nano was carried onto the ship by some sailors, knowing she mustn't sneeze or cough or let a single cheep out of her. Dada walked beside the chest. She couldn't see him but knew he was there because his voice travelled through the wood. She heard the seagulls shriek and felt herself bumped down ladders. When the box came to rest, the sense of movement didn't stop because the ship was bobbed about by the tide.

By and by, the swaying increased. She anchored her arms around her legs, desperate to see the sky, even just a sliver, but it was dim in this place where the container was stored.

"Nano, we're out at sea now and I can let you out."

Dada talked quietly to her while he pulled out nails with the claw end of a hammer, praising her for being as quiet as a mouse. Oh, thought Nano, there were no mice figures in her ark. Too bad. She hoped her brothers and sisters would be careful when they played with it.

"This is the hold, Nano. It's a place deep inside the ship where cargo is stored. You can leave the crate now but you have to stay in here – it isn't safe to go on deck. The captain knows he has an extra passenger but not all of the hands do. We can't risk loose lips."

"What are the hands?"

"That's what sailors are called."

"Why is it a hand and not a foot or an eye?"

"Now that's a question I don't have an answer for." Dada smiled for the first time since leaving home and Nano grinned back at him. "Little monkey, there isn't a bother on you."

He lifted her up, set her on her feet and knelt down beside her.

She had pins and needles. Dada understood without her telling him because he rubbed his big, warm hands over her arms and legs, kneading the flesh back to life.

"I'll stay with you as much as I can, Nano. But when I have to leave the hold you must get back into the crate – it protects you, you understand?"

That first day, she was sick because of the way the ship rocked, but Dada gave her water and sponged her down, and by the second day she barely noticed the constant roll. It was impossible to tell day from night in this place called the hold. Men's voices shouted in languages she didn't understand. Bells rang at regular intervals – curious, she asked the hand who carried food to her and Dada about them. He said they signalled time. Dada remained with her as much as possible but sometimes he had business elsewhere on the ship. Nano was nervous until he returned but kept her anxiety buttoned inside herself.

It took three and a half days to reach Brittany. Waiting to go ashore, Dada rubbed his hands. "We were fortunate this trip. The winds were in our favour — sometimes it can take five days or more. As soon as you set foot in France, Nano, you won't need to hide any longer."

"Secret places are special, though," she said.

"True. But you can't stay tucked inside them forever. Your new life is about to begin now. And the nuns will take good care of you."

Nuns? Nobody had said anything about nuns.

The Ursuline convent smelled of beeswax polish and rosewater. In their peculiar headdresses, the nuns looked like the medieval women she saw pictured in books. They were brisk, clapping their hands to hurry her when she dawdled and urging her to use her time profitably when she daydreamed. *La petite Irlandaise*, they called her, although mostly they spoke to her in Latin until she began to shape her tongue to French words.

Once, she asked a novice why she didn't want to marry.

The young nun looked radiant. "I belong to God. I am the Lamb's bride. He invited me to accept him as my heavenly bridegroom and I said yes."

Nano made a new friend, a Scottish girl called Flora Mills, and the following year her sister Ann joined her at the convent. Ann was devout, prone to talk about joining the Ursulines when she was older. But Flora and Nano ignored her. They liked to speculate about what the nuns looked like without those veils which covered their hair. Underneath the veils were bands of white cloth concealing every inch of their necks right up to the chin. Only by their eyebrows could the girls guess at hair colour.

Flora admired their white hands, kept tucked inside the wide sleeves of their habits when they weren't in use, and drew Nano's attention to their knack of walking rapidly without giving the appearance of hurry.

"Maybe they have invisible wheels," suggested Nano.

"Supplied by God," put in Flora.

And the pair of them dissolved into giggles while Ann radiated disapproval. Ann was always reading about martyred saints: their near-death convulsions and heroic acceptance of suffering. She enjoyed nothing better than to ponder about which martyr's death she'd prefer. Could she be as brave as St Cecelia, who was beheaded but lingered on for three days because her neck was not severed completely, during which time she kept on preaching? Or how would it feel to be tied to the horns of a bull and gored to death in the Circus before the roaring mob, like some of the early Christians?

Nano missed home but soon settled into the routine of school life. Watching the nuns, she grew to recognise beauty in the simplicity and dedication of their lifestyle. They prayed, read, worked and ate, all at preordained times of day according to the Rule of St Augustine which urged detachment from the world. Above all, their plain chant delighted her. In later life, she could not see the words of *The Magnificat* – that carefully noted meeting between Mary and her cousin Elizabeth, both surprised (although for different reasons) to find themselves expecting babies – without recalling the nuns' voices raised in unison.

My soul doth magnify the Lord
And my spirit rejoices in God my Saviour
For he hath regarded the lowliness of his handmaid
And henceforth all generations shall call me blessed.

In time, Nano realised it took courage to accept the cloister, as her Ursulines had. There were some who did it from timidity, but many others who chose it from a position of strength and independence. The Mother Abbess, Mother Xavier, ran her ship with the sovereignty of a captain at sea. Granted, she had to yield to the bishop should he choose to exercise his authority, but generally she kept out of his way and he out of hers.

Sometimes, Nano thought about Ita McAuliffe, chanting her lessons under the Master's eye in the barn at Ballygriffin, and wondered should she send a letter to the blacksmith's forge. Somehow she never found the time. Her family visited her in France and it was three summers later before she went home on holiday.

By the time she set foot in Ballygriffin it was too late to renew her friendship with Ita. Nano called to the forge to ask after her but Mr McAuliffe, massive in his leather apron peppered with sparks, said she had finished with school and was making her way in the world. Ita was hired out as a servant in an apothecary's household in Cork city.

When her time at the convent was over, Nano lingered in Paris, meandering on currents of pleasure between the opera, salons and supper parties. The Nagles had a wide circle of relatives and friends there and decided to rent a house in the French capital. Their mother lived with Nano and Ann, while their father travelled between Ireland and France. The younger girls, Catherine and Elizabeth, were still with the Ursulines, while Joseph was being educated by the Jesuits elsewhere in the city. As for David, soon he left school too and settled to learning about the family business. Nothing was expected from Nano other than to be an accomplished young lady. Mama hinted at marriage proposals for her two elder girls but, while there were plenty of officers to partner them at balls, no serious offer was made.

"Time enough," said Mama.

Nano knew dowries were a problem. There wasn't enough money both to set up the boys and provide dowries for all four girls sufficient to tempt someone from the same social class. Nano shrugged mentally and concentrated on enjoying the froth of her supremely indolent life.

It reached an abrupt end when she was twenty-eight and her father died. With him evaporated the money for Paris. The Nagles sailed for Ireland. Joseph would lodge with an uncle in Cork city and train as a merchant under him, looking after the family's trading interests, while David would be based in Ballygriffin and oversee their lands. Her brother had married recently and it was time for him to step in as head of the family.

After consulting with David, Mama decided she and the girls would live in Dublin, where the Nagles had a small townhouse on Gardiner Street. She could have moved them all home to that spacious riverside house in the Blackwater Valley, but said it was best to leave it to David and his wife, who was expecting a baby. Opportunities for her daughters might arise in Dublin.

By which Nano knew she meant marriage proposals. However, if dowry money was in short supply while their father was alive, how could it be any more plentiful after his death when their means were stretched? His will stipulated that each of the girls should have an income from some properties put out to rent but it was less than they had been accustomed to spending when he handled the bills.

Dublin was filthy, smelly, and elegant only intermittently – Nano disliked it at first sight and never revised her opinion. She missed the grace of Paris, its sophistication, the fashions, boulevards and carriage rides. How could anyone admire the Liffey after seeing the Seine?

The scale of Ireland's deprivation shocked her. While she had witnessed poverty in France, it had been held at a distance. Here, it was under her feet, her nose, her notice. Behind the broad streets lined with mansions lay a warren of back lanes and alleyways crammed with slums. Ragged children scampered after their carriage when they drove to the Phoenix Park to take the air. She knew some of the urchins slept in the doorways of shops because she had seen them there, returning to Gardiner Street from card parties and other entertainments.

Ann inquired about Dublin's poor from the servants, who described their wretchedness. Nano didn't want to know but Ann insisted on sharing the details. Nano was more interested in a ball they were invited to attend by the Earl of Kildare. Recently, he had married an English girl of just fifteen, Lady Emily Lennox, daughter of the Duke of Richmond. The Kildares were the leading aristocrats in Ireland and Nano was impatient to observe them at close quarters.

She had been saving a bolt of peacock silk from her Paris days – she'd have it fashioned into a gown for this premier event in the social calendar. However, when she sent her maid to retrieve it, the girl returned empty-handed. Ann had sold the cloth, distributing the proceeds among the needy. Nano howled her frustration.

But Ann was imperturbable. "They have so little and we have so much."

"You should have asked me."

"Sacrifices must be made."

"You didn't invite me to make a sacrifice. You made it on my behalf."

"You'd have said no, Nano. You're like Lot's wife. You walk on the pathway to God but the temptation to look back is too great with you. You risk being turned into a pillar of salt. In time, you'll thank me."

"Do-gooder!"

"I am a tool in the Lord's hands."

Mama brokered peace by lending Nano her best peach satin. Its train was torn in the crush. Still, Nano was stimulated by the sight of the new Countess of Leinster, who had a Roman nose and a fetching pink colour in her cheeks. Mama muttered about artifice but Nano thought her charming, although abnormally self-possessed for a fifteen-year-old.

Driving home at dawn, Nano was puzzled why she didn't feel

replete – on the contrary, a spirit of restlessness seized her. Barefoot children began loping alongside the carriage and she tossed some coins from the window. They peeled away to scrabble in the mud. One imp was toppled in the stampede, however, and let out a desolate wail. With Mama's permission, she ordered their driver to stop, leaned from the window to beckon, and handed the boy a coin.

He was stubby, with a runny nose and clothes that flapped like a scarecrow's. Speechless, he stared at the money as if at a vision. When the carriage trundled off, Nano felt happier than at any time during that overlong, overheated, overcrowded ball.

Ann developed a rash and was gratified initially because the saints endured afflictions without complaint. Her satisfaction turned to fear when sores appeared on her mouth and throat, signifying smallpox. Mama nursed her but could not prevent Ann from dying, nor herself from following her daughter into the grave. At least she ensured Nano's escape by sending her to stay with David in Ballygriffin.

Watching him presiding at table, it occurred to Nano how different her life would be if she'd been born a man instead of a woman. As the eldest, she'd have inherited the house and its estate; she'd be making decisions in her own right rather than have her brothers – both younger – advance proposals for her future.

It wasn't too late to marry, David suggested. A match could be arranged, a moderate dowry rustled up. He knew a doctor who was a decent sort. Not from their class, it was true, but gentlemanly enough and in need of a wife.

Nano felt impatient with her brother. However, she adopted a modest expression. "I don't feel drawn to marriage, David."

"In that case, there's always a home for you here. Susannah would be glad of your company and I know she'd appreciate your help with the children."

Already, there were two junior Nagles.

While Nano liked David and Susannah's babies, she wished to

do something useful with her life — and didn't count acting as companion to a sister-in-law and nursemaid to nieces and nephews as enough. No matter if she was loved, they were not roles she welcomed. Marriage meant enforced domestication, as did living under David's roof.

"I thought I might seek admission as a postulant with the Ursulines in Paris," she said.

David's relief was visible. "Mama would be delighted."

It might or might not be true. Mama had expressed no view either way.

"We'll make sure you don't enter the convent empty-handed," her brother continued. "I'll speak to Joseph."

Nano suspected Joseph would be just as thankful as David at the nunnery solution to an excess of sisters. "I'll write to Mother Xavier," she said.

In Ballygriffin she had discovered a preference for being outdoors rather than inside. Now, she excused herself and took a stroll in the garden. It soothed her to see the sky with its racing clouds and be surrounded by the scents of the countryside. Was that a patch of clover underfoot? She snapped off a stem and sniffed at the pink-tipped globe. During quiet periods outside, God's presence overwhelmed her senses and she knew herself to be enveloped by his love. Once she joined the Ursulines she'd be enclosed. She should walk about freely while it remained in her power to do so.

A few days later, prowling the country lanes, Nano spied clots of glossy blackberries. She leaned into the hedgerow and plucked one. Its inky juice spilled from her lips and fingertips — drenched in summer, it tasted extra luscious because the season was drawing to a close. She rambled along, nibbling berries, and happened upon a woman filling a billycan with them. Nano said good day and kept walking.

"Don't you know me, Nano?"

She halted. The stranger's face was lined, her frame scraggy. "Forgive me, I don't believe I do."

Two words of reproach were levelled: "I'm Ita."

Nano examined her. No trace of her childhood friend was visible. Ita's face had been vivid with curiosity and a thirst for life, whereas this woman's expression was flat, beaten down.

Ita read Nano, just as she always could. "Six births and five children to show for my pains." She rubbed the heel of a hand against one of her eye sockets. When she took it away, she would have stumbled if Nano hadn't caught her by the arm. Nano sat on a grassy bank, inviting her old friend to join her. Questions about France tumbled from Ita. So, thought Nano, her passion for learning hadn't deserted her, whatever else had been lost in the two decades and more since they sat together in the secret-school. Glimmers of the girl she had played with filtered through.

"Are you living in Ballygriffin, Ita?"

"I make my home in Cork these days. It's sorry I am that ever I left Ballygriffin but I went where I was sent. And, after all, my parents thought they were doing right by me. I'm married these ten years past. My husband works on the docks – when he can get the work. He has a broad back and he's willing. But there's more men looking for work than jobs to go round. I'm at home for a few days to see about my mother. She hasn't been well. God knows how I'll get her back on her feet, mind you, because I had to bring the young ones with me. Their racket hurts her head. But what could I do? Timothy would let them run the streets and forget they had a mouth on them."

"Do you still find time to read, Ita?"

"My brain isn't empty if that's what you mean."

"Mammy!" A thin bleat interrupted them.

"That's my Josie," said Ita, her aggravation subsiding.

A girl with Ita's nut-brown curls appeared, a yellow ribbon catching them back from her freckled face. She carried a baby of about a year jammed against her hip. "Hawley's hungry."

Without a word, Ita reached for the child and turned aside from Nano, fumbling at her clothing.

Nano became conscious of Josie gaping at her. She smiled at the girl, who edged closer. Purple stains circled her mouth. Maybe she was hungry. Should she invite the three of them back to her brother's house for a meal? She supposed it would be acceptable to lead them to the kitchen and ask the cook for mugs of milk and bread and cheese. Or bread and treacle for the children if they had a fancy for that. Except it smacked of Lady Bountiful behaviour. Ita was capable of biting her head off and she couldn't blame her.

What was it her mother used to say? *If you stick your hand into a beehive you must expect to be stung.*

She began to fumble in her pocket for a coin, reconsidering as her fingers closed over one. In her mind's eye, she met Ita's glower – resentment and necessity battling it out. She'd have to find a more discreet way to help.

"Do you go to school, Josie?"

A shake of the head caused the ribbon to slip. Nano reached out to straighten it. When she was done, she cupped Josie's chin momentarily in the palm of her hand.

"There's no master to teach school," said Ita. "Even in a place the size of Cork. We were lucky with Master O'Shea, he was the man had the learning. Dead of a fever, half a dozen years back."

"I heard that, I was distressed at the news. A fine man. Ita, Josie has a look of you about her. Can she say her ABCs?"

The girl's eyes latched onto to her mother, who nodded encouragement, and she began to recite, stuttering and missing out letters.

Ita mouthed along, prompting her. When Josie was finished, Ita sighed. "They have hungry minds as well as hungry bellies, my babies. But there's nobody to teach them. I do what I can. But the way of it is, I'm worn to a thread by nightfall." She flickered reproach at Nano. *You were carried away to France* dangled in the air separating them.

"I wish I could do something for you, Ita."

"There's nothing to be done for me. My bed was made for me and, like it or lump it, I must lie in it." Ita swallowed, her voice thickening. "If you have it in you to do anything, Nano, do it for Josie."

In that instant, an idea ballooned through Nano's mind – a wish which became a desire, the desire a burst of longing. It surged up to captivate her, even while it terrified because of the danger involved. Instead of returning to Paris and joining the Ursulines, she should open a school in Ireland. After all, giving children the gift of an education was an act of prayer. Mother Xavier had been fond of quoting St Teresa of Avila to her girls: "*There is a time for partridge and a time for penance.*" Wasn't there also a time for teaching?

Nano took Josie by the hand, guiding her onto the grass beside her. "When I was your age I had a Noah's Ark. An ark is a big boat. Long ago, a man called Noah built one and filled it with every kind of animal, two of each. The rain fell, heavier and heavier, flooding the world – drowning everything. But the storm didn't matter to Noah and the animals because they were floating in their ark, a special place which kept them safe."

Risking imprisonment, Nano Nagle opened a free school in a two-room cabin in Cork city, intending to provide a basic education for around 30 girls. However, demand was so high that she went on to open seven schools – five for girls and two for boys – developing her own system of education.

At night she walked Cork's unlit streets carrying food and medicine to the sick and needy. She became known as 'The Lady of the Lantern' and her lantern is the symbol of the Presentation order she founded.

SPERANZA

Born Dublin, 1821; died London, 1896

Nationalist poet, journalist, essayist and writer

Jane, Lady Wilde, born Jane Elgee, wrote under the pen name of Speranza, and was known as well for her literary salons. Her verses, printed in *The Nation*, were inspirational to followers of the Young Ireland political movement, while she edited the weekly nationalist newspaper in 1848 after its editor Charles Gavan Duffy was forced abroad.

She was an early supporter of women's rights and wrote numerous articles in a variety of publications supporting greater equality. She praised the passage of the Married Women's Property Act of 1883, which meant a woman was no longer reduced to "a bond slave" when she became a wife.

Her causes included the vote (she invited a well-known suffrage campaigner to speak at one of her salons); access to education – she complained the present system prepared girls only for "husband worship" and called for an all-female university; and the Rational Dress Movement, advocating practical clothing for women rather than unhealthy fashions which restricted their breathing and mobility.

She had an interest in folk tales which she helped to gather in *Ancient Legends, Mystic Charms, and Superstitions of Ireland*.

She was also the mother of celebrated playwright Oscar Wilde, jailed for "gross indecency" in 1895.

Tucked Away

"The letter's here. It's just this minute arrived, Mama," says Willie Wilde.

By her bedside, he holds it out, a tremor in his hand — he hasn't yet had a drink to steady himself. None is kept in the house. Partly because funds are tight, partly because he'd sniff it out wherever it was hidden. Once this business is dealt with, he'll slip off to a pub by the riverfront. The letter concerns his brother. Too long indulged, in Willie's opinion. However, he cares enough about his mother to carry it in himself rather than delegate the task.

Jane, Lady Wilde, is propped against a pillow tower, a glittering plumage of brooches and cameos pinned to the bed-jacket covering her nightgown. An excess of jewellery is habitual with her. But the pieces are trinkets — anything valuable has been traded for credit or ready cash.

It is a grey January morning but even so not a chink of daylight makes it past the velvet, floor-length curtains at her window. Pastilles of medicinal herbs smoulder on the mantelpiece, contributing to the general fug. Candlelight at all times is one of her idiosyncrasies. From a double-pronged candlestick, twin tongues of flame skirmish ineffectually against the obscurity.

She has not left her bedroom for two months. "The life spring is broken in me. I shall not smell this summer's roses," she predicted, when Lily kissed her and wished her a Happy New Year several weeks earlier. Lily discounted it as her mother-in-law's taste for performance.

Jane is marking time, however. Only one duty remains before she is ready to let go. Dislodging a pillow, she pushes herself upright, and meets Willie's bloodshot gaze without accepting the envelope. She finds it suspicious that he was loitering for the post. Does he hope to intercept a cheque? She is under no illusions about her firstborn. If he knew she wore a cloth bag containing sovereigns round her waist, sufficient to provide her with a modest funeral, he'd help himself while she slept and leave the undertaker's bill to chance.

"Open it, why don't you?" Willie urges. "We're all withered from you asking if the letter's come. Now it's here and you don't want to know." While she dallies, he could be posted somewhere agreeable, his elbow on a wooden counter and a glass of something to settle his stomach near to hand.

Jane ignores him. She expects nothing of Willie, and consequently is rarely disappointed. Her eyes latch onto the buff envelope. Isn't there some incantation she can recite to ensure a positive outcome? Once, she was an expert. Her *Ancient Legends, Mystic Charms and Superstitions of Ireland* was lionised. But her mind is a blank. Old age, or the accumulation of disappointment, or a combination of both, have sluiced her out.

If William were here, he'd recite something. Her husband had a prodigious memory, as well as a fondness for the country people's traditions. They needed no inducement to share their stories with the *doctor mór*. They worshipped him, knowing he'd crawl through a field of thorn bushes to attend any one of them, and no mention of a fee for professional services.

Jane moistens her lips with the tip of her tongue. Look at Willie, hopping with impatience. He's on the verge of flinging the letter onto the counterpane. Is it some vestige of decency that stays his hand?

He lumbers closer, the stench of unwashed armpit floating from him. To think that once she supervised his bath-time and pressed her lips again and again to his infant skin, comparing it to marzipan in its pink and white perfection.

"See? The sender's name is stamped on it." He rattles out a chuckle, along with a sour eddy of breath from the previous night's excess. Close to three o'clock, it must have been, when she heard him racket up the stairs. "No secrets from the postman," he wheezes.

She can't bear to let her eyes rest on the wreckage of his face. Her glance flicks back to the lettering on the envelope: *H.M. Prison Reading*. Yes, that's where possibilities for redemption lie.

As long as the seal is unbroken, she can believe in the prospect of seeing Oscar again. Her imagination reunites them in a tender scene: her younger son laying his head on her breast, while she strokes his hair. "Help me to bear it, Mama," he cries. She kisses him and explains that he has lost his way but his art awaits him. He can return to it – genius cannot be unravelled by temporary setbacks.

When he is consoled, she will speak to him about the matter weighing on her conscience. Face to face, she must beg his forgiveness for the advice which helped send him to prison. She insisted Oscar should stand his ground against those Pharisees, his accusers. Does he resent her? It wounds her that Oscar has not written to her, no, not once, since that day eight months ago when monsters seized and handcuffed him.

Her eyes drift along the envelope. The lettering is typewritten, each 'e' slightly out of kilter along the lines. So much for the supposed perfection of machinery. She prefers the intimacy of the handwritten missive, coloured inks expressing the sender's personality. In pedestrian black, unambitious black ink, impassive black ink, she sees typed:

Lady Wilde
146 Oakley Street
London S.W.

It always jolts her to read that address, despite living in Chelsea for more than eight years. Number 2, Merrion Square, Dublin should be written on her post, not Oakley Street. Merrion Square is the Mount Parnassus of Dublin — a suitable perch for the virtuoso Wilde family. Why isn't she in bed there in her stately white house opposite the park?

She gropes through the memory fog. Gone, that's why. Sold. Grabbers have it. Shameless opportunists. Have they replaced the crimson wallpaper a-glitter with gold stars that hung in her drawing room, backdrop to her literary salons? She hopes so. She ought to have scored and torn at it with her own fingernails before consenting to move out. Those stars were intended to sparkle on insights, repartee, lines of poetry so glorious they stirred the soul — not on dreary family chitchat about whether the cream was on the turn at dinner, and if one of the servants was tippling at the spirits. In widowhood, she was left in reduced circumstances. How had that odious lawyer phrased it?

"Sir William Wilde overextended himself. He had a most unwise taste for multiple mortgages on his properties. Regrettably, he lived beyond his means."

"Paltry economies are for paltry people," she flashed back at that jumped-up clerk. Her husband was not fashioned from ordinary clay — from seam to seam, greatness coursed through him.

Even so, it would have been more convenient to be fatly and

fitly provided for, instead of finding herself obliged to sell up. She took the decision to transfer her family lock, stock and barrel to London, where the streets were paved with opportunities for her two talented boys. And, while they made their way, London's journals would be honoured to publish Speranza.

If only Oscar could have avoided late hours, champagne and friendship with that idle, aristocratic pup, Boy Douglas. When he settled down to work, he was capable of producing dialogue that pirouetted and skyrocketed. But his stellar career has crashed to earth. No matter, brilliance must out. Oscar would recover his position.

Once, she had predicted a future for Willie, too. Now, she can no longer blind herself to the truth: given the chance, he'd sponge off a pauper. Willie had ability but lacked the discipline to apply himself. She weighs him up. His thumbnail is poised to slit the envelope flap. He's puzzling out how to gain some advantage from its contents, if she's not mistaken.

Willie bares his teeth like a donkey. No, like one of the camels in London Zoo. That's what he reminds her of, with his bulging eyes and humped posture.

"Better get it over and done with, Mama. Never know. It might be good news."

Now he's scratching his scalp. Willie's hair must be longer than Oscar's these days. How she wept when they told her the prison barber had shorn him. They seek to banish beauty, these soulless people who lock up others for punishment. Don't they understand loveliness can never be destroyed? It lives on in a glance, a word, an idea.

She clears her throat and speaks at last. "Not yet, Willie. First, I must prepare myself."

"No time like the present, Mama."

Wincing, she shuts her eyes. His brother speaks in perfect epigrams, while Willie dangles clichés before her.

Willie's patience is wearing thin, taunted by a vision of a

steaming brandy punch. He must escape this claustrophobic house. He has the means, thanks to a half-sovereign stolen from Lily, jammed in his waistcoat pocket and clamouring to be spent. There'll be the devil of a row if his wife finds it missing before he leaves.

"Shall I open it?" Put us both out of our misery.

Tempted, Jane considers his offer. But what if the letter's contents disappoint? She takes it from Willie, slipping it under her pillow. Soon. She'll open it soon.

"Let me read it aloud to you."

His tone is wheedling, the way he coaxes Dorothy. Nobody can settle the baby like Willie when the humour is on him.

"Here, give it back to me and I'll do it now. I need to step out on some business, you see, and I don't like leaving you with it. Letters can be dicey things."

The old trout's cheeks are flushed. If the letter proves distressing, as he suspects it will, she might take a heart attack. The family can't afford to lose her pension.

"Run along, my boy. I'll attend to it presently. You might do me the favour of finding my smelling salts before you go. They aren't on the table."

You'd be able to spot them if you'd let us open the curtains. "Here they are, on your breakfast tray." He bends over to skim her cheek. "I'll send Lily in to you when she's finished feeding Dorothy." He retreats to the door. Fingers touching the handle, he hears her muttering, and glances back over his shoulder "What's that you say?"

"I wasn't talking to you, Willie."

"There's no one else here."

She mumbles something he can't make out.

"I distinctly heard you mention your conscience. I suppose you're going on about Oscar, as usual."

Embers from the fire of former years stir in her fine, dark eyes, inherited from an Italian great-grandfather. "I wasn't, as it happens. I was thinking about two girls. Sisters." They are the ones who weigh heaviest on her mind but she daren't say anything to Willie. He'd use them against her. "But I do need to see Oscar before I pass on."

"Oscar's reaping the consequences of his own arrogance, Mama."

She bristles with reproach. "Where's your sense of charity, Willie? Oscar was too trusting. He was undone by malice."

"Oscar was bloated with vanity and conceit. Prison will purify him."

"Purify him? It will kill him! Shame on you for dismissing your own flesh and blood. Especially in his hour of need. Let others say what they like about Oscar, his family must always defend him. The Wilde name is an *honourable* one."

Willie blinks. Why must Mama persist in speaking in italics? "Honourable? You're rewriting history, Mama. You know perfectly well our father dragged the Wilde name through the muck long before Oscar took his turn."

"How dare you!"

"How dare I speak the truth?"

A howl, rooted in outrage, gushes from her. She cannot accept the idea that she coupled her life to a man unworthy of Speranza, heroine of the Young Irelanders' movement. Her pen denounced injustice. Her ballads were sung on the streets. Her poetry fired Irishmen and women's souls. She provoked Dublin Castle into shutting down the newspaper that published her. *The Nation*'s editor was put on trial because of one of her editorials.

"Mama, I'm sorry, truly I am. I didn't mean to cause you pain." Willie approaches and pats her shoulder until her heaves subside. "There, there. Let me fetch you a handkerchief. Where are they? In the drawer?"

She flaps him away and rummages for a scrap of linen under her pillows, a dangling earring catching in her grey plait. She can't have him ferreting about. He's capable of pocketing anything that takes his eye. Mopping at her face, she gestures towards the door, and he backs away.

There are days when she itches to tell him to leave for good. Willie possesses an ace, however: his six-month-old daughter, Dorothy. She can never throw him out now that Lily and Dorothy are living under her roof. Willie possesses the knack of making other people responsible for his obligations.

Jane listens to his footsteps taking the stairs three at a time. He'll tumble and break his neck one of these days. At seventy-four, her hearing is acute. Perhaps it has been sharpened by her habit of lying in bed by candlelit: "glooming" Willie calls it. Ghosts flit among the shadows but she can live with them. She won't even agree to gaslight. It's a brutality, the way it floods people's faces.

Household sounds sail up. The maid bangs the dustbin lid in the back yard. Dorothy grizzles. Willie's voice rumbles, followed by Lily's response. Their conversation transfers to the hall. The front door slams shut. Jane supposes he is loping down the stone steps, past the iron railings.

She hopes he remembered his coat. Chills can be difficult to shake off, especially in the winter months. He will have to shoulder his family duties when she is gone. Jane knows he will have delayed to lift his hat. Willie suits a hat. Oscar does, too – exactly like their father before them. William Wilde was a man who knew how to wear a hat, rather than have the hat wear him.

She gropes for the envelope and turns it over, as if to gauge its substance by touch, like a fairground medium. The prison stamp tells her it is the response to her appeal to the governor of Reading Gaol. She wrote to him herself, despite the pain in her fingers, knotted into unlovely shapes by arthritis. Lily offered to act as her secretary but Jane insisted on making the appeal in her own hand.

Grant a dying mother this one boon, I entreat you. Her exuberant penmanship dominated the page, her letter asking that Oscar should be allowed out of prison to visit her, at home. *For an hour, a quarter-hour, five minutes – for as short a term as you decree*, she wrote. The request does not strike her as unreasonable. After all, she is dying. The governor must take this into consideration.

Willie said she was asking for the sun, moon and stars. "Oscar's a convicted felon." A vulgar observation, she felt. "Why not apply for permission to pay a prison visit to Reading? Cite mitigating circumstances, et cetera. You might have a chance of success, instead of insisting the mountain should come to Mohammed."

She tried to explain she was unfit for the journey. That she'd gasp out her last breath en route. Imagine dying in a railway carriage at Paddington Station! How would that be a fitting end for Speranza? Willie told her she was behaving like a tragedy queen. But she wasn't certain she'd make it downstairs to the street, let alone to the railway station. Willie could sneer all he liked but she was positive she'd expire in the attempt. There'd be a collapse by the ticket office, or on the platform.

A thought occurred to her. The setting was humdrum, but the circumstances had drama. A mother, crawling on her hands and knees to her ruined son's side. Dazed by the cruelty of others, numbed by her superhuman effort, she perishes from the effort. She plays with the image, savouring the note of sacrifice. On balance, she ought to stay in bed in Oakley Street. Otherwise, strangers, low people, would peer at her death throes. It didn't bear thinking about.

Boots clatter outside her door. Willie is back, short of breath. "Damn nuisance. Just been collared by a tradesman. Waved the bill for Dorothy's perambulator under my nose, in full view of the neighbours. Send it in, I told him, but he said he'd done that twice already without satisfaction. Persistent sort, raised the devil of a row. I had to tell him to wait. Be obliged if you could advance me something to settle it, Mama."

"I have nothing to give you, Willie. I'm not due another pension cheque until March."

She sees the whip of temper crack in his eyes. He doesn't believe her. But the rents from Moytura, the small estate his father bought in County Galway, have dried up, and she has long since hawked any book in her library with resale value. Her only income is £70 a year from a Civil List pension, insufficient to support all four of them. Occasional sums of money from Oscar have kept the wolf from the door but that source can hardly be counted on any longer.

"Ask Oscar," says Willie.

"Your brother is a bankrupt. And you know where he is compelled to spend his days."

Jane delivers a chilling stare, hoping to shame Willie. Her son believes himself born to a life of leisure and stamps his foot when she refuses him money. He'd be the toast of London if he bothered to work rather than cadge money. His journalism has wit and bite. But he won't knuckle down. His father would never have tolerated Willie badgering her in that uncouth manner. Then again, William ought not to have died and left her in a precarious financial position.

"Even in the clink, Oscar can raise cash," says Willie. "He knows the right sort. His friends have deep pockets. Touch him for a loan."

"I hope you are not going to prove shallow, Willie. Shallowness is a singularly unattractive vice. You are a husband and father now, with Lily and Dorothy to consider."

He hoots, as if she has cracked a capital joke. "I hope you are not going to lecture me, Mama. It's not as if you know much about the ideal husband."

"You will not mock your papa!"

"How else is one to deal with him?"

Seething, she retreats into silence.

Willie sees he has overstepped the mark, which won't get the shopkeeper off his back. "Mama, don't let's fight. Lily can't take Dorothy out for air if the perambulator is impounded. Babies need air."

The air separating them bristles.

"Go downstairs. Wait until I call you."

He does as she orders. When she is alone, she extracts one of the sovereigns from the cloth bag inside her nightgown. At this rate, there'll be nothing left to bury her. She's about to give Willie proof that an emergency stash exists, and he'll hound her for every last coin it contains.

How she resents him for reminding her that William was far from being the husband she anticipated. In her prime, she vowed never to wed, despite a flock of admirers. She reached the age of thirty, almost, before consenting to take a husband. William had such charisma and eloquence — his monkey-face cavorted with life. When he proposed, he painted an irresistible portrait of their life together. They would be an unstoppable force!

But William had a secret vice. He could not control his passion for women — lowborn females in particular. It led to certain repercussions. Shortly before their wedding day, he knelt before her as a humble petitioner and confessed all. At least, he suggested it was all but possibly it was the tip of the iceberg. He offered her the opportunity to sever their engagement. However, if she could stoop to forgive, he vowed to govern the unruly side to his nature. His weakness shamed him — with her hand in his, he'd have the strength to resist his base impulses.

Exuberant now, moist-eyed at his own eloquence, he stood up, no longer a supplicant. She should know he was determined to acknowledge his offspring. Never would he disown his three natural children. They had claims on him which he was determined to honour. She thrilled to his manliness and they embraced, renewing their pledge.

It was only later, alone, that she deliberated on his admission. The number startled her: three natural children by two different mothers. There was a son, Henry Wilson, aged thirteen — born, William explained, when the impetuosity of youth lit a blaze in him. He was twenty-three then. But how to account for the arrival of his daughters a decade later? Emily and Mary were four and two years old when he made a clean breast of his past to Jane. That liaison was relatively recent. She faltered, regrouped and decided to transcend it. William would start anew, bolstered by the purity of their union.

Yet, during their marriage, persistent rumours of other children supported by him emerged. She never condescended to confront him. Should she tax her husband with fathering a child in every village in Ireland, as some said? An intolerable conversation!

William had his faults but a generous heart. As for Jane, she wonders now if her heart has been too pinched. Lately, she is beginning to recognise a breach of faith on her part. She feels she should have gathered together all of those children, the ones born within marriage and the innocents outside that protection, and sheltered them under her wing. She could have mothered all under one roof.

However, she let herself be deterred by society's narrow definition of love. By its history of punishing those who flouted the conventions. But the natural children would have ruined her husband's medical career and led to his talent being squandered. She was ambitious for the place in society which William could achieve. For those honours he accrued as Dublin's leading eye and ear surgeon, and a respected scholar, besides – the knighthood, the title of Oculist-in-Ordinary to Queen Victoria, the awards at home and abroad.

William would have risked the wagging tongues. He'd have concocted a story about the children's origins, defying the scandalmongers. But Jane preferred them settled elsewhere, with discretion.

"Mama." A tap on the door. "May I come in now? I've been waiting rather a long time, and that peasant with his bill is still loitering on the doorstep. Mama?"

"Very well, Willie." The door opens, and she extends a plump fist, fingers closed over the sovereign.

His eyes gleam. He advances, holding out his hand, palm upwards.

With a flick of the wrist, she drops the coin into it. "That's all there is. I want a receipt."

Exhausted from the battle of wills with her son, Jane dozes, the letter still unread. But her nap is fitful, the mutilated shades of Emily and Mary Wilde troublesome to her rest. The girls were Wildes only because William's brother, the Reverend Ralph Wilde, was charitable enough to accept them as his wards and give them his name. They were not entitled to their father's name. While they lived, she ought to have spoken up on their behalf. The sisters were entitled to a place in the world. Who better than her to make the case for them? She championed other women's rights – women she had no connection with, other than shared gender. Why was she silent about Emily and Mary?

William made space in his life for his eldest son. Henry Wilson – how William chortled over that flaunting pun on 'Wilde's son' – was passed off as a nephew. Educated to a high standard, he worked as a doctor alongside his father at St Mark's, the hospital founded by William. The daughters, however, were tucked out of sight.

Right was done by them – up to a point. The Reverend Ralph served as rector in Drumsnat, a remote part of north County Monaghan, and they lived in purdah with him. William used to visit now and again – she pretended it was brotherly affection alone which sent him northwards occasionally to Monaghan – and she knew from a hint let slip by the Reverend Ralph let slip that he visualised doing something for the sisters when they grew up. But he never did. Perhaps she ought to have encouraged it. If she had, it might have averted that horrifying fate crouching in wait for those girls.

All three of those natural children are dead now, and one of hers besides. Henry died the year after William. She isn't troubled by thoughts of him. He was helped to make his way in the world. Gone, too, is Jane and William's radiant daughter, Isola – the pet of the household. A fever stole away their sunbeam almost thirty years ago. Oscar remembers her with fondness. But Willie snarled when she suggested Dorothy ought to take his sister's name.

Isola no longer tugs at Jane's peace of mind. She presumes Isola is at rest, unlike her daughter's half-sisters. Yes, her half-sisters. Emily and Mary Wilde were close kin to Isola, and it took a tragedy before Jane was prepared to admit the connection. For every minute of her nine years, Isola was cherished, but her sisters were treated by a different standard. After Emily and Mary's deaths, recognition of the injustice done to them seeped through her consciousness, like a patch of spilled water, and she was unable to blot it out.

She wakens with a jolt, imagining herself in Dublin. "'Ave an 'art, mum, that ain't Christian and it ain't nice." A snatch of speech swimming in from the street puts her straight. One of her back teeth throbs.

After Isola's death, she should have channelled her grief in a positive direction, inviting her little sprite's sisters into their home. If they had lived with her and William in Merrion Square, they would have avoided that grotesque end. Jane shudders. Their ghosts must be disfigured. Are they vengeful?

Perhaps they wait by the Seat of Judgment, primed to challenge her. When she's called to answer for her life, they'll step forward and confront her about her sin of omission. Out of sight, out of mind: that was her attitude to the girls. Except, after their deaths, they took up residence in her mind and she has never been able to eject them. Even now, they hover in the shadows, watching her with reproachful eyes. In their death throes, Emily and Mary must have ill-wished their respectable Wilde relatives. A dying person's curse is a powerful one. No wonder the family is jinxed, losing their home, Oscar doing hard labour, Willie drinking himself into the grave.

1871

"William, my dear, you look ghastly. What's the matter?"

His face was puffy. He dropped onto the sofa beside her,

covering his face with his hands. To her alarm, she saw they were trembling. Above all else, a surgeon cannot have shaky hands.

"William, you're frightening me! What is it? You said you had to go to Monaghan. Is it bad news?"

From behind his hands, a low moan oozed out. "It's Emily and Mary. There's been a dreadful accident. They caught fire. They're in agony." He uncovered his face, misery, horror and guilt chasing across it. "Their screams, Jane, their screams are ringing in my ears!"

She held his hands in hers. "I don't understand. What caused the accident? Is Reverend Ralph injured?" William shook his head. "And the girls, are they terribly hurt, dearest?"

"Their lives are hanging by a thread. But even if they survive their burns, they'll be maimed beyond recognition. I didn't know them, Jane. They're bandaged from head to toe. Their hair was scorched to cinders – eyelashes, eyebrows gone."

She recoiled but he didn't notice.

"I couldn't save Isola five years ago. I can't help Em and Mimi now. And I call myself a doctor!"

"Can nothing be done for them, William?"

"I have to see a patient in the morning. But I'll cancel the rest of my appointments. Tomorrow afternoon, I'm going back to Mongahan. I can't cure them but I can give them chloroform. That's one thing I'm qualified to do." Sweat sleeked his face. "My girls! My small-little Em and Mimi! They don't deserve such punishment. When the chloroform wears off, they writhe in pain. Having their dressings changed is agony for them."

It seemed to Jane that Isola, grave and attentive, sat beside her while William spoke. She nerved herself to keep listening.

"Start at the beginning, dearest. Tell me what happened."

"There was a Hallowe'en Night dance at a neighbour's house. Emily and Mary were invited, they were dizzy with anticipation. Ralph agreed to escort them. He's a better man than me. Drinks nothing but water – no stimulants. 'Water's only good for shaving in,' I'd sometimes tease, to get a rise out of him. But he never obliges me. I can't say a word against my brother: he loves those girls. He'd prefer to have given the dance a miss, citing his clergyman's collar. He has no taste for frolics. But he went for their sake. He knew how rarely such excitements figure in Em and Mimi's lives."

Jane blushed.

"Ralph said they were ready hours before it was time to leave. They helped one another to dress, curling their hair, tying on ribbons and titivating themselves. When they were satisfied, they skipped downstairs and twirled for him to admire their finery – which my brother did, right gladly.

The gathering was in Drumaconnor House – that's a small manor house about two miles from Smithborough village. The girls were the belles of the ball, partnered at every dance. During the interval, they ate a hearty supper. They were in prodigious high spirits – everyone's agreed on it.

When Ralph decided it was time to leave, the pair of minxes begged him, with their pretty ways, for permission to stay longer. He was reluctant. But their host overheard the conversation and Mr Andrew Reed promised personally to convey the young ladies home after the dance. And so, satisfied they were left in safe hands, my brother went away without them. You can imagine the torments he's going through now.

Mr Reed could not quit his own party until the final guest had departed, and consequently the girls would be the last to leave. They assured him it was no hardship – they wanted the evening never to end. When he bowed out the last couple, Mr Reed ordered his carriage. On an impulse, he invited Miss Emily to take a final turn on the dance floor. And would Miss Mary be kind enough to accompany them on the piano?

The sitting room was cleared of furniture for the gathering but it was not a large space. As they danced past the fireplace, a spark landed on some decoration dangling from Em's gown, and in an instant her crinoline caught fire. Her cries sent Mimi rushing to help. A flame leapt from Em's clothing to her sister's. Now, both were alight.

Their host didn't knew which one to help first. Em appeared to be the neediest case. He tore off his coat and wrapped her in it, to extinguish the flames. Meanwhile, poor Mimi was left to fend for herself, and ran about shrieking until she collapsed with shock.

Mr Reed picked up Em and carried her outside. Snow had fallen during the dance, and he rolled her in it, hoping to alleviate her burns. All the while, he was yelling for his servants, frantic because Mimi needed attention. But things were slack because of the dance. Drink had been taken in the kitchen. And that loyal little girl was left to suffer – for how long, I can't establish. It rips the heart out of me! Surely, somebody must have taken pity on her?"

William groaned, the whites of his eyes rolling up. Jane kneaded his shoulder, silent for fear of interrupting his account.

"By the time a message reached me, several days had elapsed. As you know, I set out for Monaghan at once. They cannot be moved from Drumaconnor House and are being cared for there. A local doctor is doing his best for them. I don't suppose anybody could do more. But their injuries are gruesome. I forced myself to examine them. All over their bodies, their beautiful faces, the skin has melted away, laying bare the flesh beneath. The lightest touch is torture to them. All I can do is ensure heavy sedation. When they wake up, they seem to relive the horror because their cries tear the air. They howl incessantly! I can't get the sounds out of my head." He rooted through an inner pocket for a hipflask, and gulped the dregs left in it. "The best we can hope for is the mercy of a swift end."

That blessing was not granted. Mary died eight days after the dance, while Emily lingered for three weeks before joining her sister in the grave. They were aged twenty-four and twenty-two. Reverend Ralph Wilde conducted the funeral service. Afterwards, out of compassion, his superiors transferred him to a parish in another county.

The calamity changed William – left him shrunken in size. He retreated to Moytura, finding some solace in Lough Corrib's solitude. As for Jane, she tried to forget about those girls, and whether she had any responsibility for them. But there were nights when she lay awake, and other nights when she startled out of sleep. Not haunted – she couldn't make that claim. But her sense of knowing right from wrong was undermined.

She is uncertain whether Oscar and Willie are alert to the circumstances surrounding the double accident. She never broached the subject. Perhaps they are aware of next to nothing. If he was familiar with the details, Willie would be incapable of holding his tongue. He would use them as weapons against Jane, accuse her of complicity with the great Sir William Wilde, whose influence hushed up the deaths. No inquest was held – his name was kept out of the newspapers.

Jane counts on her fingers. Emily and Mary would be forty-nine and forty-seven if they had lived. They might be mothers themselves. Once, William visited the girls' grave and indulged in an orgy of weeping, mirroring his behaviour after Isola's death. She learned about it from Emily and Mary's mother. Yes, she met her, it must have been four or five years after the tragedy.

As William's life ebbed away, he asked to see the girls' mother. "I know I trespass on your affection," he managed to gasp out.

Jane hesitated for the space of a heartbeat, before deciding it would be a cruelty to refuse him. Let other women squeeze morality into shapes they were comfortable with – Speranza was above such narrowness, she reminded herself.

From behind a raised curtain fold, Jane watched her arrival. Veiled in black, the woman descended from the Wildes' carriage. Jane had sent it, thinking it appropriate to extend that courtesy. The woman, who called herself Mrs Carmody, stood looking at Number 2, Merrion Square, making no effort to ring the doorbell. As Jane peered down, trying to decipher her response, she debated sending one of the household staff to invite her in. Perhaps she was overawed?

On second thoughts, while Mrs Carmody's face was

unreadable behind the veil, her demeanour didn't suggest someone who was intimidated. She glanced towards the carriage, as though inclined to climb back in. Jane's heart sank. The woman was resentful, and disinclined to go through with it. On balance, she had every right. Jane chewed her lip while she waited. She should neither pressurise nor persuade – Mrs Carmody must be allowed to decide for herself.

Two doors up, a dog darted out and disappeared into the park. Mrs Carmody watched its progress. With marked reluctance, she transferred her eyes to the Wildes' house. Leisurely, she smoothed down her dress. Then she raised her chin and advanced towards the front door.

Jane had given instructions for her to be led upstairs to William's room. She intercepted her on the landing outside and introduced herself. It was immediately clear to her that Mrs Carmody was not from a genteel station in life. Nevertheless, she was dignified. Jane accompanied her into William's bedroom and told the nurse to go for tea.

As soon as the door closed behind her, Jane touched her husband's hand. "Mrs Carmody is here to see you, William, my dear."

His deep-set, watery eyes swivelled towards Mrs Carmody, standing behind Jane. She raised her veil, tucking it back, and stepped past Jane. His reaction was instantaneous. Animation flashed across his face. Feeling surplus to requirements, Jane left them alone together without another word.

On the floor below, in the salon with its star-spangled wallpaper, Jane waited – intending to invite the visitor to take tea before she was conveyed home. She tried to read some verses but her mind kept wandering to what the two of them might be discussing. Their daughters, she presumed. Those girls had never set foot in the house on Merrion Square but there was no doubting their presence at William's bedside.

A knock on the door, and Mrs Carmody stood there. She was handsome. Not unlike Jane, as it happened.

"Do come in, Mrs Carmody."

Mrs Carmody advanced into the salon. A huff of expelled air, quickly suppressed, registered her surprise at the drawn curtains and blazing candelabra.

"I believe daylight extinguishes conversation, which is a passion of mine." Jane offered her a seat, rang for tea, adjusted her skirts, and prepared for a tête-à-tête. "My husband was particularly anxious to see you."

"He's failed, poor gentleman. He was sleeping when I left him. But he seemed more settled. I'll remember him in my prayers."

"How kind. I hope you were able to set his mind at rest?"

"I did my best, milady. He couldn't talk much. On account of his illness, I dare say. But his eyes said what was needful."

Jane reflected. Once, William used to bubble with plans and schemes – ideas broke from him with all the joyful abandon of waves against the shoreline. But silence had settled on him long before he became bedbound.

Tea arrived, putting paid to confidences while the parlour maid was in the room. The visitor kept on her gloves and declined both bread and butter and a slice of cake. She accepted a cup of tea and sipped it with restraint. A most refined person, despite her accent, which couldn't disguise her origins. Jane knew she was a shopkeeper who dealt in black oak, presumably set up in business by William.

Mrs Carmody looked for somewhere to place her cup and saucer, and Jane indicated a side table with a gracious sweep of the hand.

"Sir William managed to say your name. I felt it was the right thing to do, sending for you, Mrs Carmody."

"He was always very good to me, milady. A proper gentleman." She gathered herself, as though in preparation for departure.

Jane took a deep breath. "May I offer my condolences on the loss of your daughters?"

"Thank you, milady." Her ramrod posture slackened. "I didn't know them well. You see, I wanted them to grow up to be ladies. It meant I couldn't be a mother to them."

Stricken, Jane searched for a response. "I lost a daughter, too."

"I'm sorry, milady."

"Isola."

"Yes."

Silence pooled.

"A mother never forgets," suggested Jane.

"No, milady. At least now I can visit them. Every November, I go to Monaghan and put a wreath on the grave to mark the anniversary."

"Do you make the pilgrimage ... alone?"

Mrs Carmody gleaned her meaning at once. "Yes, milady. Always on my own. I catch the first train in the morning to Monaghan town, and hire a hackney to take me to Drumsnat. The driver waits, no matter how long I am, and keeps an eye on the time for my train back. Some years, the weather cuts things short – there's not much shelter thereabouts. But I wrap up warm and do my best by the girls. I talk to them, tell them my news, tidy away any leaves blown onto their grave. And I never go away without giving the headstone a good scrub – I bring what's needed with me. Sir William put up a fine stone. He never did things by halves. '*They were lovely and pleasant in their lives and in their death they were not divided*.' That's what it says."

"He told me the Reverend Ralph Wilde proposed it. A verse from the Book of Samuel, I believe."

"I like to read it there, milady. In their death they were not divided. There's comfort in it."

Jane crumples the letter from Reading between her hands. William had charm. Oh, charm by the gallon. Even the woman he wronged wouldn't utter a word against him. But Jane could not deny her husband had an ungallant side, and Willie inherited it. Conscious of its taint, she watched out for it in Oscar. That's why, although there had been time to make his escape to the Continent, she goaded him to recklessness. "If you go to prison you will still be my son," she warned him. "But if you turn tail you are no gentleman."

Lady Queensberry told Jane she was a fool and wasted no time in arranging for her son to set sail for France. Instead of prison, Oscar could be in Paris – with, or preferably without, Lord Alfred Douglas. Hard labour! What they're doing to her son is primitive!

She is what the marchioness called her – she cannot deny it. She spoke out when she should have been silent, and was silent when she should have spoken. No wonder she sees Emily and Mary's faces wavering in and out of focus between the guttering candles.

"I'm sorry!" she cries. "I only did what most women in my position would have done."

Except Speranza has always prided herself on being different.

A tap on her door, and Lily hooks her head round it. "Would you like me to bring in Baby? She's full of smiles today."

Jane fastens distraught eyes on her. With an effort, she composes herself. "Do."

She is too weak to dandle her only granddaughter, as she did Oscar's boys. But she likes to watch Dorothy, who is the image of Willie and Oscar. Jane misses her grandsons, who have been sent away to shield them from the scandal.

When Lily's eyes adjust to the dim light, she notices how sadness has settled into the lines on Jane's face. She must be having a bad day.

"Once the weather is warmer, we'll tuck Dorothy up in her perambulator, and the three of us can stroll across the Albert Bridge as far as Battersea Park," she suggests. "The fresh air will do you a world of good. We can find your veil, if you like. Though the air would be beneficial to your face."

On the last occasions when she ventured out, Jane draped a close-fitting white gauze veil, doubled over, across her features.

"Her Mary Queen of Scots incarnation, pacing to the scaffold," according to Willie. He has a wicked tongue that makes Lily laugh. "Half the people used to go to her literary salons for the pleasure of tittering at her costumes," he claimed. "There was one outfit you could have sold tickets for: three parts Celtic druidess to one part music-hall performer, with a dash of opera diva for good measure."

Speranza's salons belong to the past. The present is threadbare.

Lily dandles Dorothy on her lap. "*I am His Highness' dog at Kew — Pray tell me, sir, whose dog are you?*" It rarely fails to make her daughter clap and her mother-in-law smile.

This time, however, Jane's face is sealed off, expressionless. A death mask, thinks Lily. "Time for Miss Dorothy Wilde to go down for her nap. Wave to Grandmama, Dorothy."

Jane waggles her fingers at the baby, who gurgles and flaps a starfish hand.

When she's alone, Jane decides it's time to read her letter. Sliding her spectacles onto her nose, she opens the envelope, and scans the typed sheet. It is signed at the foot of the page by the governor, Henry B. Isaacson.

I regret … not possible … interference with prison routine.

The blood slows in Jane's veins. Outside, a seagull squawks. A cart rattles past. From the Thames, the muffled horn of a barge drones. She turns her face to the wall.

Mr Isaacson must have a heart of stone to reject a dying mother's request. They warned her he was a mulberry-faced dictator. Yet she convinced herself he would yield to the intensity of her desire.

There is nothing left for her now. Even Speranza cannot hold on to hope. A rustle as the note drops from her hand. Let it lie on the floor, the ungenerous letter. She will not trouble to read it again – the rejection is an insult to motherhood. Does Mr Isaacson have a mother? He does not deserve one.

The hypocrisy of the present age is intolerable! Respectability is for tradespeople – the Wildes need have no truck with it. If Oscar has done what they say he has, how was anyone injured by it? Beauty alone, beauty always, beauty forever – that's his ideal.

A draft of air causes her candles to waver. She watches the flames flicker and right themselves, a face appearing in each. Emily and Mary. Who else? They are her constant companions. It might be that they are simply waiting. As she is.

Soon, her life force will be snuffed out. Jane welcomes the prospect. She feels herself drain away, as though her body is a cracked cup no longer capable of containing her. But in death she can accomplish what she cannot in life.

Her love for her son will penetrate his prison cell. Neither guards on gates nor locks on doors will separate her from him. The flesh that anchors her to earth will dissolve and she will become ethereal – able to waft through keyholes to where he waits for her. She will find a way to be with him, for a time, and he will know it.

Then, she must travel on to face Emily and Mary, an encounter she knows she cannot evade. Nor does she want to: she's ready to meet them now.

Oscar Wilde spoke of seeing his mother in his cell after her death, wearing travelling clothes. He invited Jane to sit down and remove her wraps but she shook her head sorrowfully before vanishing.

Oscar paid her funeral expenses. Willie Wilde was broke.

ANNA PARNELL

Born Avondale House, County Wicklow, 1852; died; Devon, England 1911

Leader of the Ladies' Land League, activist, journalist

Anna Parnell was leader of the ground-breaking Ladies' Land League (1880-82), which made an enormous impact in its own right, and acted as a forerunner to influential groups such as Inghinidhe na hÉireann and Cumann na mBan.

It was formed during Ireland's Land War to continue the work of the all-male Land League when the men were imprisoned, including Anna's older brother Charles Stewart Parnell. However, the female organisation proved to be more radical. It used funds raised in the US to build shelters for homeless families, feed Land League prisoners and support their families. Anna ran the Ladies' Land League with skill, speaking before large public gatherings, devising tactics to subvert unjust laws and occupying a highly visible role at a time when women were expected to restrict themselves to the domestic sphere.

After it was disbanded, disenchanted by Ireland's nationalist men, she moved to England where she lived under an assumed name, Cerisa Palmer. She spent her time painting and writing, and drowned while bathing in rough seas off the Devon coast. Her funeral in Ilfracombe was attended by only a scattering of mourners and none of her former comrades or relatives.

However, her account of the Ladies' Land League days, *The Tale of a Great Sham* – turned down by publishers during her lifetime and subsequently lost – resurfaced and was published some seventy-five years after her death.

In 2018, a ceremony was held at her graveside, attended by representatives of Ireland's government in recognition of her contribution to Irish life.

Somebody

The street door triggered the pawnbroker's bell. Glancing up from an inspection of his inventory, the shopkeeper saw a woman, respectable in black, reverse into his shop. She was shaking drops of rain from an umbrella onto the pavement outside. When the door closed and she turned towards him, he was disappointed to realise she was nudging middle-age – with her slender frame, he had taken her for someone younger.

The customer jammed the umbrella into a nook beside the doorframe and approached the counter, where she placed a brown-paper package for his inspection. She closed one gloved hand over the other, rested them on her midriff, and looked him full in the face. Usually, his female patrons had an unobtrusive air, if not downright apologetic. But there was nothing submissive in her stance.

She was birdlike in her delicacy, the remnants of beauty clinging to her. What struck him particularly, however, was the intensity of expression in her hazel eyes – they communicated intelligence, candour and pain. He had to look away.

The shop owner cleared his throat, preparing to speak, but she took the initiative.

"Good morning. I have some belongings to offer you as pledges. Perhaps you'd be kind enough to name a price."

"Certainly, ma'am."

He extended one hand, palm outward, inviting her to open the package.

There was a degree of predictability as regards what his customers bartered. Clocks and watches. Some silverware. The odd painting. What treasures was she ready to part with? A piece of heirloom jewellery, perhaps, or a porcelain ornament passed through the generations? He was a sound judge of character. He had to be, with the number of pickpockets who turned up, trying to offload what they pinched. This punter was genteel.

Stiff-fingered from the cold, she fumbled at the string. He knew better than to offer help. The knot mastered, she peeled back the wrapping to reveal her valuables.

Blow me! He'd guessed wrong. Clothing lay in a folded pile. Granted, there was a market for a bit of quality stuff, provided it was kosher – not supplied by a washerwoman thieving on the side. But you wouldn't expect a lady to sell her cast-offs. Ladies had maids entitled to hand-me-downs. His customer's voice hinted at time spent leaning over the embroidery frame, or practising dance steps, piano scales, elocution – that la-di-da thing his missus talked about for their daughters, the ornamental graces.

He studied her for clues about her circumstances. Her hat was plain, and in the style of several seasons ago. Even a fashion numbskull like him could see that. Her face wore the nip of hunger – there it was, by the nostrils. No disguising it. Even so, she carried herself with the assurance of inherited privilege. He had met his fair share of the quality, after a lifetime in the pawn game – the quality could get tripped up by debt, same as anyone. They possessed something that could not be sold or copied, however. It was bred into them.

Lifting the top article, he shook it out. A smell of lavender floated from the black silk dress. His fingertips travelled across the material assessing its quality. Automatically, he checked for damage, finding a rent near the hem mended with minute stitches.

She flushed. "I caught my heel. I like to go walking. I grew up in the countryside, in Ireland, and formed the habit there. The exercise helps me to think. But my clothes suffer by it."

"Still a nice piece of cloth," he reassured her. "Or it was, in its day." It didn't do to admire a customer's belongings. Always express some reluctance to take their goods – that was his policy.

A winter coat lay beneath the gown, also showing signs of wear, along with a waist-length velvet jacket, and a shawl embroidered in green thread with spindly leaves. All were black, the cut and tailoring excellent. His customer had class.

He flicked his eyes over her left hand. Bare. He'd have staked bees and honey on her being a widow. He must be losing his touch. A spinster lady, then.

"Leaving off your mourning weeds, ma'am? Too much black can dampen the spirits."

"Gaudy colours have never been to my taste. These items are surplus to my requirements."

He reverted to business. "Two sovereigns for the lot. That's what they're worth to me, ma'am."

She caught her lower lip under her teeth. "I had counted on more." Her answer was quiet but it acted as a rebuke.

His line of work left little room for a soft heart – it was a luxury he couldn't afford with a missus and twin daughters to feed and clothe. But this customer moved him. He did not desire her – she was too bony for his liking, inclined to haughtiness besides. All the same, she had something which insisted on a response from him. Courage, if he had to put a name to it.

"Two sovereigns, plus a crown for luck. That's my final offer. Take it or leave it."

Exhaling, she lowered her eyes. "Needs must when the devil drives. I'll take it."

Now, why did she want to go and spoil everything by bringing the devil into it? It wasn't proper. Vexed, he reached for a pawn ticket from a drawer in the counter. Staking her claim as a woman of the world, that's what she was doing. He disapproved of members of her sex operating outside the home – they ought to be sheltered by their male relatives.

He licked a pencil stub. "Name?"

"Anna Parnell."

Parnell. It had a familiar ring. He'd heard it before, and in dubious circumstances. "How do you spell it?"

As she dictated the letters, he chased down the memory shadows. Parnell. Not many of them to the pound. A divorce case last year, that was it. Parnell was named by the injured party, the husband. Shocking business. The newspapers had a field day with it. And the music hall comedians, afterwards. Plenty of nudge-nudge, wink-wink.

Charles Stewart Parnell, that's who he was – leader of the Irish mob in the House of Commons. For years he'd been bedding the wife of one of his own MPs. Secret assignations under assumed names. Servants' evidence about the doorbell ringing and Parnell hopping through a window just ahead of the husband. Straight out of a farce, it was. Fellow was an out-and-out bounder. Typical hypocrisy from that lot in Westminster: laid down the law for others and behaved how they liked themselves.

He stole a glance at the bone-white composure of the woman opposite. She mentioned growing up in Ireland. Was she related to that Parnell? Could be. He was landed gentry and she behaved like a blue blood with her touch-me-not air. But she had nothing to be superior about if she was one of his breed.

Captain Something, wasn't he, the husband? Belonged to the

same party as Parnell, the Irish Whatsits. Must have been a military man before he took up politics. Bet he was sorry he hadn't stayed with the regiment. Sordid business, politics. Parnell. Yes, he had a picture of him now in his mind. Tall chap, bearded. Sombre. Image of the Beak who fined him and threatened he'd do time if he caught him fencing any more stolen goods, back when he was starting out in this line. Holier-than-thou types always got his goat. He remembered seeing top-hatted Parnell toys sold after the court case, complete with tiny fire escapes – for quick getaways from compromising situations.

A spike of voyeurism poked at the pawnshop owner, who surrendered to it. "Parnell. Isn't there an Irish politician by that name?"

"Yes." Her expression betrayed nothing.

He persevered. "I suppose you know him, being Irish yourself?"

"Once. Long ago. Not now." The tone was chilly.

His better nature reasserted itself, and he tried to make amends. "Ireland. Supposed to be full of scenery. Lakes, mountains, and what not."

"There is no justice in Ireland. That's all you need to know about it. My money, if you please. I have other business to attend to this morning."

He shrugged, belonging to a school which believed a woman could be as imperious as she liked, provided she took the precaution to be a looker. Fumbling in a leather pouch, he clinked out two gold sovereigns and five silver shillings, and handed them over with the pawn ticket. It gave customers a year plus one week to reclaim any goods pledged, upon repayment of the loan plus interest – the latter mounting monthly until it reached twenty per cent.

A curt nod and she left in a rustle of skirts.

He felt chastened. She wasn't the first lady with a cad in her family, nor would she be the last. He stroked the pashmina, visualising it draped across her shoulders by candlelight. Yes, candlelight would relax the pinched nostrils and leave a trail of gold sparks across her hair.

You'd never know she was putting her clothes in hock to make ends meet. Surely a person of her refinement could find work as a governess, or a lady's maid at a push? It seemed a pity there wasn't a brother or an in-law to take her in. Mind you, if Parnell was part of her tribe, no wonder she was in a pawnshop. It was a crying shame to see someone like her reduced to trading her winter coat. And that was another thing. Today was the sixteenth of October, she'd need to put it to use soon.

You've enough on your plate, he told himself. Can't go worrying about strangers.

He'd given her a fair price for her bits and bobs. He was almost certain she wouldn't return to redeem the pledge – he had a nose for it. His gaze landed on her umbrella, puddling in the corner. She mustn't lose that after pawning her winter coat.

Rueful about mentioning the scandal, he tried to make amends. Snatching up the umbrella, he ran out to the street, scanned left and right, and saw her standing in front of the grocer's six doors down on the Bethnal Green Road.

The pawnbroker thought about calling to her, before deciding it wouldn't be right to accost a lady in that way. He hurried after her.

"Your property, ma'am. The rain's stopped but I expect you'll want this again soon enough." Uncharacteristically chivalrous, he bowed.

Gravely, she accepted the umbrella. "Thank you."

He wouldn't call it a smile, exactly, that she gave him but her lips curved into something conveying grace. With a spring in his step, he returned to his shop. He hoped she'd buy something in that grocer's with his sovereigns to put ginger into her – she looked half-starved.

It was only when he was back behind the counter that he realised the chance he had taken by leaving it unattended, something he had never done before. "Blimey! What a cabbage!" He slapped his hand to his head. A tealeaf could easily have helped himself and legged it while he was behaving like an addled youth of one-and-twenty. A quick skim of the shop's contents. No gaps, as far he could tell. Clocks ticking and chiming, bric-a-brac doing whatever it was meant to — look decorative, he supposed. No shattered glass where he kept the jewellery under lock and key.

"Who was you talking to?" called his wife's voice, from upstairs. "I saw you through the window."

"Nobody," he shouted back.

The pawnbroker's coins fattening her purse convinced Anna to enter the grocer's for a quarter of coffee. She refused to accept pre-ground coffee, despite the pimply assistant's assurance about having prepared the beans personally only half an hour earlier. At her insistence, he ground a quantity of beans afresh. Further up the street, near the Shoreditch junction, she bought two bagels hot from the oven at a Jewish bakery. The smell was heavenly and it required willpower not to eat one of them on the move. "Breeding, Anna," she reminded herself, forcing her feet to continue along Great Eastern Street.

St Paul's Cathedral lay ahead. She must paint it someday. Perhaps at twilight in a misty glow, gaslight and fog combining for an ethereal effect. It wouldn't happen during this visit. She was already anxious to return to Cornwall. A group of artists had clustered round the village where she boarded, among whom she felt a sense of community. Mrs Tregaskis, her landlady — a fisherman's widow — was a decent sort. She was storing Anna's belongings in the attic at no extra charge.

Imagine if she was on her way to Paddington Station now to catch the Penzance train, followed by a cart ride onwards to Marazion. She could breathe its crisp, salty air, instead of this soupy concoction assaulting her lungs, and take her sketchpad outdoors to be inspired by the clarity of the Cornish light. It couldn't match Wicklow's wooded hills and coastline but it mitigated the misery of exile.

Thinking of Ireland, a pain swiped at the small of her back, causing her footsteps to falter. Her banishment was self-imposed, but the ache took no account of that. She had nowhere to go in Ireland. Friends would lend or rent her a room, but she refused to be a lodger in her own country. Avondale was no longer her home. Charley was master there, although he spent hardly any time on the estate. The Palace of Westminster was the great Charles Stewart Parnell's natural habitat. What free time he had was spent in south-east London, in Eltham, with Mrs O'Shea. Mrs Parnell, she should learn to call her – they were married in June, according to her mother.

Her brother had sent word to her that she was welcome to live at Avondale, where Mama and Emily made their home with Emily's young daughter. Lord High and Mighty, dispensing his charity. She'd felt a rush of blood to the head when their widowed sister had delivered the message.

"Anna, I'm only the messenger. You look ready to snatch up a whip and drive out the money changers from the temple!" Emily complained.

"Tell Charley I'd prefer to starve than accept anything from him." While she had breath in her body she'd never forgive his public humiliation of her.

"You'd be company for Mama and me," said Emily. "And, you know, Mama can be a handful. I don't see why I should have all the responsibility."

"I'll never live under his roof again."

"But he's never there. And he means it kindly, Anna. Honour bright."

Anna shrugged, her face settling into those mulish lines that provoked Emily. Really, she revelled in her obstinacy.

Stung, Emily added, "He said if you refuse him you're a fool."

"Then I will persist in my foolishness."

A click of the tongue. "Anna, I never knew anyone more exasperating! You'll grind yourself to pieces. Besides, you're entitled to his help. He's head of the family – John doesn't count. So Charley's responsible for you. He has to make sure you're decently housed."

"Don't you dare say that! I am answerable to no one and entirely responsible for myself. I refuse to be treated as a burden on a male relative. While I have breath in my body I'll make my own way in the world."

"Well, I have a ten-year-old child to consider. I'm glad of Avondale."

"Your circumstances are different," Anna allowed. Emily had married a waster. Hardly surprising, considering how many unlucky alliances there were in the family. She had no intention of throwing in her lot with any man, whether husband or brother. Charley, in particular, she intended avoiding like poison.

"Men must work and women must weep," shrugged Emily, as though that settled the matter.

Really, thought Anna, Emily was the limit. There was more to life than accepting the status quo, resigning yourself to leaving visiting cards and making tasteful arrangements of flowers. How was it possible that women didn't boil with rage on their deathbeds, recognising the waste?

It was difficult to credit that she and Emily shared the same parents. Fanny would have understood the principles that were Anna's guiding star. She was always her favourite sister, cut from the same cloth – they complemented one another. The two had planned to live together as companions, sharing living expenses. But Fanny was buried in Massachusetts. Anna wore a lock of her hair in a locket tied by a yellow ribbon at her neck.

Old Street underground station was behind her, not far to go now. Her feet were on City Road. That pawnshop owner had recognised the name. She supposed he must have gorged on the lurid details in scandal sheets. Charley had tarnished the family with his public misconduct but he hadn't a grain of repentance in him. All he cared about was having his own way. Pigheadedness forever at war with his better nature, that was Charley. "Like two peas in a pod, the pair of you, Anna," their mother often said. Trust Mama. Delia Parnell was outspoken, one of her American traits. The Parnells tended to guard their tongues, on the whole. Well, maybe not Anna. Sometimes she had to let fly.

Anna would have to consider changing her name. She couldn't risk another bout of insolence such as that pawnshop man had subjected her to. At least he didn't come right out and say it, like the last person who put two and two together. *Is the adulterer your brother?*

Charley's ungovernable passion had split the Irish Parliamentary Party. Typical of him, plotting to have it both ways. He had a ruthless streak. She'd seen that clearly when he tried to turn her brave, resourceful, true-hearted girls in the Ladies' Land League into a bevy of handmaidens. Making a great sham of all their hard work.

She'd halted his gallop there. She wasn't having the Land League men dictate to her girls and use them, meanwhile belittling all they'd achieved. Dismissing their efforts on behalf of evicted tenants, and Land Leaguers in prison, and their destitute families. For no other reason than because the men were humiliated by taunts about hiding behind petticoats. "*Descending to, or condescending to*" female leadership, according to one editorial.

She turned right into Shepherdess Walk – you could count the shepherdesses in London on the fingers of one hand, and still have fingers to spare, she thought, tickled by the street sign – and zigzagged until she arrived at her destination. It was a terrace of redbricks that looked glued together, running parallel with City Road. By the railings at Number 24, she fished out a latch key to enter her lodgings. It was a mean house, worn out from use – its walls seemed ready to cave in from sheer exhaustion. Still, it was home. For the present.

Two flights of stairs and she'd be inside her room, boiling the kettle for coffee on her spirit lamp, using fresh coffee instead of last night's soggy remains. She'd been prodigal and bought a pack of ten pre-rolled cigarettes, too. Smoking in the evening was a treat which relaxed her. Lately, she had been trying to cut back on unnecessary expenses but London was stressful.

A bulky form materialised in the hallway. "Miss Parnell, you're behind with the rent. It ain't good enough. I can let that room ten times over to lodgers as'll pay their way."

Faint with hunger, Anna had hoped to break her fast before dealing with her landlady. Annoyance lent her strength, however. "Mrs Jenkins, my willingness to honour obligations is never in doubt. I have the funds here on my person. Kindly follow me upstairs so we don't hand money backwards and forwards in public like cattle dealers."

Mrs Jenkins sniffed. Lady or no, she was in arrears, and Mrs Jenkins's family were the losers by it. The butcher was palming off scraggy ends of meat on her because she couldn't meet his bill until Miss Parnell paid up. Her Ron said if she gave him tripe for his dinner once more he'd send the plate flying through the kitchen window. Seething, Mrs Jenkins clumped upstairs after her lodger. Typical of those high-and-mighties to put you on the back foot when they were the ones in the wrong.

Anna Parnell opened her bedroom door with a second key and stood aside so that Mrs Jenkins could precede her into the narrow attic room running the length of the house. It was as naked as a winter's garden – nothing but a single bed, a table and chair, and a bockety wardrobe.

"What's that pong?" demanded Mrs Jenkins. "Smells foreign in here."

Anna summoned up her most patrician tone. "Coffee, I believe. I find the aroma pleasing, personally." She laid her shopping on the table and produced her purse. "Now, Mrs Jenkins, let me settle up with you."

The landlady pursed her lips, wiped a hand on her apron, and held it out.

Anna took out a half-sovereign with Victoria's left-facing profile on it. It was a youthful portrait of the Queen, her hair in a loose, Romanesque bun that made her look girlish, although Victoria was seventy-two years of age now. People said she was indestructible, sure to outlast the century. Anna turned the Queen-Empress face down on her landlady's palm. "Paid in full, Mrs Jenkins. With some change due to me, I believe."

"I'll send one of the youngsters up with it. Them stairs is too steep for me to keep trotting up and down." Gritting her teeth, she added, "I'm sure I hope as how I didn't give you no offence. I always knew you was good for the rent, Miss Parnell."

"I'm grateful for the vote of confidence. And now, if you'll excuse me, I find I need to rest. Perhaps those stairs are taxing my strength, too."

"Will you want the room for much longer?"

"One more week, I think. I'll let you know by Friday."

When she was alone, weariness crashed over Anna. It blotted out the willpower which kept her upright and she tottered. Her elbow hit the portable gas burner, knocking it over. She would have fallen if she hadn't clung to the rim of the table for support. "Breathe, Anna," she reminded herself, and by and by regained her balance. She let go of the table, unbuttoned her jacket and hung it in the wardrobe. Next, she righted the toppled stove. There were matches on an improvised shelf formed by the roof timbers in the ceiling. She reached up and used one to light the burner. Some coffee would revive her. She had to guard against brooding. How about a bagel? Her appetite had evaporated. Still, she ought to eat to boost her energy. Currently, a piece of driftwood carried on the tide had more purpose than she did.

Soon, she would have to pound the pavements again. She'd need to set aside something from the pawnshop haul to meet a cobbler's bill. There were galleries to call to where she was hoping her artwork might be exhibited for sale. And she had a sheaf of articles, typed by herself, to place in the London periodicals. The cost of new typewriter ribbons was prohibitive but she judged it worth the expense. Typed work had a professional appearance. She needed to do something to distinguish it from the crowd. If she could eat paper, she'd be able to gorge on a pile of rejection letters, baldly stating there was no market for her work.

Dear sir, I enclose an article on the merits of women's suffrage for your consideration, which I believe would be of interest to your readers.

Anna was banking on a personal visit to the editors' offices to persuade some of them to publish her. London was awash with magazines and journals, a number of them aimed at a female readership. She had essays about politics and the important events of the day. There were some verses, besides. Magazines liked poetry. As a poet, she wasn't a patch on Fanny. Fanny had been well regarded, although honesty compelled Anna to admit that her sister's verses might have benefited by an occasional departure from patriotic sentiments. An endless diet of *Rise up! And plant your feet as men where now you crawl as slaves!* could grate. She didn't deny that Ireland had been misruled for centuries. It was just that poetry could cover other themes, too.

Determined, loyal, idealistic Fanny. How could she be gone? Even nine years later, it remained a shocking fact. Like hearing springtime was cancelled and winter was a permanent fixture. Her death had coincided with the death of the Ladies' Land League. The losses were interlocked in Anna's consciousness. A hole left by the sister she loved best and by her sense of purpose in life. Fanny had been Charley's favourite, as well.

The kettle whistled her back to the present. She splashed hot water into her coffeepot, emptying its contents into a bowl. Other lodgers leaned out of a window and dumped their teapot detritus into the back yard. But she made a point of scooping it out and disposing of it separately. She must never let her standards slip.

Delia Parnell had taught all six of her girls the correct way to make tea and coffee. A servant would carry a tray with the caddy and an urn of hot water to the drawing room, along with plates of cakes and knife-thin slices of bread and butter. Mama would mix the blend herself on the spot. The trick was to add piping hot water and leave it standing for four minutes precisely – neither more nor less.

Delia had many admirable traits, especially at a remove, but her company left Anna with a profound sense of irritation. Currently, her mother divided her time between the United States and Ireland, unable to settle anywhere. If Anna wanted it there was a home for her in Bordentown, the New Jersey estate inherited by Delia from her father, Rear-Admiral Stewart – Old Ironsides, a war hero on the American side. But Anna did not care to go there now, even if she could raise the funds for her passage, which was doubtful. It held too many memories of Fanny. She had died there without so much as a whimper. Snuffed out like a guttering candle.

Anna poured her coffee and inhaled the steaming brew. She took it as it came, black and unsweetened. Sugar was abandoned years ago because her conscience would not permit her to indulge in a product associated with slave labour. She sipped, enjoying the sharp tang on her tongue.

Feet scuffled outside her door. Hopefully, it was her change. She eased back the door a crack: a junior Jenkins waited outside. She allowed the opening to widen.

"Mum says I's to give you this." A hot paw frilled with bitten fingernails thrust a shilling and a sixpence at her.

"Thank you." She had an urge to hand him a penny, or even a ha'penny, for sweets but restrained herself. That transaction at the pawnbroker's was meant to feed her, buy art materials, pay omnibus and train fares, and at least one further week's rent. Still, it was niggardly not to give the little man something for his trouble. She fetched the paper bag with the bread rolls. "Would you like a bagel?"

Watching her with caution from under his fringe, he took one. "Thanks, miss." He bit in, already backing away.

"How old are you?" For some reason, she wanted to detain him. He was a grubby imp but his manners were nice enough.

A muffled, "Seven, miss."

"Where do you come in the family?"

This time, he finished his mouthful before answering. "I's number three. After our Nell and our Sally. But I's the oldest boy. 'Bye." He spun away and charged downstairs, boots ringing on the wooden treads.

Anna watched his descent, cheered by the encounter. There was something about his face that moved her. Maybe it was the way freckles clumped on the bridge of his nose.

She shut the door, drained her coffee cup, and pulled out her sketchpad, pencil racing to reproduce a small boy with an untidy fringe. She was so absorbed in her work that she forgot about eating. It was only when the sketch was finished and she tilted her head, assessing it, that she remembered the remaining bagel.

Her mouth began to water, appetite reawakened. She poured a second cup of coffee and bit into the bagel, enjoying the texture against her tongue. Invigorated by her artwork, she pulled the chair to the window, looking at the tree in the back yard while she ate. It was a scraggy runt compared with the towering oaks and firs in Avondale's parkland. Still, a tree was a tree. Its roots burrowed into the ground, drawing nourishment from the soil, while its leaves budded and unfurled, before drifting to the ground and being absorbed back into the earth. There was reassurance in the cycle. The ash tree visible from this London attic connected Anna to the Wicklow landscape she carried inside her. She'd never spend time in a city but for the need to earn enough to keep body and soul together.

If only John would pay what he owed her from the estate. Her eldest brother was legally bound to provide her with an income, according to the terms of their father's will. But the law would not uphold her rights. It accepted his explanation that he couldn't afford it. The annuities meant to take care of a family's widows and spinsters were the first charge on the land to be sacrificed when Irish landlords — their own brothers and sons — fell upon hard times.

John said the tenants on his Collure estate in County Armagh had stopped paying rent, so he had no money for Anna and her sisters. 'You can't get bl-bl-blood from a stone,' he shrugged. Only the stammer betrayed any remorse. He always reverted to his childhood stutter when nervous or excited.

In line with tradition, her father had left estates to his sons, and minuscule legacies to his daughters. Its unfairness never failed to vex Anna but her brothers' lack of any financial sense made it even more of a drawback. Charley speculated on hopeless mining ventures and loaded Avondale with mortgages, while John ran Collure in such an unprofitable way that the Parnell ladies' capital was destroyed.

So be it, she must practise self-reliance. Just as she had urged the tenant farmers facing eviction when she ran the Ladies' Land League a decade ago.

A creak in the room behind her made her turn back towards her surroundings. A mouse sniffing out the breadcrumbs? Her eyes patrolled the bedroom for movement. All was still. Perhaps it was the wood expanding.

"The boudoir has not been invaded," she told the furniture. "At least, as far as I know."

Boudoir was a word she enjoyed shaping on her tongue. She knew it derived from *bouder*, to sulk. She had enjoyed living in France, perhaps she'd go back there and rent a boudoir from a Parisian Mrs Jenkins, there to *bouder*. Typical, that women wanting to be alone occasionally was interpreted as sulking. Where was the harm in a yearning to experience solitude so your thoughts could range free?

But woman cannot live by meditation alone, which put no

bread on the table. "*Once more into the breach*," she said aloud, stiffening her resolve. She would gather up her portfolio and head for Fleet Street with her wares. Otherwise, poverty beckoned, and she'd wind up as a charity case in some pious home for distressed gentlefolk. If she was lucky. She had witnessed poverty at close quarters in Ireland. The people were in perpetual debt to the landlords and shopkeepers, barely keeping their heads above water. One poor harvest meant disaster. Irish tenant farmers endured conditions verging on slavery to remain perched on their ribbons of land.

As for her, she could have agreed to a form of slavery, if she valued comfort and security above independence. She had her chances of marriage. Lawyers, politicians, the odd officer. Irishmen, Englishmen, Frenchmen, Americans. Men who saw qualities they admired in her – and other characteristics they were prepared to overlook, imagining she would outgrow them, or they could be suppressed. Her decisiveness, sharp wit, grasp of detail and public-speaking skills – useful, but not to everyone's taste. In a Parnell male, they were assets. In a Parnell female, superfluous to requirements.

Once, Michael Davitt had been sweet on her. "You have a hare's eyes," he told her. She liked him well enough. Was moved by the empty sleeve pinned to his jacket, visible symbol of his suffering. But liked her independence more.

Their views on land ownership for the people were more closely aligned than hers and Charley's. Davitt had been the driving force behind the Land League – Charles Stewart Parnell was a figurehead. An insightful man, Davitt. He told Anna the Irish would never accept him as their leader because he was from the cabin class and they preferred their chiefs to come from the demesnes. She admired his honesty. But Davitt's manners were not quite a gentleman's and his flat Lancashire vowels grated.

A robin landed on the windowsill outside and jerked his head this way and that, admiring himself in the glass. Such vanity ought to be rewarded. Some breadcrumbs remained in the bottom of the bag. She squeaked open the sash to scatter them on the sill. At the first groan from the wood, he flew off, but she expected him to return. He was a confident city bird with an eye to the main chance.

She, on the other hand, only aped poise. But life had taught her that if something was said with confidence, there were always people who'd believe you. She had travelled Ireland telling tenant farmers what to do. *Don't pay unjust rents. Band together. There is strength in numbers. Know your rights. Even English law in Ireland has loopholes you can use.* "Miss Anna, I hear you've taken to the public speaking like an old goat to new grass," said one of the Avondale tenants, boisterous because of knowing her since she was in short skirts. She had felt herself to be a fraud but confidence grew from the way the people listened to her at those mass meetings – intent, respectful, daring to hope because she told them they should. It had humbled her. Frightened her. Reinforced her determination to speak up on their behalf.

Unexpectedly, a laugh bubbled out. *Captain Moonlight in Petticoats*, that's what the English press called her. Men – it was always men – said she was a mischief-maker, a radical and, her favourite taunt, unwomanly. That's what really got their danders up. She hadn't known her place. At her first public meeting in Claremorris, she stood on a platform behind a white banner that read *Miss Parnell to the Rescue*. Now, she couldn't save a kitten from drowning.

At least she could do the washing-up. Standing, she took a tin basin from under the bed, added warm water from the kettle, rinsed her cup and saucer and dried the china on a rag. When her hands were empty she wrung her fingers together, squeezing flesh against bone.

"*Shame on you, Charley!*" she cried out. "*Shame on you, John! Shame on you, Father! Shame on all of you!*"

Humiliated by her weakness, she dashed away a tear. She must stop talking to herself. People would claim she was losing her mind, a most convenient development from their perspective. William Gladstone, the man Charley put his trust in for Home Rule with their so-called union of hearts, had his sister locked up by the Lunacy Commission. Helen Gladstone was supposed to be unstable, addicted to opium, and to have taken lovers. Save her from herself! At least Anna's brothers had never threatened to commit her to an asylum. She should be grateful they left her alone. Small mercies.

A hoarse yell from the street signalled the arrival of the first edition of the evening newspapers. It must be lunchtime. She was delaying too long – she needed to make her rounds. She could read the headlines as she passed the news stand. She liked to keep abreast of political developments. All year, Charley had been battling for his political life. She was under no illusions about how faint were his chances.

Once, she had worshipped her big brother. In the House of Commons, she had watched his obstructionist policies hold a government to ransom. Roosting in the Ladies' Cage, a gallery high above the Speaker's Chair which cloistered women behind a metal grille, she had swelled with pride at his certainty. Now, they didn't speak. He disapproved of how she spent the money raised by American supporters – accusing her of extravagance because he wanted some held back for parliamentary purposes. As though politics could ever trump people in need.

"You carried everything too far," he told her. "You're too militant. An extremist."

A chasm had opened at Anna's feet when she understood the distance between them. He hadn't been serious about the Land League's No Rent policy of resistance against landlordism. To Charley, it was a political game. She had believed she and her brother were partners in a crusade. But, to him, they were not equals – they were not even marching in step.

An unbroken sovereign in her modest hoard remained. Anna

wrapped it in a clean handkerchief and pushed it into the tin caddy containing her coffee. There, it was hidden in plain sight. Like the rebel in her.

She rinsed her hands in the few remaining drops of water in the kettle, buttoned her jacket and pinned on her hat. Ready at last, she gathered a file of her articles. One editor after another would receive a visit today. As many as she could reach. She had no appointments but would sit in their outer offices and weather their indifference, shaming them into giving her a hearing. She had dealt with their breed before.

They tried to make her feel invisible. They'd rush past, pretending not to see her, implying they were in the middle of urgent business. But she'd stand up, address them, block their exit if necessary. "Excuse me," she'd say. She wouldn't simper, although they'd like it if she did. She'd be businesslike. "I believe my articles would appeal to discerning readers. I have them here if you could spare a few minutes to read them. I've been published before."

"Leave your work," one or other of them would say. "I'll glance over it later."

But she wouldn't let them off the hook. "I understand you're busy. But couldn't you kindly take a look now? I'm happy to wait for an answer. You're a weekly magazine, aren't you? Your circulation is impressive. But there's room for improvement. Have you considered including the female perspective on the issues of the day?"

They'd make some condescending remark about etiquette or gardening columns, perhaps mentioning the sanctity of the home and a woman's dominion there. Milk and water stories, that's what they wanted. Hers were composed of sinew and gristle. She'd stand her ground. "I understand how the world works," she'd insist. "And, after all, women are affected by decisions taken outside their homes, just as men are."

Sometimes, they suggested she write a novel. She tried to read some examples, to see if it was possible, and found herself bored by details of the gowns worn by characters, the lists of dishes served at dinner and the wanton use of capital letters — excess of any kind repulsed her.

Simplicity, that's what she craved. In London, she missed the cry of the wild geese overhead, the blackberries you'd happen across out walking, the brooks that frothed like the foam on top of a milk pail. But the city had opportunities if you knew how to pass through the doors that led to them. She must go back out into the city and keep knocking.

On the landing, key in hand, examples of her work packed into a satchel hanging from her shoulder, she paused. She'd forgotten her umbrella and it was sure to rain again. Round the doorjamb she stretched to collect it. The sketch of the Jenkins boy caught her eye. She'd caught his puckish quality — she could work that into a composition when she was back in Cornwall. Pleased, Anna pulled the door shut behind her, straightened her back and went out.

Some miles to the east, the pawnbroker's wife watched him eat his dinner.

"Who was you talking to on the street earlier? I saw you with a lady. Skinny sort."

"I already told you. Just a customer. Nobody."

But he knew that was untrue. Anna Parnell was somebody.

In 2002, the Parnell Society put a plaque on Anna Parnell's grave with her own, perceptive words on it:

The best part of independence,
The independence of mind.

SOMERVILLE AND ROSS

Edith Somerville: Born Corfu, 1858; died Castletownshend, Co Cork, 1949

Writer, artist, suffragist

Violet Martin: Born Ross House, Connemara, 1862; died Cork city, 1915

Writer, suffragist

Edith Somerville and Violet Martin, who used the pen name of Martin Ross, were among the most successful Irish writers of their era as the Somerville and Ross duo. The second cousins co-wrote three collections of their celebrated *Irish R.M.* stories and a number of novels including the literary classic *The Real Charlotte*.

In their writing lives the pair pushed against gender boundaries, contributing to public discourse with newspaper articles. The writer Molly Keane saw them as forerunners in trying to escape the rigid limitations of class and era. Business-minded and keen to earn a living from their pens, Somerville and Ross employed one of the first literary agents, who represented a Who's Who of writers including Henry James, Oscar Wilde and Joseph Conrad.

The pair worked for female suffrage in the Munster Women's Franchise Association. In 1910 Edith Somerville became its president and Violet Martin its vice-president.

On the political front, Martin never deviated from her Unionist background and opposed Home Rule for Ireland, regretting the disappearance of the landlord class. By comparison, Somerville, although she also belonged to the landed gentry, developed a more broadly nationalist position.

In addition, Somerville was a talented artist, had several successful exhibitions and illustrated all of their work.

Out of the Foxhole

"The pony and trap's at the front door for you, ma'am," said Bridie Ruane.

"Tell Jeremiah I'll be out presently," replied Mrs Martin. "Don't dally, Violet, Bridie needs to clear the table. Bridie, run along and tell Jeremiah he mustn't give Killola any sugar lumps while they wait. That pony's too fat by far." Mrs Martin reached into the sugar bowl and filled a pocket with the forbidden cubes. "Right, m'dear, I'm off to see Father Fitzgerald at the presbytery. A crashing bore but needs must." She nodded at her daughter and sailed out of the breakfast room after the housemaid.

In the corridor, Mrs Martin paused, returning to balance on the saddle board. A pup used the gap to skitter in. He made a dash for Violet's chair and skulked beneath it, trusting to her protection.

"There was something else I meant to do today. Can you remember?"

"You promised to write a reference for Nora Ruane, Mama."

"Isn't she happy here? Why is she leaving? They're flighty as hens, these girls."

"She's Bridie's sister. Nora never worked here, Mama. She's in a grocer's shop in Oughterard but wants to go to America. She thinks a reference from you might help her chances of finding work in Chicago."

"What do I know about her ability to weigh tea leaves and slice ham?"

"You can write that she's willing and quick to learn. All the Ruanes are."

"If you say so, Violet. Personally, I'm convinced the girls we take on are caught in the wild on a turf bog and imported raw into the house. Perhaps you could draft a letter for me, m'dear, and I'll sign it after I deal with Father Fitzgerald."

It was a compliment to the priest that Anna Selina Martin of Ross was calling on him in person. Once, she would have summoned him to an audience with her. But the century was winding to a close and, in the spirit of changing times, she had decided *noblesse* should occasionally *oblige*.

"Whether we like it or not, it's politic to court the Roman Catholic clerics," she had told Violet, over supper the previous evening.

"Surely, Mama, we need only trouble with the bishops?"

"I think not. These priests have an extravagant level of influence over their flocks. It's positively feudal how the people – poor, simple souls – defer to them."

Violet had been obliged to stifle a laugh. No one could queen it like her mother. Her saving grace was her willingness to converse with every man, woman and child in the barony regardless of who they were.

Today, Mrs Martin was preparing to follow through on her

theories about the duties imposed on her by breeding. "Tick-tock, time and tide wait for no man. Before you write that reference you might check on the woodpile, Violet, it's simply melting away. We shall have to put it under lock and key at this rate."

"Of course, Mama. '*Every man looks at his woodpile with a kind of affection.*'"

"What on earth are you babbling about, child?"

"Thoreau. He meant there was security in a woodpile."

"Just so. What else do you have on this morning?"

"I thought I might try my hand at an article on Irish politics for one of the London periodicals."

"Gracious me, no, the household can't spare you to your scribbles. The chimney sweep is due to call and I'm depending on you to supervise him." A ripple of her fingers and the stately Mrs Martin – incongruously known as Nannie within the family network – swept away.

With the coast clear, the pup emerged to snuffle about the breakfast room, alert for scraps of dropped food. Violet stretched out her legs and poured herself the remains of the coffee. The woodpile could wait, as could the chimney sweep.

She addressed herself to the little dog. "So this is depravity, Cousin. Not truffles by the dozen, or a magnum of champagne at my elbow, but lollygagging at the breakfast table when I should be instructing chimney sweeps."

Luxuriating in her idleness, she watched him, nose down, following a marmalade trail. "I know what you'd like." She buttered her palm, the yellow grease thick on her left hand, and extended it in his direction. He shot across and licked her skin clean. "A filthy habit, I know," she remarked. But the rasp of his tongue against her flesh pleased her. She had to gather her rosebuds while she may.

When he was finished, Violet scratched the sturdy little fellow behind the ears. He writhed in bliss, eyes closed, his tail a speeded-up metronome. Cousin was a West Cork foxhound. She had carried him away from Castletownshend at eight weeks old, tucked into her carpet bag. "A keepsake from Drishane, to warm your feet in bed," Edith had said. Violet was glad of his company in her bedroom on the third floor. Everyone else slept below her, and his steady heartbeat was a comfort when the house creaked its groans in the wee small hours.

Violet cleaned her hand on a napkin, positioned her pince-nez on the bridge of her nose, and read over Edith's letter again, written in purple ink. The scrawl indicated a hurry to catch the post. Generally, the artist in Edith formed her characters with grace.

Drishane House
Skibbereen
County Cork
8 May 1897

Dear Violet,
The house has been like fair day in Skibbereen, with some howlingly tedious guests who can't tell one end of a horse from the other, and haven't the wit to cry off when we go out riding. One of them clung to his mount's neck, looking positively green for the entire time he was in the saddle. He was jolly lucky it wasn't hunting season and there was no jumping because I'm certain he'd have been bucked off. When a horse throws his rider it's because it knows that person doesn't deserve to be on its back. I was on tenterhooks during the entire ride, watching for the tell-tale tightening of its quarters under the saddle. That always betrays a horse's intention to bolt.

Violet allowed herself a smile. Edith lived for her horses, with the hounds a close second. She was almost convinced the smell of leather and animal sweat wafted off the pages she was reading. Skimming through family gossip, she reached a passage about business which she read closely.

Mr Pinker continues to harry me about a hunting book and I presume you are receiving similar communications. As I mentioned after my meeting with him in London, he believes we could round up a cast of characters and thread them through a series of comic hunting stories. His advice is to fashion them after 'A Grand Filly' which so pleased the Badminton Magazine. It would be most lucrative — the magical word! We'd be paid serialisation money by the magazine and afterwards could collect the stories into a book — win-win! Publishing houses won't mind prior publication because it builds audience, according to Pinker. Gratifyingly, he says hunting yarns are our "own stuff" and nobody else is doing anything like it. We must buckle down, Martin, or someone else who can hunt and write will steal our thunder. That would be too maddening for words. We ought not to let ourselves be jockeyed aside.

The house will be quietish from the middle of this month which is just as well because I've been going at full gallop. I haven't had a chance to slacken the reins since I don't know when. Do say you'll come. Pinker says we need to push on while the public is clamouring for our books — and he has a point. If he shows his usual flair for treating publishers like oranges ripe for squeezing, we'll have the shekels for a jaunt afterwards. I am absolutely, positively, flat broke at the moment and desperate for some readies. I'm longing for the chance to take some more art classes in Paris. Also, I need to order a new riding habit for next season but daren't risk it at present until payment for 'The Silver Fox' arrives. If a cheque doesn't come soon, we'll have to instruct little Pinker to send the publisher a stand-and-deliver letter.

Send a wire telling me when to expect you, Martin. It feels as though we're hors de combat, what with you trapped by interminable domesticity in Galway and me cornered by a houseful of guests in Cork. If we could just seize some time together and put our heads down, I'm certain we'd make cracking progress.

No time for more. I feel as if I have forgotten to tell you something important.

Yours ever, Edith

Violet reflected on the elegant austerity of a riding habit, nun-like in its simplicity. Nothing suited Edith better. Even the bowler hat she wore in the saddle was perfect for containing her untidy hair. Edith had been taught to ride as soon as she could walk, virtually. Violet enjoyed riding, too, but she wasn't a natural horsewoman like her cousin and her short sight made it a somewhat hazardous pastime.

Just then, another Cousin caught her attention. The pup had scrabbled onto the sideboard, nudged the lid off a silver salver, and was gobbling leftover strips of bacon.

"You know you ought not to do that," she scolded. "Mother would have you banished to the barn if she caught you."

His ears twitched, eyes registering momentary trouble at her tone, but he was too excited by the breakfast room to be crestfallen. He licked his chops, sizing her up, before returning to the bacon scraps.

She wondered what it might be like to be a dog. Edith always insisted she'd prefer to be reborn as a horse, preferably a hunter, if she had any say in the matter, during one of their conversations which rambled over every topic under the sun. Invariably, they dissolved into fits of laughter. Neither of them wanted to return as a woman. Ladydom was overrated, they agreed.

Violet did not yearn to be a horse. Nor a dog, although she appreciated their devotion. How about a cat, with its independence and sense of entitlement? The cook tolerated a couple of black-and-white pusheens, as she called them — a law unto themselves. A few swipes of their claws had taught Cousin respect and he gave them a wide berth.

Violet fell into a wandering train of thought. Cats quickened at night, metamorphosing from pets to predators. There was an eerie charisma to the after-dark time which attracted her. Or maybe it was the idea of being a predator ... instead of a submissive daughter.

Imagine stalking through the undergrowth, ears pricked to every crackle and rustle. Imagine eyes adjusted to night vision, beneath the opulence of the night sky. Imagine scenting other creatures who shared the gloom with you but were as insubstantial as smoke to human sight.

She reflected. A cat wasn't the smartest of animals. If cleverality was her preference, she should be a fox. Granted, the country people were convinced foxes were vermin, indignant at their knack for burrowing under walls and penetrating henhouses, which they treated as larders. Foxes knew every ruse in the book. And how they could run! They outpaced the wind when the need arose.

A memory ambushed her. A summer's evening when she was a child, the heather warm beneath her body, its sweetness mixed with the fragrance of the nearby bog. She must have nodded off, because she regained consciousness with a start, to find a fox appraising her at close quarters. It was russet with a black muzzle, sharply defined, and she could make out the bushy white hairs in its ears which were pricked forward. But what stamped itself on her notice were its eyes. They were unknowable. Intelligent. Not likeable as a dog's or some tamed animal's. The fox's eyes were intent, searching, gauging. A whiff of something rank floated across to Violet but did not repulse her. Nearby, another fox barked. The fox bared its teeth and gave a dainty whisk of its brush before gliding away.

Recalling that encounter, Violet was struck by the animal's fitness for purpose. Shadowlike, it roamed where it chose, its independence a given. Foxes played by no rules but their own. Except she'd hunted often enough to know how it ended. The drawn-out note of the horn, the headlong tumble of the hounds at full cry, the thudding of hooves in pursuit. The fox might jink sideways, double back, go to ground – do all sorts of things to give the hounds the slip. But one day they would flush it out and run it down. Sooner or later, the chop was waiting for the fox – a quick kill with a broken neck if it was lucky, its body used in a tug-of-war tussle between the lead hounds if not. Sooner or later, its bushy tail was cut off for a trophy. Sooner or later, its blood was smeared on a novice hunter's face. Sooner or later, its mask was mounted on a wall.

Violet shuddered. Save your sympathy, she told herself. The fox was paying the price for freedom – that was the bargain. Wasn't it worthwhile, even so? Hadn't she climbed trees as a small girl to experience a sense of liberty? Her brother, Robert, had shown her how to take a running jump at the trunk, latch on to a low-hanging branch, and claw her way up, toehold by toehold.

An urge to climb a tree again stole over her. She shook the thought out of her head. "Violet Martin cannot climb trees, she's a grown woman, with responsibilities," she said aloud, speaking about herself with detachment, as if Violet Martin was a distant relative. "Violet Martin needs to use her free time for writing."

She considered Mr Pinker's advice. Humorous short stories weren't nearly as important as novels but it sounded as if they could be lucrative. He was shrewd about negotiating royalties, securing serialisation rights and forging connections that might lead to overseas sales.

Peace to work in Drishane seemed too good to be true – Castletownshend was always teeming with Somervilles and Townshends, their relatives and friends. They were tremendously sociable and liked nothing better than to rustle up all sorts of jollies, from sailing trips to picnics. Even though the very word *picnic* made the weather weep. Undeniably, it was topping fun. But sometimes you felt like burying a tomahawk in their skulls. Or at least threatening them with one. People took it as a personal insult when you said you couldn't go sailing because you needed to push on with your writing. They stared, as if you'd just told them you were busy operating the guillotine in revolutionary Paris.

Edith was accustomed to them – hardly surprising, being a full-blown Somerville squaw herself, as her brothers called her. But even she struggled in vain against the family's escapades. Once, she'd hidden in the wardrobe to avoid paying a social call, smothering her giggles as her mama, Cousin Adelaide, had wandered the house attempting to summon her. Violet found them all a shade rambunctious at times. Their welcome was warming, of course. Blood mattered to them and Violet was treated like a surrogate sister, although technically a second cousin. But their teasing, squabbling and general noise levels took some adjustment. It felt exhilarating. But also draining.

There was no such thing as a room of one's own to work in. At any moment, the door might burst open and in would fly some Somerville or other insisting you share in a hare-brained scheme to dress up as a Greek goddess, or play a practical joke on a victim they'd lined up, or some equally delicious slice of nonsense bound to gobble up her writing time.

A crash returned her attention to Cousin, still perched on the sideboard. A salt cellar knocked over. No harm done, apart from possible tribulations caused by the spilled salt. Cousin's bad luck, or free-floating misfortune?

He was trying to make a nest on the sideboard, uncongenial as it looked to human eyes. Violet considered leaving him to his own devices. Bridie Ruane would soon root him out with a brush. The servants were unsentimental about animals, except in terms of eating or selling them. She knew they considered the Martins to be ridiculously profligate in their affection for pets.

But Cousin looked thwarted and she couldn't help herself: she knew precisely the spot he'd like. Rising from the table, she opened a drawer padded with felt in the sideboard, where oddments for dinner parties — fancy cruets and candlesticks that had been in the family for generations — were stowed. There were few left, compared to previous years: the agent who had mismanaged Ross during their sixteen-year absence must have been selling them, or using them for target practice, or doing something irresponsible with them. As though by accident, she left open the drawer and returned to her seat.

Alert, Cousin surveyed this new possibility. He scampered into the space, which just about accommodated him, sniffing at the green material lining it. Yes, it would do. Neat as a properly trained housemaid handling a feather duster, the little foxhound sank his face onto the baize, covered his eyes with his paws, and dozed off. How easy it was to make a pet happy. Her desires were more complicated.

A longing seized Violet to lift a pen and write to Edith, a hankering to say, *I'll be in Skibbereen the day after tomorrow. Can you send the pony and trap to collect me from the afternoon train? Let's knuckle down to an omnium gatherum of rip-roaring hunting stories, earn our fortunes, and run away to heavenly Rome or divine Tuscany!*

However, her mother needed her. The Martin family needed her. Ross House needed her. It was almost impossible to manage on a skeletal staff, all they could afford nowadays with rents collapsed and the family's income pinched. The domestics hadn't a clue about their duties unless she gave them hourly instructions, while the outdoor staff were an even greater trial because they took it upon themselves to do things without consulting anyone. How could she justify abandoning Ross? Even on the basis that the money from finishing another book would pay to mend a house in a running state of disrepair?

Technically, keeping the house shipshape was Robert's responsibility, having inherited Ross, but the landlord was earning his living in London where leaks in Galway caused him no hardship. When he visited, he didn't engage in much by way of hands-on management. Unlike the women of a household, a man was free to shut his study door until he chose to open it again. Nobody knew what went on behind that closed door. Probably, he was indulging in the bliss of a whiskey and soda while communing with *The Times*, without unpaid butcher's bills and housemaids' complaints to distract him.

A knock at the breakfast-room door. Violet whipped off her pince-nez. Oh, it was only Bridie, tray in hand. She put the spectacles back on.

"Will I clear the table, Miss Wi'let, or are you still 'atin'?"

"I'm finished, thank you, Bridie. How are things at home? Your mother must be missing your grandfather."

"Ah, God help him, he was taken from us sudden, the dacent man, and wouldn't you miss seein' him noddin' there by the fire with his pipe. But Father Fitzgerald says he'll have gone through purgatory like a flash o' lightnin'. Sure he was the next best thing to a saint. Not like some I could mention, livin' in this very townland. Demons hot from hell, they are."

Demons hot from hell — what a perfect slice of dialogue. She must add it to her commonplace book of useful phrases. Edith kept a similar log. Their notebooks were worth many times their weight in royalties.

"Send my best regards to your mother, Bridie. Is she well?"

"She does be gettin' a pain in her side at times but I'll say no more about it. Speak of misfortune and misfortune will come."

Violet made a clicking sound with her tongue intended to convey sympathy. "Oh, by the way, his nibs is hibernating in the drawer there, try not to bother him. He'll be like one of your demons hot from hell if he doesn't catch up on his sleep."

"Sure, I wouldn't vex him for all the tea in China, Miss Wi'let. Not a chick nor child in the house but knows you dote on the crathur."

"I suppose the local people must think me a sad specimen, lavishing all my affections on a puppy?"

"Well, indeed, some of them say you must be fierce hard to please that you never wed, and the many foreign places you traipsed about, meetin' with all sorts of high ginthry and the like. But says I to them, why should you be 'asy to please and you a celebrated authoress, with letters pourin' in from them that reads your books and wants to congratulate you on them? You've earned the right to do as you choose and answer to no man."

While she spoke, Bridie piled the plates and cups onto the tray with a reckless attitude to the law of gravity. Bridie was better suited to the kitchen, where her potential for wreaking damage was limited to spilling the contents of saucepans and tramping mud into floors. Still, her chatter could be entertaining.

Look at her now, with the crumbs still littering the tablecloth and the sideboard yet to be cleared, leaning her elbow on the mantelpiece to handle one of Mrs Martin's French porcelain ornaments. Not to dust it but to examine it, and without so much as a by-your-leave. She didn't know her place. Ought Violet to remind her? On balance, she thought not. Bridie Ruane had sat up with her the night she'd doctored a terrier after it caught its paw in a rabbit trap set by the gamekeeper.

Besides, she found herself in agreement with the maid. She *had* earned the right to answer to no man. As the youngest of sixteen children by her father's two marriages, there was no shortage of older sisters to watch deferring to imbecile husbands without one-tenth of their brains. She and Edith had settled between them never to put their heads in the matrimonial noose. "A husband is Caesar and must be obeyed," they used to remind one another, rolling their eyes at the idea of it.

Children were a reason to wed, of course, apart from the risk of dying in childbirth and the tedium of devoting your life to blowing runny noses and sewing labels on school uniforms. Nieces and nephews would have to compensate. Between them, Violet and Edith had scores.

She noticed Bridie slide her hand into her apron pocket, and pop something into her mouth. "I say, Bridie, you shouldn't be eating in here. Mama will go through you for a shortcut if she finds you chomping like a milk cow while you're carrying out your duties."

"I'm not 'atin', Miss Wi'let."

"Come now, Bridie. I distinctly saw your jaws move."

"'Tis only Robin Starch. I find it keeps me from pickin' at food between meals. I do be pilin' on the weight fierce fast these days. 'Tis on account of Cook. She's a marvel with the dinners."

"Not eating is the best appetite suppressant. And you really oughtn't to chew that stuff — who knows what it's doing to your insides?" Violet squinted at the carriage clock on the mantelpiece, trying to decipher the time. Good heavens, the morning was half gone. She must fly.

Yet Bridie's chatter made her pause, hand on the doorknob.

"If it wasn't for Sean Joyce from the forge, I wouldn't mind fattenin' up a bit. But I couldn't abide anyone sayin' he might do better, and only keeps a-courtin' me because of us growin' up together."

"He'd be lucky to have you, Bridie," said Violet, regretting her sharp tone over the Robin Starch.

She didn't think there was any danger of Sean Joyce from the forge letting Bridie slip through his fingers. She had met them out walking. Violet had been on horseback, letting her mount crop grass while she idled, listening to a curlew's cry. From her vantage point, she had observed how Joyce was as sticky as scrambled eggs on toast in the girl's company. Which reminded her: could she make time to take a ride today? The exercise was invigorating. She knew every inch of the Ross demesne, although some said you familiarised yourself more closely with a place on foot.

"But I hope you aren't thinking of settling down with him just yet, Bridie," she added. The responsibility of training up another housemaid would fall to her.

"Ah, not a-tall." Bridie gave an airy sweep of the arm. "I've a half notion to take my lead from you and not step out with any fellow. There's great independence in bein' answerable to no man and havin' the freedom to go about sayin' women, childer and madmen is treated alike in this counthry and given no rights. Mind you, Dada's threatened to skin me alive if he finds me repeatin' the things you do be sayin'. He says too much freedom for women is a bad thing entirely. 'Tis unbridled."

"You tell your father from me I am not a horse to need bridling."

As if she hadn't spoken, Bridie continued, "And then, you know, it's not every girl has a curly-haired man like Sean Joyce, so fine he'd take the sight from your eyes if you looked at him long enough, blushin' at your smile and tremblin' at your frown. I cannot deny it, Miss Wi'let. Not for the world would I deny it. And that's the holy truth of it."

Stifling a laugh, Violet bolted for her bedroom to capture Bridie's speech. She pulled the cork from an ink bottle and made rapid notes in her spiky handwriting. That done, she pondered a reply to Edith's invitation. Except – for all her talk about being beholden to nobody, she had responsibilities as Miss Martin of Ross.

The tenants had charm, like Bridie Ruane, but there was no substance to it. They had broken her father's heart, after all his charity and care for them, excusing rents during the hard times. Not one of his people had died during the famine years. His own family had been obliged to practise demeaning economies, shutting up the house eventually. What thanks had he? Disloyalty that lashed him to an early grave. The faithless tenantry had refused to vote according to his instructions, throwing its support behind Parnell and his wolf pack of Land Leaguers baying for landlords' blood.

England had been ridiculously tolerant of the Land League, that was the long and short of it, and the loyal landlord class had suffered. Despite their deference to his face, his tenants had betrayed the Master of Ross and Violet would never forget it. All their 'your honouring' to her mother and 'Miss Wi'leting' to her was a sham. She'd shake off the dust from Galway in a heartbeat if her mother didn't rely on her. A spasm shook Violet's hands, and she laid down her pen.

She was trapped here in Ross House. Part of her loved it as her family home, part of her recognised the place was handsome but pointless – like an expensive suitcase that nobody wanted to risk using because of an unreliable lock. It wasn't as if she had much right to be here. The roof over her head was provided by a brother's mercy and a sister-in-law's tolerance. The emptiness of this large house crouched about her. Its demands were beyond their means, if they were honest. It offered her nothing in return that could compare to her literary career with Edith. Now that promised self-sufficiency, autonomy, fulfilment – but its joys were dangling just beyond her reach.

Violet lit an Egyptian cigarette. To smoke was a new accomplishment and she was not yet proficient, blowing out when she meant to suck in, which caused coughing fits. Still, she gloried in it because it seemed modern.

Was that her mother's voice in the front hall already? She hadn't tackled any of her jobs. Some judicious fibbing would be required. Violet stubbed out her cigarette, slid a peppermint in her mouth, and ran downstairs, pausing only to tap the barometer on the lower landing. *Rain* was its promise. As usual.

"Ah, Violet, I've just spoken to the chimney sweep, who is drinking tea in the kitchen without a care in the world as though his brushes can lie there cluttering up the back yard till Doomsday. Weren't you supposed to deal with him?"

"I didn't know he was here, Mama. I was attending to something else. I'll send for him right away."

"No need, I've given him his instructions. Though I was depending on you to do it. There's only so much a woman of my age can be expected to accomplish."

"Sorry, Mama. Did everything go well with Father Fitzgerald?"

Ms Martin turned a bland face on her daughter. "No, m'dear, I haven't left yet."

"But wasn't Father Fitzgerald expecting you at ten? To see about our picnic for the village children?"

"He may expect all he likes. I will not be made to keep time like a clock, especially not by a man with a face as shiny as a pair of Sunday boots. If I am late it is because I have pressing matters to attend to. I had to talk to Jeremiah about the vegetable garden. It simply could not wait. He won't plant according to my directions – he behaves as though the garden is an egg he laid himself and only he has rights to it."

So much for her mother's intentions of placating the clergy. If Father Fitzgerald chose, not a single child would attend their event. No parent would thwart his authority. Violet must proceed with care or there'd be a tiresome scene with her mother.

Swallowing back any hint of criticism, she asked, "Would you like me to see Father Fitzgerald on your behalf, Mama?"

"That would be most helpful of you, Violet. Tell him we intend laying on a treasure hunt so the little ones can have a splendid romp in the woods, followed by a tea they will remember until their dying days. The Martins of Ross have never been accused of a niggardly act. We have always known how to do things in style."

"Should I invite Father Fitzgerald, too, Mother?"

"If you must. I warn you, he will talk about the weather ad nauseam."

"An invitation might make him more amenable. You know how these Roman Catholic clerics worry that we'll try to convert poor people's children in return for cakes."

"I suppose he should be present, if only to demonstrate that we have no designs on children's souls. But I had counted on you taking charge of the treasure hunt. Who will keep Father Fitzgerald company? Perhaps we could leave him in the library with a glass of sherry while you deal with the children. Later, you may read aloud to us."

"What do you suggest, Mother? Some poetry? Mr Wordsworth?"

"I detest poetry, particularly good poetry. But Father Fitzgerald may not share my sensibilities. And I dare say he can nod off if it becomes too tedious. Very well, some poetry. Is that a letter in your hand?"

"Yes, from Cousin Edith. She has invited me to pay a visit to Drishane. Naturally I am too occupied here to take her up on the offer."

"Always gadding, those Somervilles, and inciting others to do likewise. It's rather an uncouth habit. Besides which, I wonder if Castletownshend's wet fogs aren't unhealthy for someone with your weak chest? Very well, I suppose I could spare you for a week or two after the children's treat. Your sister Winifred and her brood are due to spend a fortnight at Ross from the last week in May onwards, and I shall have them for company."

"Thank you, Mother. I should be glad to see Edith again. She's a tonic for the spirits."

"I expect you will spend the entire time running the length and breadth of West County Cork."

"I expect so."

"Still, young people have the constitution for it. Remember to bring some raspberries from the kitchen garden when you go. Jeremiah says there'll be an early crop this year. They should be ripening shortly. Cousin Adelaide has a weakness for them and Ross produces much sweeter raspberries than Drishane. We must make certain to keep the village children out of the canes during their treasure hunt. Does Edith have any news in that letter?"

"She says Cousin Adelaide thinks our latest novel, *The Silver Fox*, is quite the thing and will make the critics sit up and take note. She disapproved of the way *The Real Charlotte* ended. Edith says her mother believes characters should leave a story in the same way the animals exited the ark, two by two."

"Stuff and nonsense. Adelaide is an admirable woman but a literary critic she is not. Your ending was exactly right, Violet. But I meant family news."

"Edith sprang a muscle in her right calf playing tennis and is now lame – an awful nuisance to her."

"They play an excessive amount of tennis, those Somervilles. And when they aren't on the tennis courts they're hunting or shooting. How are the boys?"

"Leaving soon to join their ships. The family are reading *Hamlet* aloud after dinner, with a view to staging some scenes from it at a farewell party for the boys."

"Shakespeare was a coarse man, Violet, but I suppose my cousin will supervise her brood to restrict crudities to a minimum. Hurry along, you mustn't keep Father Fitzgerald waiting. A lady is always punctual."

Except for Mama, who makes her own rules and carries them off with her ruthless charm, thought Violet.

"While you're in the village you might order some supplies," continued Mrs Martin. "Check with Cook to see what we're low on."

Couldn't you go, Mama? By now, Violet's thoughts ran mutinous. She didn't feel like dealing with the grocer today. He was far too obsequious, with an equally unpleasant habit of lolling on his fleshy bare arms on the counter, a low-grade newspaper spread out in front of him.

However, she did as she was told. Retrieving her hat from the bedroom, she slipped on her pince-nez to check her reflection in the mirror. The Paris hat was becoming, while her collar and cuffs were pristine, but nothing could disguise her snaggle teeth and the lines bracketing a drooping mouth. It occurred to Violet that she did not resemble an independent woman. Not in the slightest. No matter what Bridie Ruane said. Not because she was doll-like – seven stone four pounds in full hunting rig – but because she was subject to her mother, despite being thirty-five years of age.

Violet turned aside. A shadow moving across the looking glass caused her to glance back. She had taken off her pince-nez and pocketed it but, oddly, the reflection was not blurred. Open-mouthed, she stared. The eyes were unknowable. They were intelligent but not likeable as a dog's were – they seemed intent, searching, gauging. Below them, a sharp nose and an even sharper chin jutted out.

Appearances could be deceptive, she realised – a thought brimming with possibilities. Satisfied, she bared her teeth and gave a dainty whisk of her skirts before gliding away.

After Violet Martin's death, Edith Somerville continued writing books using the dual signature, insisting that the grave made no difference to their collaboration. She mined their letters and notebooks for inspiration, and relied on séances and automatic writing sessions to shore up her belief that Somerville and Ross remained in constant communication — whether alive or dead.

ALICE MILLIGAN

Born Omagh, County Tyrone, 1866; died Tyrcur, Omagh, 1853
Playwright, poet, theatre producer, journalist, political activist,
Gaelic League supporter

Alice Milligan was an important figure in the Celtic Revival era and closely connected to many of its key figures. From a Methodist background, she stood for an inclusive nationalism which recognised the value of other traditions. She wrote plays, poetry, novels and journalism and was a tireless activist throughout her adult life. In particular, she believed that Wolfe Tone and Emmet showed how the cause of Ireland was not simply a Catholic one.

In Belfast, she founded and ran two nationalist publications, *The Northern Patriot* and the *Shan Van Vocht* (which had a global distribution) with her friend, the poet Ethna Carbery, also known as Anna Johnston. They were first to publish the political writing of James Connolly in Ireland.

Alice was a talented playwright and theatre producer before the Abbey was started and her play, *The Last Feast of the Fianna*, helped to inspire a national theatre in Ireland. She travelled the country with lantern slides and tableaux, staging productions with historical subject matter which fostered interest and pride in national identity. A supporter of the Irish language, she also gave Irish language lectures.

Written on her gravestone is *Nior car fód eile ach Éirinn* – She loved no other place but Ireland.

No Other Place

"White roses for this year's bouquet, with ivy for remembrance. What do you say, Willie?"

Alice bends to sniff a rosebud, while a tabby cat weaves figures-of-eight between her ankles. She is slight – a breath of sudden wind could whirl her high above this overgrown garden.

"I know, Willie, I know. You want your milk. Just let me get these flowers gathered up."

As she straightens, pain catches at her and she gasps, pressing the heels of both hands into her lower back. With an effort of will, she heaves her mind back to the flowers.

White roses for hope, she thinks. His hope and hers too. She must hold tight to hope. This roof over her head might be lost. The flow of words reduced to a trickle from her pen might vanish.

Even Willie might disappear – tempted by a household with more titbits. But hope she can carry on her back, like a tortoise with its shell. So long as she stays true to hope, it stays true to her.

She looks away from the garden, with its jungle of foliage, towards the house – a Church of Ireland rectory without a rector. It's a substantial building, impressive enough in its time. But the shabbiness of neglect undermines its claims.

So many addresses over the years. Always on the move. Yet here she is, back where she started, near enough. She was born a handful of miles away and grew up in a house that sat fair and square beside a crossroads. How she wishes she was rooted by a crossroads again. A world of possibilities beckoned at them. Out here, the world keeps its distance: holding her at arm's length.

Alice turns back to the rosebush, one hand cupping a bloom. The penetrating blue eyes examine it for imperfections before she takes a pair of kitchen scissors from her cardigan pocket and guillotines the stem. With the whisper of promise, the rose lands on a spill of ivy in the basket at her feet, followed by eight of its sisters.

"Morning, Miss Milligan." A police constable advances, his moustache as stately as the bicycle he is wheeling.

She hasn't heard him approach and is peeved by this proof of her deafness. However, she doesn't let it show. "Good morning, Norman. Isn't it a glorious summer's day?"

"Aye, glorious is the word for it. It's set fair to be a scorcher the-day." He looks for somewhere to prop the bike, finds nowhere suitable, and lays it flat on the laneway. "I have somethin' for you, ma'am." One pocket after another in the dark green tunic is patted until paper crinkles in the fourth and a letter is withdrawn. "You forgot this yesterday when you called tae the barracks tae sign for your post. I'm just headed out on me rounds, an' thought I'd save you the trouble. You took the Free State one wi' you. But you left the one from England behind."

Heavy-hearted, she accepts the brown envelope and sees her

name and address typed on the front. It must be another bill. No matter how she economises, or how hard she works to reduce the backlog, she can't keep pace with them. She hasn't bought a new hat since — when? It must be the green felt one when Mr de Valera took office more than seven years ago. Really, it's beyond her pen's power to earn enough to hold these bills at bay. The half-year's rent is always a particular worry.

She had to borrow the most recent instalment from one of her brothers. The shame of it — her independence undermined.

She turns the envelope over. At least it hasn't been opened, unlike yesterday's letter from Dublin. Whoever has oversight of her post is scrupulous about leaving bills unread. Perhaps he regards it as ungentlemanly to cast an eye over her unpaid accounts, whereas scanning her private correspondence is a question of duty. With an expulsion of air halfway between a snort and a giggle, she tucks the offending letter into the waistband of her skirt — bad news can keep.

"You look warm, Norman. Would you like a cup of tea?"

"A drop o' tae wud be just the ticket, ma'am, but on'y if you're makin' it anyway. I'm parched, so I am."

"The kettle's on the boil for my breakfast. Come in, won't you?" Today was usually a day she spent quietly, reading and praying. But there was time enough for that.

Alice makes her way through grass that hisses underfoot, towards the front door lying ajar. She looks to see if Willie is following them but he has melted away. Cats have a gift for invisibility. Unlike overheated young policemen. Norman follows her into a porch with rust-coloured tiles and on into a wood-panelled hallway from which a staircase ascends.

"Shall we be informal and use the kitchen? Everything's to hand there."

Her quick step leads the way past a drawing room on the left, a dining room and a study on the right. His boots sound a tattoo on the floorboards, their racket embarrassing him.

In the kitchen at the back of the house, she lays the basket of roses on a deal table. The kettle is bubbling on the range kept lit, winter and summer, for cooking. She lifts the kettle and splashes water into a metal teapot, swooshes it twice clockwise with a twist of the wrist and empties the contents into the sink.

"Why, you're still standing, Norman. Sit down, please."

He removes his peaked cap and sets it on the chair alongside his seat. The range is too close for comfort. Should he offer to open the back door? But she's as old as his granny, she probably feels the cold. Taking out a clean, ironed handkerchief, he mops his forehead and neck. He fingers one of the silver buttons along the middle of his tunic, each disc stamped with a harp topped by a crown. If only he could undo them. But he ought to leave them fastened up – he is on duty, after all.

Alice, who misses nothing, observes his dilemma. Her invitation to shed the jacket withers on her lips. Let him swelter, him and his buttons! The crown has no business with the harp, to her way of thinking.

Tea leaves added, she returns the teapot now brimming with boiling water to the range. "I'll just put these roses in water while the tea draws." She opens a press and stretches on tiptoe for a Belleek china vase. Are the shelves getting higher or is she shrinking?

Too late, Norman realises he ought to have offered to hand it down to her. Not that she'd accept help from him or anyone else in a hurry – a headstrong one and no mistake. He watches her arrange the flowers, puzzled by the close attention she devotes to the job – placing them stem by stem, moving some an inch one way or another.

"You've green fingers, Miss Milligan. Them's fine roses." On a surge of emotion, he adds, "Like queens, they are, the way they hould up their wee heads." Mortified, he halts. It's only a jug of flowers when all's said and done.

She nods. "'*And these I gathered at the dawn – Remembering you –*

Wet in the gleam of morning' … the garden is gone horribly to seed. I haven't the time to see about it, with the house to keep straight too. But I've always loved flowers. When I was just starting out, and felt a pen name was more appropriate, I chose a flower. Iris. Iris Olkyrn."

"The brother is married tae a woman be the name of Iris. He used tae be a corporal in the Inniskillings. On'y left last year, when he got married. Thon Iris, she's powerful afeard o' war comin' an' he havin' tae enlist again. Experienced men wud be expected tae offer theirselves. But the brother says to her, says he, 'Iris, you shud know better nar tae go lookin' for troubles – they come lookin' for you soon enough'."

"He's right, Norman. I hope Mr Chamberlain is right as well and war can be avoided. Too much blood has been spilled already this century." Her eyes fasten on the roses, a shadow settling on her face.

"I've no doubt war's on the way, so it is. An' it grieves me I won't be let join up. The sergeant says the police is a reserved occupation. So if it's tae be war, I'll spend it in uniform, but not a sodger's. If you don't mind me askin', why did you choose Iris, ma'am? For tae be a poetess an' that?"

"She was the Greek goddess of the rainbow. I can never see one without stopping to admire it."

"I can never see one wi'hout wishin' for a pot o' gold!'

Her smile is polite. Wealth has never interested her, although freedom from this perpetual anxiety about paying bills would be a relief. "Iris was a messenger of the gods – she rode on a rainbow between heaven and earth. Like Iris, I used to travel about a fair bit myself, back in the day. I thought nothing of flitting from Belfast to Dublin or Cork. The railways were my chariot – I had the timetable memorised. My father was the same, he knew the times upside down and inside out. Happy days! Now, I hardly ever leave Mountfield. I count myself lucky if I get the length of Omagh."

"I'm a bike man meself. I love mine. God bless the Royal Ulster Constabulary and His Majesty the King for supplyin' it."

"Hush, Norman, today's no day for blessing kings! If you only knew —" Repenting her sharp words, she stops abruptly.

Shock has immobilised his face.

Alice covers her mouth with the back of her hand, almost laughing aloud. The young are so quick to take offence.

He clatters to his feet, intending to leave. She's a Fenian to the core – just as the Sergeant said. The silver hair could fool a man if he didn't keep his wits about him. But she's betrayed her true colours.

"Don't go. Forgive me, I know you have your line of business to consider. You're Constable Gibson, as well as Norman, all grown-up now. Do, please, sit. Let's have that tea. Truly, I meant no offence. I spoke out of turn. Today's a sad day for me, you see. An anniversary."

Half against his will, he resumes his seat, although tempted to replace his cap in a show of authority. However, Norman's granny, who lives with the family, has impressed on him that only yahoos keep their heads covered indoors. She was in service in her youth and remains an authority on etiquette.

From the same press which housed the vase, china decorated with peacocks is produced.

The young policeman finds its near-transparent fragility as alarming as his hostess's anti-monarchy sentiments. "A beaker's good enough for me, ma'am. I wud'n want tae break one o' them delicate wee boys."

"They're sturdier than they look, Norman. I'm afraid there's only bread and butter to go with your tea. No jam."

"Ach, a cup in the hand is all I want, Miss Milligan."

She pours the strong tea and sets it in front of him, along with a jug of milk and a bowl of sugar. He serves himself only one spoon of sugar, although his preference is for three. Everybody in Mountfield and beyond knows how she's fixed. Poor as a church mouse, for all her highfalutin ways. Meanwhile, she takes a breadknife to the loaf, butters the slices and lays them overlapping on a plate, devoting as much attention to their arrangement as to her floral display.

"I've noticed ladies is powerful fond o' flowers," he offers, between mouthfuls. "Me ma grows away at them. Though me da says there's no eatin' in a dahlia. A head o' cabbage wud be more tae the good."

Alice sits opposite, her tea untouched. "Flowers serve many purposes, Norman. I like to cut them as an act of remembrance, to keep faith with those who've gone ahead. I make what you might call a ceremony of it."

"Oh aye, you mentioned an anniversary earlier. I'm sorry for your loss. A relative, I take it?'

"The bond was comradeship, not family ties. But a loss, undeniably. This bouquet" – she indicates the roses and ivy – "marks the death of a fine man. An honorable man. I was privileged to know him."

Norman relaxes, at ease now. A spinster mourning a lost love – sure they're ten-a-penny since the war twenty-odd years back.

She realises how he is interpreting the flowers but doesn't correct him. People prefer to elevate romantic love above loyalty, fellowship and a common cause. Let the boy make his assumptions.

"Is he long dead?"

She frowns at the freckled hands on her lap. Involuntarily, their fingers reach out and interlace, one hand seeking comfort from the other. But her voice is steady. "They killed him twenty-three years ago today. It happened in London. I was there. On the pavement outside. Waiting. With other women from our circle who believed in him. When the bell tolled that morning to say it was done, the crowd bellowed its approval. Not words – just a thunderous roar. Of victory, I suppose. The power of might. I can hear it chiming still." She shudders. "I felt as if the human heart was beyond all understanding, that day. To cheer at another person's death — it left me hardly able to put one foot in front of the other to leave that place. I tried telling myself his ordeal was over: he was at peace, finally. But it took me a long, long time to find any peace, myself. Those were wild times. Frightening. They ran out of control." A clock ticks and she gives her head a quick shake. "Yet I never felt more alive than I did back then. They were exciting times too, you see. Dense with dreams. Overflowing with possibilities." Unexpectedly, she smiles. "I always gather flowers on the third of August. In honour of him. And the dreams and possibilities we shared."

Norman scrapes a tea leaf off his lower lip. He supposes the old lady must be talking about one of her rebels. Hanged or shot for disloyalty — and good riddance to bad rubbish. Which one of those traitors she's commemorating, he doesn't know and doesn't want to know. They were a nest of vipers, trying to murder away the link with Britain. Wasn't the British Empire the last word in magnificence? Envied by other countries with piddling wee empires? It was a privilege to be born British. Those renegades were rotten to the core — they were better off dead.

He's not prepared to listen to any more of this rebel nonsense. His granny always says he should make allowances for her and his ma backs her up. But he's had enough of Alice Milligan. There's no excuse for it, with her from good Protestant stock. Not even a papist who knows no better.

Seizing his cap, he pushes back his chair from the table. "Thankin' you for the hot drop, ma'am. I'd best be on me way."

She pays no attention, engrossed in her own train of thought. "Sure he's dead now, Alice, for better or for worse." That's what her brother used to say about her shrines, as he called them. "Is he?" she'd answer him back. "I wouldn't be so certain. There's an alchemy that sparks between memory, belief and imagination — in that space, he's alive. He always will be."

Just then, the cat noses in round the doorjamb and assesses the lie of the land. Tail aloft, he parades towards his saucer. His disgruntled mewls at its emptiness penetrate her reverie.

"Poor Willie, you must be starving." She lifts the milk jug from the table and empties it into the chipped saucer.

Norman hovers by the door, cap under his arm. Despite being vexed, he is naturally courteous and reluctant to leave without a pleasantry. "The size of him! You could harness thon cat to a cart and get a day's work out of him."

"Handsome, isn't he? There's great companionship in a puss."

"I dare say you call him Willie for your brother, the captain, God rest him."

"No, in fact, it's for Mr Yeats, the poet. He visited our house in Belfast and sat opposite me in the library for hours on end, discussing poetry. We always had cats about the place. Mama was partial to them. The day he came, one of the pups was teasing a couple of the cats and Mr Yeats decided enough was enough. He lifted the two cats onto his lap – both black, I remember – and petted away at them as we talked rhyme and reason and everything in between. He's another one gone, just a matter of months ago. But I can see his long fingers, as clear, as clear, stroking the cats, and that dark wing of hair flopping into his eyes. Mr Yeats it was who advised me to write plays. He never thought much of my poetry. Didn't come right out and say it, of course, but I knew. You can always tell with another writer. My work was too effusive, I suppose you might call it, for his taste." She slants a glance at him. "Goodbye, Norman. Be sure and give my regards to your grandmother." His grandmother worked for her family, donkey's years ago. Back when they lived in Omagh in a house with fir trees in the garden. The games she played in that garden, with her sisters and brothers! And his grandmother, not much older than them, busy in the kitchen. They could hear her singing while she worked – Heather had a voice to shame a thrush. "Does she still sing?"

"Ach, not for a brave while now. Her breathin's not the best. She likes to tell the odd story when the humour is on her. There's nobody like Granny for givin' you a tale wi' skin on it. I'm sure she'd wish tae be kindly remembered tae you, Miss Milligan. I'll tell her you were askin' for her. Well, I'll bid you good day." He catches at the door handle, intending to pull it shut behind him.

"Leave it open. There'll be nobody coming or going, apart from the bould Willie here. Still, I would not wish to have barriers of any kind erected this day. Amid the free flow of air, of thoughts, of memories – that's how today should spend itself."

She doesn't live in the real world, thinks Norman, sliding away.

As though the ghost of that judgement filters through, she lets fly a peal of laughter, clapping her hands together. Cheerful again, she carries the flowers into a drawing room impregnated with accumulated years' worth of turf smoke. A framed pencil sketch of a bearded man stands on a handsome marble mantelpiece, once white but somewhat yellowed by age, and she places the vase next to him.

"God bless you, *'verray, parfit, gentil knight'*. You waved me into a seat beside you in the Ulster Hall the day the news broke about your knighthood. I was late for the meeting, delayed by a thunderstorm. You wouldn't go up onto the platform for fear they'd announce it. I thought you altered-looking – strained, weakened. And no wonder. You were just back from the Putumayo. Even so, you insisted on putting yourself out for people. Always first on your feet to offer your chair when a lady needed one. And you'd take no end of trouble checking train times for delegates to our conferences. I could never get permission to visit you in prison. Another Alice had that privilege. But you waved at me in the courtroom and sent your counsel over with a message. 'Write a poem about this, Alice,' you said. I suppose you meant it as a joke. But I took you at your word."

Head bowed, she leans against the mantelpiece. Through the years she wrote and wrote and wrote. Verse, stories, drama, journalism. Did any of it make a jot of difference? His words lit a flame. But hers? Did anyone hear her? Or was she just talking to herself? Perhaps it's irrelevant if they listen or not, she thinks –

maybe what matters is the act of writing.

Returning to the kitchen, she pours her cold tea down the sink and refills the cup from the pot. The cat has had the last of the milk. She'll have to take it black. A sip to brace herself. From her waistband she retrieves the dreaded envelope delivered by Norman Gibson. Two stamps on the top right-hand corner, one for a penny and the other a ha'penny. She looks at George VI's profile. The bicycle-provider, she thinks. Among other roles. A figurehead, of course. Kings reign, they don't rule. Bicycles are supplied only in their name.

He's her fifth monarch, imagine! None of whose rule she accepts. But whether she assents to them or not, each one has been a reality. Victoria, then Edward VII, followed by George V, succeeded by the short reign of Edward VIII, who abdicated for the love of Mrs Simpson. Such a burden for Mrs Simpson. And now this George, his brother, reigns in his place. Which tells her that kings and queens endure.

As she must.

Fancy! She has something in common with those British kings and queens. They persevere and so does she.

To give up is not in her nature. Here she was born and here she'll stay in this territory they say is theirs. And, after all, they have the crowns on postboxes and policemen's uniforms to support their case. But by living here she's planting a counter-claim. *Planting.* She half-smiles at that. A word with more than one meaning in this northern pocket of Ireland.

Her amusement pinches to a pucker at the envelope in her hand. Whose bill is this George-with-his-crown conveying? More to the point, how will she find the wherewithal to pay it? Breadknife in hand, she slits the flap.

The Lost Property Office at Paddington Station regrets to inform her that a handbag she wrote inquiring about, left behind on a train from Bath to London, has not turned up.

Thank goodness it's not a demand for money. As for the

handbag, it was on its last legs. Besides, all her life she has mislaid possessions. Memories she can retain, and friendships, even minute details about events. But not objects. When she went to hear Mr Parnell speak in Dublin, back in the last century – she couldn't have been more than twenty-four – she lost her purse. Fortunately, it contained nothing more than a stamp and a pen nib. She used to have a flower from a wreath left on Mr Parnell's grave. For years, she kept it carefully but now she can't lay her hands on it. That's what comes of all her gipsying about. A life spent on the move.

She only tried to trace the handbag because of some poems left inside it. One of them showed promise, although it could use some reworking. She ought to have polished more – she lacked the patience for it, preferring to tumble words out of herself in the exhilaration of inspiration. Letting them fall where they might.

"There's no call to go hoking in handbags for your poems, Alice," she tells herself. "You have them inside you."

She opens a drawer in the table, finds a pencil and turns the communication from Lost Property face-down on the table.

Willie, who has been stalking imaginary prey between the table legs, springs onto her lap. Round and round he circles, flexing his claws, and she waits until he settles – listening for the noise, midway between purring and humming, to rise up. Only then does she place the pencil point on the back of the letter. The hand holding it is knobbed with rheumatism. Yet still it works for her. A prickle along the back of her neck. A rushing in her ears. Letters form into words and words shape into phrases.

Alice writes.

When Alice was a schoolgirl, the Milligan family moved from Omagh to Belfast. Among servants in their new home was "Old Jane" – formerly employed in Mary Ann McCracken's household. The Milligans looked after this link with revolutionary Belfast until her death at an advanced age. She was loved by them for her loyalty and ready tongue. When a distinguished clergyman knocked on the front door and set the dog barking, Alice recalled Jane telling him, "You may be the Dean of Down but the dog thinks you're the postman."

Note:

This story also appears in *The Glass Shore: Short Stories by Women Writers from the North of Ireland* edited by Sinéad Gleeson (Dublin: New Island, 2016)

COUNTESS MARKIEVICZ

Constance Gore-Booth, later Countess Markievicz,

born London, 1868; died Dubllin 1927

Revolutionary, suffragette, politician, socialist

The Countess came from a privileged Big House tradition in Sligo, growing up in Lissadell House. However, she identified with the people and became a founder member of the Irish Citizen Army, as well as Cumann na mBan. She was also a co-founder of the youth group Fianna Éireann. She took part in the 1916 Easter Rising and was condemned to death as a leader. However, her sentence was commuted to life imprisonment on the grounds of her sex.

On 28 December 1918, she became the first woman elected to the British House of Commons. Sinn Féin's abstentionist policy meant she did not sit at Westminster, instead joining others to form the first Dáil Éireann. In another first, she was the world's first democratically elected woman to hold a cabinet position (1919-22). While a woman had been appointed to the Russian cabinet before the Countess became Ireland's Minister for Labour, she had not run for public office.

Known for her gallantry and spirit, Countess Markievicz served several terms in prison. She joined the newly formed Fianna Fáil party in 1926 and was re-elected to the Dáil as one of its deputies. However, she died in the public ward of a Dublin hospital before taking her seat.

What Would the Countess Say?

The present day.

A first-floor apartment in a redbrick terraced house on the South Circular Road, Dublin.

Aoife Blanchard, in her late twenties and wearing jeans, enters the living room drinking from a bottle of water. She stops short, splashing water onto her T-shirt.

Another woman is in the room. It is Countess Markievicz, tall and imposing, with a strong-boned face. She is in her fifties, dressed in a brown tweed skirt and jacket and wearing a broad-brimmed hat.

"Kindly stop staring at me, young woman. Don't you know it's rude to stare?" The Countess pulls off her hat and fans herself with it. "Could someone please open a window? There's no air in here."

Aoife knows she's gaping — those crisp, parade-ground tones have just told her so. With a visible effort, she recovers her powers of speech. "Forgive me, I wasn't expecting it to work. Especially not the first time. I've never attempted a materialisation before. But here you are. It is you, isn't it? Countess Markievicz?"

The older woman's eyes rest on the younger's. Behind the commanding veneer, a faint air of bewilderment is perceptible. "You are addressing Constance de Markievicz. Have we met?"

"I'm afraid not. You've been dead for more than ninety years."

"Really, this is too ridiculous. My head's pounding — I can't concentrate. I say, why hasn't anyone opened that window yet?"

She's closer to the window than Aoife but it seems easier to do it for her. Aoife sets down her plastic bottle and tugs at the sash. Fresh air gusts in and begins to cool the room. As she steps back, the Countess holds up a warning hand.

"Watch out! Don't tread on Poppet!"

"What's Poppet?"

"My dog, of course."

"I don't see any dog."

The Countess checks under the coffee table and peers round the back of the sofa. "Oh, Poppet isn't with me. How disappointing. Little scamp's generally at my heels. I wonder where he's taken himself off to?" She extends her hand. "Since there's no one to introduce us, we must do it ourselves. How do you do?"

Aoife takes her hand and, surprising herself, bobs a curtsey. Later, she rationalises it on the basis that it just seemed to be the right thing to do. "Aoife Blanchard. It's an honour to meet you."

"Why on earth are you genuflecting? Shoulders back! Stand up straight, young woman! The Irish bend the knee to no one."

"So sorry, Countess. The etiquette for interacting with titled people isn't one of my strong points."

"No need to stand on ceremony. And you address me as 'madame', not 'Countess'." She tosses her hat onto the sofa. "Miss

Blanchard, I really think you might stop gawping. You look like you've seen a ghost."

"But I have, madame. You're one. A ghost, I mean. I've summoned you up from the dead. I do hope you don't mind. I didn't hold out much hope, to be honest, but I thought it was worth a try. And here you are — just as real as if you're flesh and blood!"

"Steady on with the name-calling. Of course I'm real."

"Actually, you aren't. I can prove it. What's today's date?"

"July the fifteenth, 1927."

"How interesting. That's the day you died. Rather a long time ago, I'm afraid, Countess — I mean madame. Here's today's newspaper. The date's on the front."

The Countess takes it between her hands, forehead ruffling.

Sensing she's wavering, Aoife continues, "Look outside. It's a completely different world to the one you knew."

The Countess crosses to the window, sticks out her head and shoulders, and gasps. Hurriedly, she draws back her upper body into the room. "Gracious me, what a lot of motor cars. And they're positively whizzing along! Where are all the horses?"

"Replaced by the engine."

"No harm, I dare say. Some of the poor beasts were treated abysmally." Trying to make sense of her situation, she gazes into space. "I'm finding this rather a lot to take in. I wonder if I'm in the middle of a dream? Could I have eaten something which disagreed with me? I seem to recall a horrid bout of indigestion. And someone saying I was as white as a sheet and ought to see a doctor. Naturally I said I was far too busy. But they're not terribly substantial memories. May I?" Without waiting for an answer, she flops into an armchair, plucks at her collar and undoes her top button.

Aoife walks to a desk in the corner, where a laptop rests. She clicks it into life and taps a few words into a search engine. An image appears on the screen. She checks the caption, then carries the laptop to the Countess. "Look, that's a photograph of your funeral. Here's the newspaper account."

Agitated, the Countess sits bolt upright. "What is that malevolent-looking object? Remove it at once!"

"All right, I'll read it to you. '*Large numbers of people marched in the funeral procession of Madame Markievicz, T.D., yesterday afternoon. Several thousands lined the route through the city. A guard of Fianna Éireann boys dressed in green uniforms led the way. They were followed by the brass band of the Irish National Foresters and a detachment of the Citizen Army.*'"

The Countess begins to rally as the account goes on and looks over Aoife's shoulder.

"'*Members of the 1916 Club came next. They carried a floral cross with the inscription 'In Loving Memory of Our Old Comrade'. A big contingent of girls and women represented the Cumann na mBan, the Clan na nGaedheal and the Women's Defence League.*' That's some photograph, madame. Shows the city at a standstill."

"I must admit, it *is* rather gratifying." A neighing laugh erupts. "I'm feeling ridiculously puffed up. Though it's somewhat unsettling to see my funeral there in black and white. Tell me, did Casimir manage to attend?"

"He certainly did. It says here your husband's in one of the mourning coaches. I understood he saw you before you died. I seem to remember reading that he brought an extravagant amount of roses."

The Countess rubs at her forehead. "This is starting to return to me. Perhaps I might be dead. Unlikely though it is. Could I be under an anaesthetic? I've heard about people having the most vivid hallucinations during surgery."

"I'm afraid you're dead and buried, Countess. You're lying in the Republican plot in Glasnevin, surrounded by people you used to know. De Valera, Collins, Casement, Cathal Brugha, The O'Rahilly — it's a top-of-the-range line-up. I can call up a picture of your headstone if you like."

"Stop! You're like one of Dickens's monstrous ghosts summoning images from other Christmases. I have no desire to see my headstone. Just supposing what you say is true ..." She trails off.

Aoife gives her a few moments' respite before speaking again. "I know it's a lot to take in, Countess."

"Yes, well, I'm an adaptable person. Nil desperandum, and so forth. Though do try to remember. You address me as 'madame'. This countessing is rather tiresome."

"Sorry. You're my first titled person. I'm a little star-struck."

The Countess gives a regal wave of dismissal. "*If you prick us, do we not bleed?* I say, how did you convey me here? From wherever I was, I mean?"

"It was a fluke, really. I knew I needed something you owned for the – well, I don't like to call it a séance. Sounds so spooky. For the process, let's say. *For best results, an item that belonged to the subject is recommended.* That's what the online guide to raising the dead said. Well, I knew there were exhibits in museums with your hats and revolvers and so on, but museums are unbelievably touchy about lending them out. Unless to other museums. So I went to Lissadell, thinking there might be something I could buy in the gift shop. But there was nothing suitable for raising the dead. Bit of an oversight on the part of their stock-ordering manager, if you ask me. Anyhow, quite by chance, when I was mooching about in Sligo, I came across an old pair of gloves in a charity shop. I'm not sure why I picked them up. They were pretty manky, between you and me. But something told me to take a closer look and I found your initials inside. At least, they're the same as yours. CGB, for Constance Gore-Booth. I took a chance and bought them to use. I think they must have been the clincher. In making the, um, process work." Aoife points to the coffee table where a pair of yellowed, elbow-length silk gloves are lying inside a ring of tea-lights. "To be honest, I only used the candles for atmosphere. I don't think they advanced the materialisation."

The Countess stands up and lifts the gloves, examining them. She lays them against her cheek. "Shabby old things. But you're quite right, they are mine. My sister Eva gave them to me and embroidered my initials inside. How very enterprising of you, my dear. So, I'm dead. What an inconvenience!" She paces about, slapping the gloves against her palm. "I do hope I didn't conk out in prison." All at once, she stops walking. "The Free Staters didn't execute me, did they? I know I antagonised them dreadfully. Nearly as much as I riled the British. I was condemned to death after the Rising, you know, by that pompous little twerp, General Maxwell. Not only that but he had the cheek to reprieve me, too. Really, I said to the officer communicating the stay of execution, I do wish you chaps would make your minds up, instead of flip-flopping back and forth."

"You can't have wanted to face a firing squad!" cries Aoife.

Nonchalant, the Countess shrugs. "I didn't like being treated differently because I was a woman. Mind you, it's something I share in common with Éamon. Being let off, I mean."

"Do you mean de Valera?"

"*Mr* de Valera to you. I don't think much of your manners in the present day. And do stop biting your nails, my dear girl. My nanny, Squidge, would have rubbed a garlic clove on my fingers if she'd caught me at that."

Blushing, Aoife jams her hands into the front pockets of her jeans.

"Much better for your posture if you stand like this." The Countess demonstrates a military at-ease position, hands behind her back. Aoife copies her. "Jolly good. You show promise. Would you mind awfully telling me, how did I die?"

"Don't worry – you weren't shot while you were on the run, or executed by the Free State government, or anything like that. It happened in hospital. Peritonitis, according to the history books."

"I am not in the least bit worried, Miss Blanchard. Information is what I seek, not reassurance." Countess Markievicz rebukes her with a tap on the forearm.

Aoife jumps. "*Ouch!* That was weird – it made my stomach flip!"

"Yes, a peculiar sensation came over me, too. Chin up. Ride the fear, don't let it ride you. That's what I told my men when we were under machine-gun fire from the Shelbourne roof." The Countess gnaws her lower lip. "I'm starting to remember things. I suppose I must have died in Sir Patrick Dun's. I had a pain in my gut. Ignored it for as long as I could. Said I'd drop in to Kathleen Lynn and have her give me the once-over. But before I could, I passed out. Next thing I remember is waking up in hospital with Éamon de Valera beside my bed. Between you and me, it quite gave me the heebie-jeebies – he looked exactly like an undertaker. Always did. After that, I don't recall anything. What rotten luck! I was counting on an afterlife. Converted to Roman Catholicism to be on the safe side. Ho hum, so much for an eternity of camping trips with my Fianna boys." The Countess sits down, squashing her hat. "I see from your clothing that women are wearing breeches now. This is normal attire? I approve. Those ill-mannered separation women catcalled about my breeches when we were marched away from the College of Surgeons, after the surrender. What larks it would have been to shout back, 'Your granddaughters will be wearing them one day!' Incidentally, young woman, what am I doing here in the future?"

"I conjured you up. To ask your advice."

"Proceed."

"It's about political representation. Irish women have hardly any. It's utterly depressing. I belong to a group of volunteers working to overturn that."

"I say, good show! Like the Irish Volunteers?"

"No, we don't drill, or practise shooting. We're not volunteers in a military sense. We're pressing for political change but progress is unbelievably slow. I thought you might be able to suggest ways to speed it up."

"Have you considered a revolution?"

"The problem with guns is they just aren't acceptable any more. They create an increased set of risks. The other side always gets its hands on bigger guns and ups the ante. No offence, madame, I know you were out in 1916."

"No offence taken. Like many revolutionaries, I am a pacifist by nature and inclination. What can I say? Events overtook me." She studies the sitting room, furnished from Ikea. "If this is the future, it looks decidedly empty. How many people live here with you?"

"I live on my own."

"How courageous! But you have a live-in maid, I presume?"

"No maid. Couldn't afford one, even if I wanted. Which I don't. I'd feel I was exploiting her. I use a cleaning lady now and again."

"But who sets your fires and cooks your meals? Places your weekly order with the butcher and greengrocer? My dear, who answers the door for you?"

Aoife nibbles her lip. She hardly knows where to start explaining the future to this vision from 1927. "We have modern conveniences nowadays."

The Countess scans the room. "It doesn't look especially different." Her eyes fasten on some intricately embroidered cushions. "I'm glad to see people still do embroidery. It kept me sane in prison. I was sentenced to hard labour, you know. Scrubbed floors. Sewed nightclothes for prisoners. But I used to pull threads out of the rags they gave me to clean with, and save little patches of white cloth from the nightgowns. I used them for embroidery. I think I'd have gone mad with frustration otherwise. Ruins your eyes, of course. Still."

"Countess, would it be very rude of me to crack on? The problem is, I don't know how long you're allowed to visit from the other side – there might be a curfew. You could vanish in a puff of smoke when the clock strikes the hour. So would it be all right if we talked about the reason I called you up?"

"Very well."

"Let me bring you up to speed. When you were part of the revolution, it looked as though there'd be real political change. I mean to say, you were the first female MP, first female TD, first female minister in Europe – second in the world. It looked as though the old order was about to topple. But the new order was just as much of a closed shop. With women on the outside. We got the vote. And then, stop right there! Reverse gear engaged!"

"Haven't any of your female Taoisigh made a difference?'

"I'm sorry to say, Countess, I mean madame, there hasn't been a single, solitary female Taoiseach."

"Not one? Not even one? In an entire century?"

Aoife shakes her head. "We've had a few women in the number two slot, but we can't seem to climb any higher than Tánaiste. Neither of the two major parties has ever had a female leader. At least there's a push-back happening now. Women are fed up of being sidelined. Change is finally happening. But the pace is glacial. So I thought if I materialised you, madame, you might have some ideas we could use. To make a breakthrough."

"Disgraceful! The future is quite a disappointment! And to think I was a minister in 1919!"

"The trailblazing stuttered to a halt, I'm afraid."

"Outrageous! In my day, we believed change was not just inevitable but irreversible. Full equality for all the children of the nation was simply a matter of time. Where did it all go wrong?"

"Madame, men wouldn't share. They still don't really want to – not in their hearts. The majority, I mean – it's not fair to tar them all with the same brush. After the Anglo-Irish Treaty, that was back in 1921–"

"My dear, I was there, in the thick of it."

"Sorry, of course you were. Anyway, a counter-revolution happened. Not all at once, but gradually. Women were exempted from jury service, banned from state jobs after they married, and paid less than men when they were allowed to work. There was no contraception available, which didn't help. Basically, women were forced out of public life and into the home. In fairness, some improvements have happened in recent decades. We have the same legal rights now. Barriers to education have gone, apart from financial — a hurdle for both sexes. We're entitled to the same pay for the same work. In principle, at least. But promotion in your job? That's slow. Participation in government? They see that as an overreach. We're told they'll give us opportunities to lead if we're good enough. But we never seem to be. At least, not in their eyes."

"Damn and blast! How infuriating! I didn't risk bullets for a two-tier Ireland! What kind of man is your current Taoiseach?"

"Photogenic. Media savvy. Handsome."

"Handsome is as handsome does. Is he kind? Hardworking? Effective? It's a frightful waste to have a duffer as Taoiseach."

"I wouldn't call him a duffer and I'm sure he does work hard. We're still waiting to see if he'll be kind."

"Kindness is an obligation on all of us. Everyone should be a little kinder than we truly care to be. I learned that during the Lockout, running a soup kitchen at Liberty Hall. I suppose you don't need them any more."

"Actually, we do. We still have soup kitchens. And homeless people."

"What? Did Britain invade us again?"

"No, we're a republic. Since 1949."

"How splendid! That's news worth rising from the dead to hear. But wait, you say we rule ourselves, yet Irish people still go hungry? That's not the Éire I dreamed about and worked for with James Connolly and the others."

"I'm afraid there's a great deal of unfinished business, madame."

'Indeed.' Thin-lipped, the Countess leans against the mantelpiece, meditating. By and by, she raises her head. "At least there's been reintegration with the North by now, I presume?"

Aoife shares the bad news. "The six North-Eastern counties are still in Northern Ireland."

"You mean to tell me partition hasn't been overturned?"

Aoife pulls a sad face.

Countess Markievicz buries her face in her hands. A muffled voice emerges. "Let's not be daunted. We must focus on continuing the good fight." She inhales and marshals her courage. "We must reach out the hand of friendship to our Unionist brethren. Rome wasn't built in a day. On second thoughts, perhaps I oughtn't to mention Rome and Unionism in the same breath, riles them up, don't you know." An idea strikes her and she wheels about, eyes alight. "I have a topping idea, young woman. You could try a hunger strike. Always a useful tool, in my experience."

Aghast, Aoife blurts out, "People die on hunger strike!"

"If you believe in a cause, you must be willing to do whatever it takes to advance it. Sacrifices will have to be made. There's no alternative."

"But a hunger strike is way too radical!"

"Do you suppose I said to myself 'revolutions are too radical' when I buckled up and reported for duty on Easter Monday?"

"I'm grateful for your suggestion, madame. Truly I am. But is there any chance you might have a Plan B?"

"Oh, very well. Though I must say, your lack of grit is disappointing. If you're representative of the calibre of women today, it doesn't inspire much confidence. Let me think." She lifts her hat and twirls it on a forefinger. "I have it! Women must become activists again. Take the suffrage movement as your model. You should run a campaign along suffragette lines. They understood how to be effective. Here's what you do. Heckle senior politicians in public. Chain yourself to the Leinster House railings. Make placards and banners. Go on marches with them. Blowing whistles. They'll loathe that. The ruling class has no tolerance for noise, except when they're making it. I learned that in the nursery. Old Squidge was always telling us, *stop causing a disturbance*. Mama and Papa were fixated on silence. I expect your

Taoiseach and his Cabinet like everything nice and quiet, too."

"I suppose we could try some rallies. We've been too ladylike. Asked politely for our rights instead of demanding them."

"If I may say so, Miss Blanchard, it sounds as if you've grown complacent. In my day, we didn't mind raising a row. If you want something badly enough, forget about the courtesies. The time for being genteel is long past."

"I think my generation has just forgotten how to protest."

"A dash of turbulence never goes amiss. I remember the time the suffragettes filled their pockets with stones and broke windows the length and breadth of Kildare Street."

Aoife gulps. "Wouldn't that lead to a court appearance?"

"And your point is?" Impatient, the Countess pushes her hair back from her face. "Dramatic public gestures direct attention to a cause. They attract criticism, of course, but they also draw in converts."

"I don't want to seem like a total wuss, madame –"

'Wuss?'

"Coward. But I can't see my committee agreeing to a stone-throwing campaign. You could put someone's eye out. Besides, it's illegal."

"Fiddlesticks! What a tame lot you are today. You need to nail your colours to the mast. If you genuinely believe in something, it's worth fighting for. Whatever the cost. When the Irish nation was conjured into being, we trusted it would mean equality for all. You can't let some selfish men get away with scaling down the revolution. You must organise. Strategise. Agitate! Centre your campaign around a mass movement of women. Here's what you do – call a women's strike. Have all your female followers withdraw their labour from the workplace and the home. That won't go unnoticed, believe me."

"I'm not sure we have the support for action on that scale."

The Countess grasps Aoife by the shoulders, only to drop her hands at once. Both of them shiver. "I keep forgetting I shouldn't touch you. But I want to shake you, my dear, honestly I do. What are you, women or cry-babies? Stand up for your rights – nobody will serve them to you on a bone-china dinner plate! You're not some tiny bulbs buried deep beneath male rule, struggling to access light and air. You're educated. With opportunities women could only fantasise about in my day, from what you say. You must use your collective strength. Show the Government you have a grievance and don't be afraid to make yourselves disagreeable until you have what's rightfully yours.' Bristling with decision, Countess Markievicz slaps a dent out of her hat and jams it on her head. "I shall meet this Taoiseach of yours and give him a piece of my mind. Let us find an omnibus stop and pay him a call immediately."

"You can't just arrive on the Taoiseach's doorstep, madame."

"We'll see about that. I'd like to meet the minion who'll stop me!"

"What will you say to the Taoiseach?"

"That inequality wrapped in the flag of a republic remains just that. Inequality. Shape up, my man, I'll tell him. And if he tries to give me any lip, he'll be sorry. I'm too long in the tooth to take it from any man."

"I shouldn't think he'll give you any lip, madame. Actually, I have it on good authority he has lovely manners."

"Never mind that old courtesy palaver. I don't want men standing up when I enter a room, I want them listening to what I have to say – that's the best kind of respect. Not fetching our wraps and escorting us to tea-parties. Frankly, my dear, I find it vexatious to be dragged into the twenty-first century – without my Poppet for company – to deal with your Taoiseach. But deal with him I shall." She tosses her head, colour flooding her cheeks. "I faced down a court martial of army officers drunk with blood lust. I faced down officious prison governors and their meddlesome warders. I faced down former comrades when they chose a different path and the country was plunged into civil war.

And I faced down hostile crowds at public meetings on both sides of the Irish Sea. An Irish Taoiseach holds no terrors for me."

Aoife resists an impulse to kneel, although it's a close call. "You're magnificent!" she gasps.

"No hero worship, if you please! It's unseemly. Fetch my coat. Oh, I didn't bring one from the afterlife. Very well, let us go as we are. Follow me."

"To the Taoiseach's office?"

"Where else?"

Aoife wrings her hands. "Is this wise? I don't even know if you can go outside, madame. What if daylight shrivels you up? What if you turn to dust?"

"I am not a vampire. I am a revolutionary. Chop-chop, time's a-wasting. Fall in! Left-right, left-right!"

Outside the Department of the Taoiseach, Upper Merrion Street, Dublin

A security guard folds his arms, facing down Countess Markievicz. "I don't care if you're the Queen of Sheba, you can't come in here without a pass."

"I am a former Minister for Labour. I have permanent access to the seat of government."

'Show us your ID, missis."

"It's 'madame' to you. I don't appear to have a calling card about my person. Nor should I require one. My name is my calling card. Kindly inform the Taoiseach that Madame de Markievicz requests an appointment."

"Is he expecting you?"

"He is not. Nevertheless, I insist on seeing him. If he is a gentleman, he will not refuse me."

"No seeing the boss without an appointment. He's a busy man."

"And I am a busy woman. I have travelled an extremely long way to see him, thanks to the ingenuity of this young person beside me, Miss Aoife Blanchard. Now, I insist on you informing the Taoiseach's people that I am waiting."

"Will he know who you are?"

"My name ought to ring a bell." Turning to Aoife, she whispers in a clearly audible tone, "Perhaps I ought not to presume?"

"He'll know you, madame," says Aoife. "You're on the school curriculum. And there's a bust of you in The Green, as well as a statue in Townsend Street. You haven't been forgotten."

"Really? I wonder if it would be too conceited of me to go and examine those memorials after I've finished with the Taoiseach? I do hope they've spelled Markievicz correctly."

"I'm sure it's right. We have spell-check now." A happy thought occurs to Aoife. "You'll like the Townsend Street statue. There's a little dog at your ankles."

"I say, I wonder if it's Poppet? How kind of the sculptor. Really, it's not much of an afterlife without either my spaniel or my Fianna boys. But, actually, I wish I could remember what the afterlife *is* like. It's all a frightful blur."

The security guard makes a flapping gesture. "That's enough gabbing. I need yous to leave right now."

"Kindly be silent. I'm thinking," snaps the Countess.

"Yous can do your thinking someplace else. Government property's no place for thinking."

The Countess stands her ground. "You will not batter me into submission, you bully. I am staying put."

"Nobody's laying a finger on you, missis. I'm only asking you politely for to leave the premises."

"Politely? I was treated with more courtesy by Captain de Courcy-Wheeler when I yielded my gun to him!"

"Jaysus, do you have a gun on you?" He signals to a *garda* standing at nearby railings. "Guard, over here, quick!"

"I am unarmed, my man. Stop putting words in my mouth."

"We're pacifists," Aoife intervenes. She wavers, casting an anxious glance at her companion. "At least, you are now, isn't that right, madame?"

The garda joins the trio outside the security hut. "What seems to be the problem?"

The security guard puffs up. "Your one here in the hat is using threatening language – she mentioned a gun."

"Don't talk poppycock. There are no weapons in the afterlife. Besides, I told you. I was forced to yield my Mauser to Captain de Courcy-Wheeler. He was on General Maxwell's staff." In an aside to Aoife, she says, "Remind me, later, to ask you what happened to the general." A curl of the lip. "I presume the British heaped him with honours and gave him a seat in the House of Lords."

Aoife makes eye contact with the garda. "There's been a misunderstanding, guard. My friend here has an appointment with the Taoiseach but his office has forgotten to notify the security staff. We're trying to sort it out now."

The garda shrugs and walks away.

Just then, a black Mercedes pulls up and the pair of ornate metal gates beside the security hut begin to open.

"Madame, that's him!" Aoife tugs the Countess by the sleeve. "The Taoiseach's in the car!"

Countess Markievicz steps in front of the vehicle, raising a hand. "Halt! I have a bone to pick with you!"

The rear window of the car winds down. "Hi, good to meet you." A hand emerges and shakes hers.

"My name is Constance de Markievicz and I have returned from the dead to tell you that the women of Ireland are extremely disappointed in you."

"A, I don't believe in ghosts, and B, I'm a feminist: I like women. So fair's fair, they should like me."

"A, I don't care whether you believe in me or not – the important thing is I believe in me. B, we're indifferent to being liked. We want you to give us our due. Your government needs more women on the inside making decisions."

"Is this a candid camera set-up?" The Taoiseach leans out of the window and scans the gates, looking for a lens. "Are you one of those 1916 actors off the tour buses? I have to hand it to you – you look exactly like her. We could use you for our party *árd fheis*. You'd be a super interval act."

"That's enough of your impertinence! You are addressing the first female minster in the inaugural Dáil Éireann. Resist the impudence to call me an actor. Or to suggest me as an – an – an –" – in her outrage, she begins to stutter – "interval act!"

Nonplussed, the Taoiseach fiddles with the mobile phone in his hand. "Why don't we do a selfie? Then I need to press on. Work's piling up."

"I haven't the foggiest notion what a selfie is. Nor will I be diverted by your reference to it. And kindly desist from fidgeting with that object in your hand while I address you."

"You sound a lot like my mum when you use that tone."

"A worthy woman, no doubt. We shall invite the good lady to join our struggle."

"Not sure I like the idea of a struggle."

"Ah, but there's rapture in the struggle!"

An aide's head emerges from the front passenger window. "*An Taoiseach* has a full itinerary and there's no space for rapture in it."

"Whoever you are, have the common courtesy not to butt in. You are not party to this conversation. I presume, Taoiseach, you can spare the time to discuss the Irish Republic – which is failing to fulfil its potential, from what I understand."

"We're a work in progress,' says the Taoiseach. "But we'll get there. Afraid I have to go to my office now. It's time to record my weekly address to the Irish people. Hashtag #puttingpizzazzintopolitics." The car window starts to close.

"Wait one moment!" says the Countess. "As Taoiseach, you have won a place in history. If you want history to look kindly on you, however, you need to show you've earned that place."

The window stops halfway up. "What do you have in mind?"

"Cancel your appointments for the rest of the day. You and I have a great deal to thrash out."

"Sorry, the logistics make that impossible."

"Don't bandy logistics at me. We'd never have stood out for the best part of a week against the might of the British empire without some grasp of logistics."

The Taoiseach clears his throat. "I suppose I might be able to squeeze you in for some face time next week. Have your people call my people."

"Look here, I haven't a clue where I'll be next week. Has nobody instructed you in the merits of *carpe diem*? Do you, or don't you, want to enter the history books as a visionary Taoiseach?"

A pause. The Mercedes idles. Then a click sounds and the rear passenger door opens. "Guess I could spare half an hour."

A hand emerges to assist Countess Markievicz into the car. She bats it away.

"I can manage, thank you." She ducks inside and the door shuts behind her.

"Madame, will I wait here for you?" Aoife calls after her.

A hand flutters at the window and the car drives through the gates.

Desolate, Aoife watches it disappear. "I don't think she heard me. I hope she'll be okay."

The security guard throws his eyes heavenwards. "No better wan! She's some piece of work. Which of the tour buses is she off?"

Aoife scuffs the pavement with a trainer toe. "Why can't she be who she says she is?"

He treats himself to a snort before withdrawing into his hut.

She looks left and right along Upper Merrion Street, considering whether to stay or go. A side gate opens and the aide appears, pen and notebook in hand.

"Your friend told me get your address off you and you're to head on home. If she can join you later she will. But it might be out of her hands, she says."

Aoife dictates her flat number and the street.

He reaches into an inner pocket. "Just in case, she asked me to give you this. It's a souvenir, your friend says."

He reaches an envelope to her and vanishes back through the gate.

Inside lies a folded-over square of cloth embroidered in brown and gold thread. It shows a bouncy dog with floppy ears, tongue out, tail in the air. Poppet is spelled below in chain-stitch, and in a corner, the initials CM.

Carefully, Aoife returns it to the envelope. With a jaunty wave at the security guard, who affects not to notice, she starts walking in the direction of St Stephen's Green.

Countess Markievicz was beloved by the Irish people. The Free State government refused her a state funeral but the people gave her a de facto one: an estimated 100,000 filed past her coffin, while crowds thronged the streets when she was taken for burial. Among flowers at the funeral was a nest of three eggs: a countrywoman had promised her some fresh eggs when she was in hospital and felt Madame should have them anyway.

Note:

An earlier version of this story was written as a fundraiser for the Women for Election lobby group. I take the view that the Countess would approve of its aims.

MAUD GONNE

Born Surrey, England, 1866; died Dublin, 1953

Civil rights activist, feminist, advocate for prisoners, champion of Irish culture and independence

Maud Gonne was the daughter of a senior British officer stationed in Ireland but felt an affinity with the Irish people and decided to work on their behalf. An heiress, she used her wealth for a variety of causes.

In 1900 she founded *Inghinidhe na hÉireann* (Daughters of Ireland), whose achievements included feeding school dinners to undernourished Dublin children, and setting up the first women's newspaper, *Bean na hÉireann*. In 1918 she was jailed in London's Holloway Prison on trumped-up charges of being complicit in a German plot to overthrow British rule in Ireland. During the War of Independence, she publicised atrocities and worked on behalf of victims. In 1922 she co-founded the Women's Prisoners' Defence League – a lifelong advocate for prisoners, she had campaigned on behalf of IRB prisoners in English jails as a young woman. In 1923 she was arrested for parading with an anti-Free State placard and jailed in Dublin's Kilmainham, where she spent twenty days on hunger strike.

She had two children by her French lover, Lucien Millevoye. Later, she was married briefly to Major John MacBride, who was executed after the Easter Rising; they had a son, Seán MacBride, who founded Amnesty International.

Maud was W.B. Yeats's muse, and many of his poems were inspired by her. Speranza was among those to whom he compared her.

The Lost Boy

The waking nightmare rides Maud.

Her lost boy is trapped in the afterlife. She glimpses him from behind, frantic to return to her. He stands by a closed door, stretching for the handle, but his arms are too short to catch at it. He drums his tiny fists against the wood, making a high, whining noise at the back of his throat. She finds the sound intolerable and covers her ears with her hands but his cries continue to penetrate. They dwindle to hiccoughing sobs that rack his toddler's frame.

The focus shifts and Georges's face is visible now. He is scarlet from exertion, his cotton-wool curls slick against his forehead. He attempts to speak. "*Mm-mm!*" he wails, again and again. It's the noise he makes when he's trying to say Moura. "*Mm-mm!*" His wretchedness is tidal, its flow will drown her.

She must help her son to turn the doorknob. He is waiting to be reborn.

August-October 1891

Immediately after Georges died, she was a whirlwind of activity. She would allow no one else to touch him. With her own hands, she stripped off his nightgown, sponged him, coaxed his limbs into a sailor suit, combed his golden hair. Under his arm she tucked Pierre, the rabbit he always slept with, sewn from scraps of brown velvet. Throughout, she talked to him, telling him his Moura was with her Georges. That's the name she gave herself especially for him.

"Moura's going to look after her pet-lamb," she promised. "Moura will keep him safe."

Except, of course, she hadn't.

She ordered him embalmed, to preserve his dimpled flesh from the indignities of deterioration. It was the month of August and Paris sweltered – there was no time to spare. Men in top hats, crepe fluttering from the hatbands, entered her apartment to carry out the process.

She lingered, reluctant to hand him over to others already. "I'll be back soon, Georges." Her forefinger touched his cheek. How cold he was already! Yet fever had overheated his skin during his illness.

"Sometimes, madame, a lock of hair is kept. For sentimental reasons," suggested one of the men. "Should we …?"

"No, I'll do it." She took the scissors he produced and snipped off a curl, before leaving them to their work.

She had not worn black while preparing her son. But now the sight of those sober-suited undertakers reminded her and she changed into full mourning. Ceremonial in her movements, she draped a veil over herself. She would keep it on indoors so that not even her household could look at her ravaged face. Lucien Millevoye arrived while she was giving orders for every member of her staff to be issued with a black armband. She was not at home to callers but made an exception for him.

"Where will you bury him, Maud?" he asked.

She registered the pronoun with a thinning of the lips – Georges was his child but her responsibility. Even in death. Later, reflecting on their relationship, she dated the ebbing of Lucien's hold over her from that moment.

She did not know what answer she would give until the words left her lips. "In Samois." Samois-sur-Seine was where Georges had lived.

Immediately, she set about commissioning a memorial chapel in the country graveyard there. Georges's nineteen-month-old body would lie in a vault beneath it.

When everything was in train and Georges had been taken away, her willpower snapped. It happened as suddenly as fog rushing in from the sea. Where once she was efficient, now she could barely speak – her knowledge of French vanished and she could not instruct the servants, leaving them to guess her desires. Tears seeped incessantly from her bloodshot eyes. Sleep eluded her and she began to rely on chloroform to snatch periods of respite. Sometimes, she laid her head on his tiny bed and napped there.

His nursery was the only place where she could settle. In her lap, she held his comb with strands of baby hair glinting among its teeth. She crawled inside his wardrobe, lifting her face to the dangling hems of his little dresses. She held the scrap of blond hair she had cut off, inhaling it, searching for his scent. Already, his essence was fading.

Her powers of concentration were fractured. She would start to do something and forget what she intended halfway through. It troubled her that she lacked a photograph of Georges, a painting or pencil sketch. She could have attempted one herself – she had some artistic talent. But it never occurred to her to preserve his infant perfection. She rebuked herself for her complacency.

Embracing seclusion, she refused to leave her apartment. Visitors left gifts of *sal volatile* or posies of flowers but she acknowledged none of them. Letters went unread. Her curtains remained drawn because the sunlight offended her eyes. When she was alone, she brooded. When Lucien visited, she picked over the details of Georges's final days, seeking a way to have altered the outcome.

"It was God's will," said Lucien.

Eyes dilated, she gazed at him, aghast at his failure to understand how Georges's death was not part of a divine plan but an appalling mistake. How could she ever have believed that Lucien shared the sensibilities of his grandfather, a celebrated Romantic poet?

Registering her distaste, he captured her hand and trailed a column of kisses on it. "Such a slender sliver of life," he sighed. "Not even two birthdays. *Petit* Georges was a gift. On temporary loan to us. And now he has been gathered back to the Almighty's side. Where he watches over his Moura, like a guardian angel."

Did he think to comfort her with platitudes? She left her hand limp in his and he dropped it. Nevertheless, she valued Lucien's sombre presence, strongly etched eyebrows knitting together to convey sympathy. Her baby had his father's heavy-lidded eyes, the same shape to their ears. The parents were united in their loss.

However, as weeks passed, the desire to rail at him fizzed beneath the surface. Those soothing pats on her back didn't fool her. She knew what he was thinking. His thoughts were goldfish circling in the glass bowl of his head. She could read them like ticker tape. Here was one now. *Her misery's excessive.* There was another. *It borders on hysteria.* His solution? *She should set it aside and look to the future.* "I have no child – you have another son," she itched to hurl at him but retained enough restraint – just – to avoid a scene.

Her resentment manifested itself in a way he could not misinterpret. She refused to allow him back into her bed. He accepted her rejection with good grace but his daily visits to her apartment slackened off. Perhaps he sensed she was breaking off their relationship and had no desire to dissuade her. Still, he gave her some useful advice: a change of scene. Yes, that's what she needed. He did not offer to accompany her. During her last week in Paris, he developed the habit of leaving on his coat and remaining for not longer than ten minutes.

Winter 1891– Summer 1893

In the second month after Georges's death, she travelled to Ireland in search of respite. It was a false hope. The Irish people were surrendering en masse to grief – Charles Stewart Parnell's body was carried on the same vessel in which she sailed, returning to his birthplace for burial. Recognising her, onlookers imagined her head-to-toe black was worn in honour of the man they called "Ireland's Uncrowned King". The sense of national mourning tallied with her mood – let the world mirror her personal loss.

Willie Yeats, who met her off the mailboat at Kingstown pier and breakfasted with her, was puzzled by the extravagance of her weeds.

"I mourn my nephew," she told him. It pained her to disguise Georges but she could not admit to a son because the loss to her reputation would be irretrievable.

Once Georges's name was spoken between them, she couldn't stop herself talking about him. "We had a special bond. He called me Moura, or at least he tried to say it. It's how I would have been known to him," she said. "It's an anagram. From *amour*." It was her compromise name. *Maman* was impossible.

Willie stroked her hand, glad of an opportunity to touch her although confused about why the bereavement flattened her. She seemed possessed by melancholy. "Death is a human invention," he suggested. "No one is lost. Individuals continue to exist beyond the veil. Our reality remains interlocked with theirs."

"What good is Georges to me there? I can't touch him or talk to him."

He rubbed at the tracks left by his spectacles on the bridge of his nose. "There is a way to make contact, Maud. I know a sensitive whose powers never fail. If you like, I could arrange a séance?"

She was optimistic when she met the medium. But Georges could not be persuaded to use that channel. There was a queue of people from the other side clamouring to pass on messages to the select group attending the séance – but none was a nineteen-month-old French boy missing his mother. Instead, Maud was told she had been an Egyptian priestess in a previous life. It was meaningless. She brushed it aside. She wanted Georges, not handmaidens from earlier times. Willie urged her to keep trying but she had no patience. "What, and discover I was a Babylonian slave girl? Maid Marion running through Sherwood Forest?" she snapped.

Meanwhile, her sorrow was as constant as her shadow and she fed it daily. She could not meet a perambulator without dipping her head to examine its occupant. She could not share a park bench with a mother and child without begging to hold the baby. She saw the puffball of her boy's curls when she raised her eyes to the clouds. If she looked at a fountain, she was reminded of the bubbles he blew trying to shape words.

One day, an idea took hold. A notion so compelling that when it wormed its way into her it swamped her sorrow. Georges was not consigned to oblivion – his nineteen months of life were not the end. Something further might be possible.

Reincarnation.

It was in Dublin that the seed was planted. Willie Yeats introduced her to the idea during a conversation about the astral plane, where he was always trying to *rendez-vous* with her. Possibly, it occurred to Maud, because he believed she might be more amenable there. Almost casually, he said, "Sooner or later, your nephew will be reincarnated. It's probable you'll meet him again in this life. After all, you say we were brother and sister in a previous existence."

Face vivid, she latched onto his remark. "Will I know him, Willie? Will he know me?"

"Yes, you'll recognise each other, Maud. People always do, at some level. Their sixth sense tells them. That's why, at our first encounter, we two were drawn towards each other."

A note of desolation entered her voice. "But someone else will be his mother! Who will it be?"

"I don't know. Does it matter?"

"Yes, it matters! I am his mother!"

Willie pretended not to hear. He preferred the myth that she was the child's aunt.

He led her to A.E. Russell, stately with wisdom, both instinctive and acquired, about the spirit world. His was the face of an early Christian martyr suffering unspeakable torments with pious resignation. His friends called him George – she regarded it as an omen. To Russell, Maud confided the truth about Georges. He was unshocked.

His words were manna: rebirth could be consciously directed, rather than left to chance. By approaching conception with intent, she could take steps to have Georges reincarnated in her womb. Another child would be born in whom her son's spirit lived on – a host body for the lost boy.

"Go to where he lies," said Russell. "Call to him there. His shade will hear your summons – a mother's voice can pierce the cloak between this world and the spirit sphere. First, you must beckon him, so that he hovers nearby. Then, you must couple in the act of love with Georges's father. It is essential that it happens in the place where your infant is resting."

A shudder twitched at her. "In the crypt? Beside his coffin?"

A curt nod. Scruples were for the unenlightened. "Miss Gonne, I can't stress this enough. Proximity to the child's bodily remains assists the process of metempsychosis – transmigration of the soul."

He had a deliberate way of speaking which impressed his hearers. Maud was no exception – she was convinced by his certainty.

"And Georges's soul will be reborn?" she asked. "I'll be his mother again?"

"It's possible. As the act of love reaches its climax, your son will be able to seize the opportunity to transmigrate. With the life force quickening inside you, he can leap across the divide between his world and ours. It can happen, Miss Gonne, but only if your courage is matched by belief."

Independent means, and no husband or guardian, allowed her to travel freely. She returned to Paris and laid her plans with care. Sending a message to Lucien, she invited him to supper. His eyes were guarded as he kissed each cheek. "Exquisite," he pronounced. Yet she knew she had changed. Lucien, by comparison, was untouched. Once, she had thought those sorrowful eyes hinted at hidden depths. Now, she knew they masked shallowness.

She gestured him to a seat by the fireside and listened while he indulged in some political gossip. When he expounded, he became as self-absorbed as a cat. She had nil interest in France's political intrigues at this point in time but it was no hardship to pretend. Since meeting him, she had grown accustomed to wearing a mask. He had explained the necessity of camouflage to her: a man prominent in political circles could have a mistress but the couple must be discreet.

Gratifyingly, she was all attention while Lucien spoke about Patrice de MacMahon, former President of the Third Republic, who had died a few days earlier and was to have a state funeral. "Your countryman," he called the Marshal. The family were Wild Geese who had left Ireland after James II's defeat by William of Orange in the late 17th century. It was a deliberate compliment – Maud could be touchy about the shallowness of her Irish roots. She remembered meeting the MacMahon. He told her she had the eyes of a tigress and must have prowled the jungle in a former life.

It was supper à deux. She had sent the servants away, intending to serve Lucien herself. She allowed her hand to rest on his shoulder as she poured his wine. She brushed against him when she passed the cheese board. She chose a peach for him and kissed its voluptuous contours before handing it over. With every touch, she was intimating a readiness to resume their physical relationship.

She would need to be wily, however. He was no admirer of spiritualism – his Catholicism left him wary of it. This first night, she must not betray her hand. She should concentrate on demonstrating that her health was recovered, her beauty heightened rather than by diminished by loss.

Only once was Georges mentioned. "Do you ever go to Samois?" she asked.

She had bought a home for Georges in the riverside town thirty miles south-east of Paris, leaving him in the care of a sensible widow. It was an attractive villa with a walled garden. He would grow up healthy there – his limbs made sturdy by fresh air and nourishing food. The trains were frequent and she could visit often from her Paris apartment. When she was absent in England and Ireland, he would be in safe hands.

"Never," answered Lucien, making a throwaway gesture with one of his hands. Belatedly, he tacked on, "I find it too sad to go to Samois. A surfeit of memories."

"We don't want to forget, surely," she protested.

"Forget? No. But to live in the past is unwholesome."

She ground her teeth together, glad of the distraction when her parrot cawed at them from his perch on top of the mantelpiece. Always, her rooms were filled with caged songbirds, but the parrot was free to fly where he chose. Lucien kept a wary eye on the jewel-bright creature. Once, the parrot had defecated on one of his patent shoes. It might be plotting to target the other shoe.

Several days later, when she shared her plans with him, Lucien's response was belligerent. He told her she was delusional. It was an unhinged fantasy springing from over-indulgence in chloroform, which she continued to rely on to help her sleep.

"Maud, you must put aside this insane idea and accept that Georges is gone," he insisted.

She faced him down. "Think it over, that's all I ask. Don't dismiss it at once."

"It's monstrous! A crypt is a place of death. A charnel house."

"But from death will spring life, Lucien! Our son will be like the phoenix resurrected from the flames!"

He shuddered. "I insist you stop dabbling in spiritualism. Such ideas are hideous – unnatural."

Normally, she would challenge him. What right had he to be dictatorial? Theirs was a voluntary treaty beyond the reach of church or law. She had natural rights which outranked religious or legal ones – the right to love whom she pleased, for as long or short a time as she saw fit, and to replace that lover with another if she chose. No law was entitled to interfere with those privileges.

Nevertheless, she must tread with care. A wisp of linen was dabbed at her eyes. "To a mother, only the loss of her child is unnatural."

"I know it's hard, *chérie*. Grieve, of course, but don't dwell on the past." He touched his fingertips to his luxurious moustache, as black as a chimney sweep's face. She suspected he dyed it.

Stoicism was never her way – she believed in making things happen. But to bring Lucien with her, she must proceed in baby steps. She made a show of considering his words and finding them persuasive.

"You have such wisdom, Lucien. I'm fortunate to have you for my guide." As an apparent afterthought, she said, "But think about my little idea. Its symmetry is enchanting. What could be more natural than to welcome baby Georges back into our lives?"

Summer 1891

In the months before he died, Georges was attempting to walk. Words were harder for him but he was impatient to be mobile. His first steps were a milestone she missed, campaigning in Ireland against evictions. Accounts of his day were posted regularly. But it wasn't the same as holding him beneath the armpits, his legs flailing, toes touching the rug, wriggling and slipping in his eagerness to be mobile.

She had missed his first efforts to crawl, too – forging strategic connections in London, including drawing Willie Yeats into her net. Her loveliness had an impact on both men and women, dazed alike by its impact. Yet she had a distance that held them on the point of a pin: this far and no further. Willie was among those speared and she intended to keep him there – his genius bent words into powerful shapes, a talent that would prove useful to her causes.

She must not allow herself to believe that her absences failed Georges. He wanted for nothing. When she was a girl, her own father was away often on army business but she never doubted his care for her. If her focus drifted from her child at times, it was not through want of love but because the Irish people's need was impossible to refuse. She must learn to forgive herself – Mr Russell said so.

When Georges had fallen sick, a telegram had recalled her from Ireland. At once, she set off, fear pecking at her. She would not have been summoned unless her boy was seriously ill. This was her punishment for resisting motherhood initially. She had not wanted a baby and Lucien had promised it would not happen. She should trust him, he had said. And she had yielded. But on a summer's day, in a doctor's consulting rooms, she had learned to doubt her lover. Her loss of appetite and dizziness were not due, after all, to overwork. In the winter of 1889, she had gone to ground in France, and in the snap of a January morning, Georges Silvère Gonne had arrived.

How could she have wept when that doctor told her she was to become a mother? Now, she quailed at the prospect of losing her son.

She went directly to him in the house in Samois-sur-Seine. Lucien was in Paris but she did not delay to meet him. Twenty days she spent with Georges. Twenty days to croon lullabies. Twenty days to tell him Moura was here and she loved her pet-lamb best in all the world. Even then, she could not risk calling herself his *maman*, in case he repeated it. But her presence gave him no relief. He was unsettled, whimpering in his sleep.

Dissatisfied with the medical attention available in the small town, she swept him back to Paris and hired two nurses so that one was always with him, day and night. The doctor who had delivered Georges looked in, morning and evening, his black bag bulging with remedies. "It's a fever in the brain, madame. Unfortunately, children sometimes develop them. Who knows why? Everything humanly possible is being done. You must pray now."

She was convinced Georges would pull through – he was a robust child, tall for his age, well nourished, accustomed to fresh air. The nurses assured her his chances were excellent. But her son was lethargic and wouldn't eat.

Lucien visited often, chewing his moustache ends. One evening, he urged her to sleep. "I'll sit with him, chérie," he promised, and she consented to take a few hours' rest. Shortly after dawn, she rose and joined Lucien beside the small wooden bed. It was clear their child was struggling for life and they were reduced to bystanders at the battle. It felt as if she had never been closer to her lover than during those hours when they kept vigil together. But at breakfast time, Lucien said he was obliged to leave. He returned to his other life.

That night, Lucien was unable to join her. She sat up with the nurse, dozing a little. Shortly before dawn, Georges heaved out a shallow breath and his hands appeared from beneath the covers, palms outwards, fingers curled. He gave a second sigh, soft as melted wax. All at once, the sheet no longer stirred to his heartbeat. She did not react at first. It would move again in a moment. But the nurse stiffened, felt his pulse and blessed herself, which caused Maud to rise to her feet. At the nurse's murmured *le pauvre petit*, a scream was torn from her.

Even in death, she could not acknowledge him as her child. Her name was not written on Georges's death certificate for fear of scandal. *Parents unknown* was entered.

October 1893

She laid siege to Lucien, who resisted her pleas. An obstinate man. No matter. She would bend his will to hers. She wept, ordered, bartered, seduced. If necessary, she'd cheat – she felt at liberty to do whatever was required.

"Maud, you must guard against these false hopes," he scolded. "Spiritualism attracts charlatans, like flies to uncovered meat. They prey on the vulnerable."

She swore an oath never to let him lay a hand on her again if he refused her. She threatened to subvert his political career by exposing his adultery in the press. She vowed to lay bare every secret he had shared with her. Exile would be his only choice.

"Let Georges go," he advised her. "If you hold something too tightly, you arrest the blood flow. You crush it."

She lowered her eyelids to conceal the truth that she no longer cared for him. Her love had become a husk. But woven through it was her need for him. "Lucien, if ever you cared for me, do this – I'll never ask you for anything again."

"Even if I did it, it wouldn't work. Surely my lack of faith undermines yours? My disbelief would block this transmigration you talk about."

"I have belief enough for both of us. Mine is limitless."

He made a small explosion of sound, midway between regret and reprimand.

"No one need ever know," she said. "It can remain another of our secrets. We have so many already."

He snapped his fingers with unexpected violence. "You and your absurdities. You are as ridiculous as those inept Irish revolutionists you champion."

Her eyes smouldered but she held back. "This is between you and me, Lucien. Nobody else. We have the power to guide Georges home to us."

For weeks, they argued back and forth. Finally, she knelt before Lucien. It was then he wavered. Her vulnerability could not be ignored. Always, there had been an aloof quality about her. Now, the goddess was human.

"Look at me." Her voice, which moved crowds at public rallies, had only to persuade one listener but she could no longer rely on her charm. Even so, she persisted. "I cannot sleep without medication. I cannot speak without wanting to scream. I cannot eat without stomach pains. I take no ease or pleasure in anything. In your mercy, grant me this boon. Help me to waken Georges to life again."

And he agreed.

November 1893

Shortly before midnight, they arrived at the graveyard. They came on foot in case a carriage idling outside attracted attention. Lucien was a sleepwalker beside her, stumbling along the unlit path, and she transferred the lantern to her other hand so they could link arms. He must not stray beyond the ambit of her spell. Earlier in the evening they had dined together and she had been profligate when pouring cognac, submerging his doubts. Lucien was superstitious about the vault. Had she miscalculated the quantity? Alcohol could stimulate men but an excess rendered them incapable.

They passed a line of sullen trees, the path slippery with moss. She could detect the white stone of the mausoleum ahead. Hard against a boundary wall at the back of the plot, it dwarfed its surroundings – a temple in miniature, modelled along Grecian lines. Moderation was not in her nature.

Before going inside, at her suggestion, they each smoked a cigarette. Tobacco would settle him. She needed no calming but was a habitual smoker, blaming her intermittent cough on weak lungs rather than dependency. The twin tips were friendly glowing stars, below a night sky entirely without stars, kindly or otherwise. The moonlight was fitful, obscured by drifting clouds. From a treetop overhead, an owl hooted and another responded.

The lantern illuminated the jet twinkle of Lucien's shirt studs. He was always well turned out, even for an engagement which he found distasteful. Inhaling on one of his Turkish cigarettes, she contemplated him. The hunch of his shoulders betrayed his unease. That stooped posture reminded her of Willie, who would have had no reservations about joining in this endeavour – treating it as an adventure, if not source material for a poem. But it had to be Lucien, no matter how grudging his participation.

A flap among the branches in one of the elms, and Lucien's head jolted in the sound's direction. "Was that a bat?"

"An owl. Didn't you hear his call?" She could not allow him to be unmanned. "It's all so Gothic with a capital G, isn't it? Moonlight, owls, the witching hour, and so forth. Thank goodness you're here to protect me, Lucien. I've always admired your *sangfroid*." A sidelong glance to establish if he had regained his self-control. She must risk no further delay. Exhaling smoke, she ground her butt underfoot. "Come, *mon amour*. It's time." From her pocket, she produced a ring with two elongated metal keys attached. Catching him by the hand, she led him to the door. "Take the lantern. Hold it up so I can find the lock." Into the mausoleum door, she inserted the key. A momentary resistance before it creaked ajar. Forging ahead, she entered a memorial chapel, Lucien at her heels. "Foolhardy," he muttered, but she pretended not to hear.

Shadows gloomed on every side. The chapel was in on the conspiracy. *Keep going, Maud. If you hesitate, Lucien will turn tail.* She knew what to look for – beneath a slit of window, a pair of trapdoors was set into the floor. Down she hunkered. The smaller key fitted inside the padlock on the double doors. This lock opened readily. She uncoiled the chain and pulled at the handle on the nearest door. It was heavy and Lucien had to help her. Together, they threw it open. The clang as it dropped startled an echo through the chapel. Lucien retreated a step, looking back towards the outer door left slightly ajar. She considered returning to close it but decided to press on. She heaved at the second trapdoor and he had no choice but to give her assistance.

A smell of mould rushed out. Underpinning it was the smack of decay. A metal, eight-rung ladder led down to a cavern beneath the chapel floor. She regarded the darkness rising towards them: her lost boy was waiting there for her. Seizing the lantern from Lucien, she directed a shaft of light into the hollow. Her eyes burrowed into the shadows, searching for the trestle table on which his coffin lay. An oversized fist squeezed her heart. *Poor Georges, sleeping there by yourself for so long. You're not alone any more. Moura's on her way to you, pet-lamb.*

By her side, she sensed a shiver of resistance from Lucien. Perhaps the nip of decomposition was unravelling him. She turned her face to him, knowing the lantern beam was her ally. Her smile was radiant. A gilded sheen glanced off her skin. "*Allons.* Fortune favours the brave." She lifted her arm high, directing light towards the ladder. "You first, *mon amour*."

Even now, she did not trust him to follow her if she descended before him. She observed his crab descent, clinging to the ladder. As soon as he was on the floor of the vault, she set her feet on the ladder. She took her time on the rungs, her descent hampered by the lantern she carried. Near the bottom, she pretended to wobble, allowing him to stretch up and relieve her of the lantern. "Well done, Lucien. I don't think I could have managed without you." Holding the light source would give him the illusion of being in control.

This lower room was claustrophobic. The stale air dragged at her throat, causing her breath to scrape. A cough tickled and she forced it back. Any coughing bout filled her with dread, fearing it signalled tuberculosis – the disease that had killed her mother, she was convinced. She preferred to believe it was the culprit rather than childbirth. Another cough gurgled at the back of her throat. This place was inciting her to hack her lungs to shreds. She moistened her lips and focused on controlling her breathing.

When she was able to speak, she laced her fingers through her lover's. "Our beloved son sleeps here. Soon, he'll be with us again."

Maud led Lucien the few paces that separated them from the coffin. Dried garlands of flowers disintegrated on the lid. Once, fresh snowdrops were scattered over it. She knew the box contained a second one. French bureaucracy had insisted on an inner and an outer casket before the tiny body could be transported by rail from Paris to Samois-sur-Seine.

She bent her neck to the coffin, intending to commune with Georges as A.E. Russell had advised, but was distracted by Lucien. Eyes bulging, he was jumping at shadows flaring on the walls. She caught him blessing himself, the rapid pant of his breath filling the crypt. She curled her lip. He lacked backbone, this man who had fathered a child on her. She suspected he was on the brink of flight.

"Lucien!" Her voice was parade-ground crisp. "Find somewhere to set the lantern."

He shrugged, at a loss. She snatched the lamp and positioned it on their baby's coffin. There was no other shelf – they could not risk placing it on the ground to be kicked over. Lucien would most certainly bolt if they lost their light.

The beam exaggerated rather than minimised the blackness, shadows massed at its outer perimeters. She looked upwards toward their exit, remembering that Lucien had left the mausoleum door open a crack. Possibly, a pale strip of light might show through.

On the floor above, she noticed other patches of darkness detach themselves from the mass and flutter into movement.

Perhaps, it occurred to her, they were spectral witnesses to what she was about to set in train.

She considered closing the chapel door before deciding it was irrelevant. The verger, who lived nearby, had been bribed. He would not arrive to investigate. She had told him she wanted to kneel there and pray for a child's immortal soul, place flowers on his coffin. An envelope containing a wad of notes had been slipped into his hand.

"There is no risk to your livelihood or reputation, *monsieur*. I will spend perhaps half an hour. Everything will be left exactly as I found it. I will trouble no other grave." His fingers had caressed the envelope, acknowledging its bulk, while her charm had lapped against him. He had tapped his nose in a complicit gesture.

Lucien was still goggle-eyeing the coffin, his distaste visible. A sense of purpose enveloped her. Quickly, before he refused to go through with her plans, she walked between his line of sight and the rectangular box. A tug and her hood lay on her shoulders, another yank and she stripped off her cloak, allowing it to drop on the ground. She shimmered in a low-cut evening gown, ink-blue satin threaded with silver embroidery and beads. Her arms and shoulders were bare. Diamonds nestled in her ears, formed a rosary against her throat, glinting starbursts in her hair. The lantern gleam exalted her, points of light refracting in all directions, but nothing was more dazzling than her crystal-sharp willpower.

Always, when she needed it, her beauty played its part. Tonight, it faced an exceptional challenge – it must outmanoeuvre death. Winding her arms about Lucien's neck, she pressed her body against his. She had been liberal with the scent bottle and her perfume enveloped him. Down she sank, drawing him with her to sit on the cloak.

Her amber eyes were trained on his, liquid with intent. His gaze travelled along the arch of her throat, the curve of her shoulders, the swell of her breasts. She saw desire flare in him. He stooped over her, taking her face between her hands. She allowed a low moan to escape and tumbled onto her back. Her shoes, trailing in the dirt, dislodged some tiny stones and sent them rattling away. But Lucien was caught within her web. He knelt over her. They kissed.

He seemed to be in no hurry — content to fumble at her nipples. Impatience pecked at her. *Careful, Maud, don't scare the horses.* Gently, she reached under his waistcoat and unbuttoned his braces. "Lucien ..." Her voice conjured a caress from the syllables.

Responsive to her advances, he pushed her skirts above her knees, groping among her petticoats. She sensed a reaction when he realised she had left off a key item of clothing. Would it incite him? Or repulse him? She did it for convenience but perhaps he'd find it too contrived. He preferred to be the assertive partner.

He groaned. "Are you a devil in female form? We're underneath a chapel. Fornicating on blessed ground is sinful. We'll be punished for it!"

"This is an act of love, not fornication. We're making life, Lucien. What could be holier? Ours is a sacred purpose." She leaned up on one elbow and extracted some hairpins, allowing the fragrance of her hair to spill down, creating a tent for the two of them within its masses.

He thrust inside her. She lay beneath him, trapped by his weight, her eyes on the coffin. Her mind detached from what was happening to her body and filled instead with Georges. One hand slid inside her pocket. She stroked the talisman she had carried to the crypt with her — a baby's sock bootee, white, softest cotton, a whisper of pale blue ribbon threaded through its neck.

Afterwards, walking home to her house in the Rue de Barbeau, he was quarrelsome. "Why must you always be so theatrical?"

She wanted to be alone with her plans. Tonight, he'd sleep in the spare room. She knew, as he did, that their coupling in the crypt had activated a process of uncoupling. Languid, she gazed at the night sky, wondering at the variety of stars. Some sizeable and some pinpoints, some bright and some dim, some ancient and some merely elderly – all spending their glow in a profligate splurge.

"Maud, are you listening to me?"

"I heard you. Why can't I be dull? Isn't that what you're saying? I have no use for passivity, Lucien. I must make things happen. It's the way I'm constructed."

"There will be consequences. There always are."

"Good."

Iseult Gonne was born in August 1894, nine months after Maud Gonne and Lucien Millevoye made love in their son Georges's crypt in Samois-sur-Seine. Maud always held fast to the belief that Iseult was Georges reincarnated.

KATHLEEN LYNN

Born Mallaghfarry, Killala, County Mayo 1874; died Dublin 1955
Revolutionary, political activist, doctor, co-founder of St
Ultan's Hospital

D r Kathleen Lynn was one of the first female medical graduates
from a Dublin university – previously, Irishwomen had to go
abroad to train. After experiencing discrimination in applying for
hospital positions, she engaged in suffrage activities, which she
later said converted her to the nationalist cause.

She and her lifelong companion, Madeleine ffrench-Mullen,
were both out in 1916 and imprisoned for their activities. They
were members of the Irish Citizen Army, where Lynn was Chief
Medical Officer and held the rank of captain. As the highest-
ranking surviving officer in City Hall, she tendered her unit's
surrender. Her surgical bag was found to contain iodine, lint,
bandages – and ammunition.

She was elected as a Sinn Féin TD for Dublin in 1923 but didn't take her seat in accordance with the party's abstentionist policy. Later, she left politics to concentrate on public health.

In 1919 she co-founded Saint Ultan's Hospital for infants (*Teach Ultain*) in Dublin with ffrench-Mullen and Sinn Féin activists. A female-run hospital, it focused on children's health at a time when paediatrics was a fledgling specialism. Despite opposition by the State and Catholic Church, Lynn and ffrench-Mullen established a vaccination project, inoculating thousands of impoverished children who otherwise might have succumbed to tuberculosis.

A Bitter Pill

Mayo 1891

"Shoulders back, Kathleen. A lady never slouches. Straight and tall, please, the way the Good Lord fashioned you. I believe I'm going to have to stand on a footstool to do this. For the first time, I can't quite reach. Either I'm shrinking, or you're shooting up, sweetheart."

Kathleen is being measured before returning to Alexandra College after the Easter holidays. Her mother has marked a series of height lines on the linen-cupboard door for each of her four children. Conducting the height ceremony with pencil and ruler is an annual ritual.

"Why, just look at the difference from last year!"

Compliant in small matters, which not only makes life easier but can disguise larger disobediences, Kathleen turns to the ghost marks of her former self on the white gloss paint. Kathleen aged twelve – they have just moved into the rectory in Cong. Fourteen – she's learning how to cycle and is elated by the freedom it promises. Now here she is at seventeen – away at school, having outstripped her governess at lessons, and measured in the holidays rather than on her birthday. Between the ages of sixteen and seventeen was when she experienced an epiphany and knew what she intended doing with her life. She's anxious to discuss it with Mother, who's not paying attention because of some fuss about whether Fardie will like the trout she's ordered for dinner.

The chart runs from left to right. First Nan, then Kathleen, followed by Muriel and finally John. Kathleen Florence 28th January 1874, reads her column. She was born during a snowstorm and had to be carried to the fire to warm her up. Family lore has it this was the first and last occasion when she felt the cold – Kathleen has been on a fresh-air crusade ever since.

Mother charts their annual progress, reporting back to Fardie, who is more interested in his children's retention of Latin declensions than their height spurts. "Robert, Kathleen is taller than me now, imagine," she will tell Fardie tonight at table. Her father will gaze at his daughter in mild surprise, as though bemused by who she is and why she is dining with them, although too well bred to inquire.

He would never say so explicitly but Kathleen knows he finds three daughters excessive. One has her conveniences, two are company for each other, but no man has use for more. The only way to compensate for Fardie's disapproval of daughterly surplus is by embracing obedience. It is implied rather than stated. But all of them know that submission to Fardie's will is the best guarantee of his affection.

Shortly before bedtime she has a few minutes to herself with Mother. Fardie is cloistered in his study with his sermon, a labour which will occupy his entire evening. He prides himself on being magisterial – being learned is taken for granted – when he mounts the pulpit of St Mary's church, nestling among a copse of trees on the Ardilaun estate. From him, Kathleen is learning the importance of preparation. But Mother has taught her to see what lies beneath her nose.

"Mother, I know what I want to do with my life. After I leave school, I mean."

"You're like a daisy, with those pink cheeks. Tell me, sweetheart."

"I mean to lead a useful life."

"I can't imagine you being anything but useful. Do you hope to train as a teacher?"

"I intend," Kathleen takes a deep breath, and rushes on, "to study medicine, become a doctor and treat the poor."

She is prepared for shock or disbelief. Instead her mother looks grave.

"Gracious me, what a large ambition!" She taps a finger against her mouth. "Doctors who care for the needy do godly work. But I'm not aware there any women doctors in Ireland."

"I've spoken to some of my teachers about it, Mother. There are a few. In time, there'll be more. Trinity College won't admit me but I can take classes at the Royal College of Surgeons, and the Royal University of Ireland has authority to award me a degree if I pass the examinations. There are places where I can study abroad, too. In Scotland, perhaps."

Her mother is meditative. Kathleen watches as she weighs her words before speaking. "It will require a great deal of perseverance. You will face obstacles. More, I imagine, than you or your teachers foresee. But being a doctor is a noble vocation and if it is what you feel called upon to do you must persist. Your brain was given to you for a reason. Your school reports are excellent – Fardie is extremely pleased – he told me so."

Why doesn't he tell me himself, thinks Kathleen? Always, he guards against vanity. She knows better than to criticise him. Her mother will be her best ally in persuading Fardie to give permission for her attendance at university lectures.

Mrs Lynn slides a forefinger under Kathleen's chin and tilts it, scrutinising her. "Why a doctor?"

As a daughter of the manse, it is taken for granted that Kathleen should consider the needs of others. But her idea of practical help is not limited to errands of mercy, distributing warm clothing or bowls of soup. Why should men be at liberty to extract the marrow from life: all the effort and responsibility, colour and excitement, achievement and reward? She refuses to be one of those women who spend their lives sewing and doing good works, with concerts and tea-parties to enliven the tedium. As if ghosting on the surface of existence is sufficient. She knows better than to share this with her mother, who might interpret it as reproach for her own life.

"Medicine can make a difference, Mother. When the people are ill, they can't work. When they can't work, they don't eat. Not unless people like us bring them food."

"You're thinking of the Brogans and Kerrigans."

Kathleen nods. "And the Hegarty place."

On Easter Saturday they visited three cottages bringing supplies. Every time she sets foot in their homes, she registers how impoverished many of their neighbours are. But Fardie insists Lord and Lady Ardilaun are benevolent landlords with their tenants' best interests at heart. He tells her it is God's will that people occupy different stations in life. As a small girl, when she was troubled by the bare feet of the village children, he said, "They don't feel the cold on their feet any more than a lamb or a calf does."

Kathleen knows this cannot be true. If it were, why did Mother parcel up their outgrown boots for the Brogans and Kerrigans and Hegartys, whose cabins are cosy but teeming with children? Kathleen can't help wondering where they all sleep. Like puppies, piled on top of one another? And in Dublin, walking to and from church service, she notices how the children of poor people are barefoot there, too, or clump about in boots that don't fit and must chafe them.

"On the last day of term, we had a holiday from lessons. We were allowed to go to St Stephen's Green and feed stale bread to the ducks. A group of children darted out and snatched it from our hands. They jammed it into their mouths right there in front of us. They were hungry, Mother."

Her mother strokes her cheek. "Life is harder for some than for others, Kathleen. We must share what we have."

"On Easter Saturday, did you notice a length of red flannel wrapped round Mrs Hegarty's neck? She said it was for a sore throat. How is that meant to cure her? Wouldn't medicine be more useful?"

"The country people are convinced red flannel is effective, Kathleen. And perhaps it is, because of their belief."

"No, Mother. They need medical treatment, not superstition. Some of their ailments are preventable. Take chilblains – I know lots of the old people here complain about them. But I've been reading up on how to avoid chilblains. If your feet get wet, you must remove your stockings at once and massage the feet near a fire until warm. Then put on a dry pair of stockings. Rubbing feet and hands sets the blood racing and prevents chilblains, you see."

"My clever girl."

"If a chilblain looks like developing, you should rub a little camphorated oil on the spot and take plenty of exercise so the blood circulates. Might I be allowed to explain this to people when we call to their cottages?"

"Certainly, sweetheart. It's good sense."

"But, Mother, I'm only Canon Lynn's daughter. They'll be polite to me but nobody will pay attention. That's why I have to train as a doctor. So when I explain to them how to stay well, they'll listen. I need to go to the university. Do you suppose Fardie will consent to it?"

A shadow flecks her mother's eyes. She lowers her eyelids, smoothing away the wrinkles on her dress. By the time she looks up again, hesitation has been put to flight.

"I'll speak to him. If it's God's will, it's bound to happen. But if not, you must accept it, Kathleen. Yes?"

"Of course, Mother." Kathleen crosses her fingers behind her back. In this matter, God's will finishes a poor second to hers.

Archbishop's Palace, Dublin 1935

"I cannot consent to this hospital," says Archbishop Edward Byrne. With the air of a man throwing down his trump card, he adds, "It is not God's will."

At that point, the meeting begins to slide into belligerence. Kathleen feels colour pump through her skin.

"You are on close terms with God's will, your grace?" she inquires.

He stiffens. "I have prayed and reflected on it. His will has become clear to me as a result of my prayers, Miss Lynn."

Actually, it's Dr Lynn. She thinks of the children and resists the urge to correct him. Every time he calls her Miss Lynn, she'll make a point of addressing him by his archbishop's title. Kathleen has a preference for the niceties. She is also a believer in concrete evidence for arriving at a decision, rather than praying and reflecting.

From her bag, she produces a sheet and offers it to him. "The infant mortality figures, your grace. Dublin fares worse than the rest of Ireland by a country mile."

He leans across the table separating them and accepts the page, the amethyst in his episcopal ring glinting like a plump grape. She knows Roman Catholics kiss the ring as a sign of piety – and because they believe it earns them time off from purgatory, according to her friend Helena Molony. Helena has a mischievous streak, and Kathleen's leg is easily pulled. When Helena mentioned the superstition, Kathleen turned to Madeleine to see if she was being teased. Could people really believe that? "Don't worry, you won't be expected to kiss it when you meet him," Madeleine reassured her. Kathleen was aghast at evidence of yet another medieval delusion holding sway in twentieth century Ireland, even in the capital city where modernity was beginning to stake a claim.

She stares at the ring now, wondering how many lips have brushed it. Meanwhile, the archbishop reads intently. At least he is paying her statistics the attention they deserve. She notices his finger joints are swollen, while his left hand trembles holding the sheet — possible corroboration of the rumour that he suffers from a muscular wasting disease. As if aware of her observation, he lays the page on the table, drops his hands out of sight on his knees, and continues reading.

She withdraws her gaze and examines the table — elm, she thinks. The red streaks through the brown wood are the telltale sign. Her eyes wander about the room. A bookcase with glass doors, its frame constructed from the same wood as the table, occupies an entire wall. A magnificent silver crucifix hangs on the wall behind the archbishop's chair. There is little else of interest in this ground-floor reception room. Presumably dozens of similar rooms, imposing but sterile, are to be found in this red-bricked barn of a place.

Dr Byrne finishes reading and meets her gaze, noncommittal.

Kathleen takes the initiative. "As you no doubt know, your grace, the tenements are riddled with poverty and disease. One in ten children in Dublin is doomed to die before its first birthday. Some from malnutrition, others from illnesses that are entirely preventable. Our new hospital would give these children a chance to grow up strong and healthy. They are the nation's future."

"The tenements are a blot on the city but a government housing programme is under way. Progress is being made. The Catholic Church fully supports any initiative to move families out of the slums. We, too, are engaged in the construction business — our focus is on building churches for these new communities to ensure their spiritual wellbeing is met. To keep the lamp of faith burning."

"Hospitals are needed, too, surely?"

He gives her a sidling look. "Provided they are run according to the Catholic ethos. What use is a strong, healthy child if it is wooed away from its faith? Far better for a Catholic child to die in the cradle than to grow up lost to Mother Church."

Kathleen keeps her face shuttered, taking her time about answering. Her nostrils dilate, and she inhales the scent of furniture polish and old books, calling to mind her father's study. Her eyes drift to the window, through which she can see a skeletal chestnut tree where some blackbirds are clustered. Springtime is some months away but it's biding its time. Progress cannot be halted. Leaves will bud on the chestnut's branches, birds will nest there.

She tries to strike a conversational tone.

"Come, now, your grace. Is your religion planted so thinly that you expect patients and their families to convert as soon as they set foot in a non-Catholic hospital?"

He bridles and she realises she has erred.

"The people are poor," he says. "They may be prevailed upon. We do not forget how they were offered food by your co-religionists if they abandoned the faith of their fathers during the Famine.'

So, battle lines are drawn. Kathleen swallows, at a loss about how to make him understand she has no designs on anyone's religious affiliation. Her only interest lies in curing their bodies. It feels as if all the air has been sucked out of this stuffy room. She glances toward the window – if only she could ask him to open it. Just then, a flicker of movement catches her eye. A bird has left the safety of the chestnut tree and is swooping directly towards them. Blinded by a shaft of sunlight, it thuds against the glass.

Simultaneously, they rise to their feet and walk to the window. The bird is lying on the gravel outside.

"I'll send someone out to see if anything can be done for the poor creature," says the archbishop. "It may simply be winded."

"Its neck is broken," Kathleen raps out. "Burial is the only thing that can be done for it." She turns towards him.

Until now, there has been a piece of furniture between them but at this moment only the space of a hand separates the two.

"I cannot stress enough, your grace, that the merger is not my idea. I have no ulterior motive. The proposal comes from the Hospitals' Commission. They're the ones suggesting St Ultan's and Harcourt Street children's hospital should combine resources." Unable to resist a sly reminder of who he's dealing with, she adds a sprinkle of Latin. "And, *mirabile dictu*, the money is available to make it happen. Do, please, reconsider. We need your support."

The archbishop returns to his seat, one of his legs dragging fractionally. Something in the way he carries himself, some act of willpower that shivers the air as he parts it, reveals a human being in pain to Kathleen. However, as she sits back opposite him, no trace of discomfort is visible on his face. She considers suggesting that he might ring for a glass of water – surely he must have some medication he can take? Or she may have suitable pills in her bag depending on the nature of the pain. On the point of offering help, she catches his eye. At once, she understands it would be treated as a violation of his privacy. She is not meant to detect his struggle.

His tone is firm, as if to compensate for a momentary weakness. "This hospital you envisage is impossible, Miss Lynn. It would create a monopoly on the south-side of the city. Ninety-nine per cent of the patients would be Catholic but you are a non-Catholic institution. I could not possibly cede control to a body whose attitude to the Catholic viewpoint is suspect, in my opinion – if not downright hostile."

"Dr Byrne, I must protest. That assessment is unjust. After all, St Ultan's matron and most of our nurses are Roman Catholics."

"Ah, but I understand the majority of your doctors are Protestants."

Temper flares in Kathleen – as much at her own slip, which gave him an opportunity to pounce on it. She has pandered to his prejudice by mentioning the religion of staff members. Unguarded, she exclaims, "In all conscience, your grace, how can you refuse a new hospital?"

His eyes flash. "I have a solemn responsibility to do right by the Catholic faith and by my flock. You, on the other hand, are a member of a religious minority, Miss Lynn. You can no longer expect to crack the whip in *Saorstat Éireann*."

His stress on the final two words suggests her Latin tag was resented. Kathleen's right leg begins to jiggle. By a force of will, she steadies it. Is he using Irish to put her in her place, presuming to know her cultural hinterland? And how dare he brandish the Free State at her? There wouldn't be a Saorstat Éireann if people like herself, Madeleine and Helena hadn't been out in 1916. Where was he when the bullets were flying?

Kathleen's group of volunteers had occupied City Hall, where they were sitting ducks for an attack from Dublin Castle next door. She remembers how, on that Easter Monday, time sped up and slowed down, seemingly at random. Some events hurtled along. The death of their brigade leader, Seán Connolly, for example. Volunteers were ordered onto the roof to watch for an attack from the Castle. She had gone up, too, bringing some of her medical equipment. It was hot there, crouched among the chimneypots, and everyone was jittery. Suddenly, she saw Seán approach along the roof. Why is he making a target of himself, walking upright, she wondered? No sooner did the thought take shape than a sniper's shot whistled out and Seán fell. She crawled towards him but he was beyond help, dead by the time her fingers felt for his pulse. Time appeared to stop then. Morale would be affected by the loss of their leader on the first day, she knew.

She gives herself a few moments to regain her composure now. "Dr Byrne, my surgery is crowded by the poor and needy. Religion is never mentioned. But here's what does matter — better prospects for the people. Better healthcare. We can give them that. But we must have space and amenities. We must have —"

"*Must?*" The archbishop chops her off in mid-sentence. "You are in no position to make demands." He leans forward, pressing a bell on the table. A priest opens the door. "Miss Lynn is leaving. Please show her out, Father."

Realising they have reached the end of the line, Kathleen allows herself to be ushered away. At the door, resistance surges up and she whirls back to the archbishop. "I leave you with this thought. The infant has no politics and no religion. It is a child of God – nothing else. But while people in authority bicker, helpless babies die. Preventable deaths. They're dying right now, today, a few miles from this palace. *Slán agat*, Dr Byrne."

The street lights flicker on, lifting her mood, as Kathleen climbs the steps of Number 9, Belgrave Road. No matter how black things appear, there are reasons to be grateful. She turns her key in the lock and drops her medical bag on the hall floor.

"Madeleine?"

"In here. Trying to do something with a useless fire. It's nearly out."

Kathleen follows the voice into a sitting room furnished with an eye to comfort rather than style. Madeleine is on her knees on the hearth rug, adding pine cones to the grate, and they crackle and smoke.

"Just in ahead of you, Kathy." Madeleine coughs, eyes running, but keeps layering on the cones.

"I thought all the pine cones were used up."

"Last lot. I've been saving them for a grey day. Plenty more in Wicklow. But who knows when we can spare the time to go back and gather some? A woman came to St Ultan's today with her baby grandson. When I told her he'd have to wait to see a doctor, she said, 'The man that made time made plenty of it, my dacent lady'. Such patience! I never seem to have enough hours in the day." She lays the poker on the hearth and rubs soot onto her cheek. "The child didn't need to be admitted – luckily, because there were no free beds."

Kathleen sinks into an armchair, allowing Madeleine's voice to wash over her. The pine cones are food for her soul. As, indeed, is the sight of Madeleine ffrench-Mullen. Her face is as comforting as an everyday dinner plate: round and plain and exactly fit for purpose. The cones remind Kathleen of daylong tramps together over springy bracken, hedgerows with their fuchsia tutus and the lingering blue shadows of evening.

All at once, the cones flare up and ignite the wood. There is nothing to match them for kindling.

"*Abracadabra!*" Madeleine sits back on her heels. She is on the point of crowing about her pyrotechnics but pauses at something closed-off in Kathleen's face. Her jaw is slack. She looks — not beaten, you could never say that about her, but as if she has suffered a setback. Madeleine stands up with a creak. Her rheumatism is getting worse. She'll have to go to a spa when work eases off. Maybe a German one.

"You should have told Winnie to see about the fire." Abstracted though she is, Kathleen has noticed the spasm clotting Madeleine's face.

"Fire-lighting is one of my special talents, as you perfectly well know, dear heart. Besides, it's Winnie's half-day. She's gone to the pictures. With a twist of pepper in her pocket in case of assailants. Our Winnie believes in precautions. She'll have left something in the oven to be heated up but I haven't gone down to inspect the rations yet."

A bottle of port and two glasses are sitting in readiness on the sideboard and Madeleine fills the glasses.

"You look like you could use a splash of Didn't Ought. I know I could do with a pick-me-up."

The two women drink in companionable silence, the pine cones carrying the forest into their home. Madeleine pats her hair, scooped into a nest at the back of her head. Her fingers tell her it's beyond tidying and she abandons the effort. Kathy, by comparison, never has a hair out of place. She's worn two plaits coiled on top of her head since the day they first met. Back before the Rising, it was. Even then, Kathy owned a car, almost as impressive to Madeleine as her medical qualifications. Madeleine attended a lecture on first aid given by Dr Kathleen Lynn and that was that. They've been together ever since, twenty-odd years now. They even shared a prison cell after the Rising. It feels as if those heady days of revolution were only yesterday, but she knows the twentieth anniversary is a matter of months away. She and Kathleen are resigned to the prospect of speechifying and posturing from well-upholstered men whose insights into nationhood could be fitted on the back of a postage stamp.

Madeleine peers at Kathy through the yellow lamplight. She has the secret of eternal youth. But something is bothering her. No point in asking, she'll talk about it in her own time.

"The air's stale in here, we should open a window," says Kathleen.

"We'll freeze. I've only just got the fire started. You and your fresh air."

"It's healthy, Maddy. You know it is."

"There's a time and a place for fresh air and cold baths. Glenmalure in July, for instance. Rathmines in January? Roaring fires all round."

Kathleen pushes out her lower lip and pings a thumbnail against her glass.

She's tetchy this evening, thinks Madeleine. Rarely without good reason. Perhaps some music might soothe her. She plods over to the gramophone and considers their records. Brahms? On second thoughts, too secular. This is a job for Handel's *Messiah*. Kathleen has a weakness for anything smacking of church music. Comes of being a canon's daughter. Madeleine slides the record out of its sleeve and lays the needle on the vinyl. Orchestra and choir hiss into life and the power of repetition begins to weave its spell.

Hallelujah, Hallelujah, Hallelujah, Hallelujah, Hallelujah!

Mind you, she reflects, her own father was a ship's surgeon and she can take *H.M.S. Pinafore* or leave it. But *Messiah* is a rousing piece of music, regardless of the listener's background.

Kathleen's twanged nerves settle. By and by, she stirs, drains her glass, and sets it on the hexagonal table beside her chair. "Maddy, how do you fight with an archbishop?"

"With great difficulty."

"Is that another way of saying I'm bound to lose?"

A shrug. "Grappling with ecclesiasticals isn't for the fainthearted. Doesn't mean they shouldn't be tackled. As to losing – I suppose that depends on whether the politicians and civil servants will support you."

Kathleen snorts.

"All right, I know the faithful tend to fall into line," Madeleine says. "Have you heard any more from the Archbishop's Palace? Is that what this is about?"

"I saw the Archbishop of Dublin today."

"I'd have wished you luck at breakfast if I'd known you had an appointment."

"It was an informal meeting. Just the two of us. I drove over to Drumcondra on the off-chance. He left me cooling my heels for nearly an hour but I brazened it out and was granted an audience eventually. His manner was decidedly Olympian." She considers. "I think I can safely say it was a peevish encounter."

"Dr Byrne gave you a roasting?"

"I gave as good as I got. Much good it'll do the new hospital."

"What made you beard the lion in his den, Kathy?"

"I didn't know myself. It was a spur of the moment thing. There was a letter from him waiting on my desk in St Ultan's. Saying his position was unchanged and I should regard the subject as closed – he'd met our delegation last month, given us his formal response, and that should be taken as his final word. It riled me that he's opposing the hospital merger on religious principles solely. So I thought I'd have one last crack at him – see if I couldn't make him understand this is about healthcare, and the common good. But he doesn't give a fiddler's about the common good. What he cares about is absolute control. Do you know, he more or less implied I had no business treating Roman Catholics because I'm not of their faith? And if I persisted it must be from ulterior motives?"

Madeleine clears her throat. "No help for it but to take Helena up on her offer."

Kathleen raises her eyebrows.

"Didn't she volunteer to make a waxwork doll of the archbishop and stick pins in it? He shuffles off his mortal coil. A successor is appointed. You start over with the new man. He couldn't be any worse than Edward Byrne."

Kathleen kicks her soles against the fender. "I'm surprised at you, Maddy. It wasn't amusing when Helena said it, and it's even less funny now. Besides, I wouldn't bank on an improvement. I haven't noticed any modernisers in the Archbishop's Palace."

She's in a foul mood and no mistake. Madeleine holds up the bottle of port invitingly. A shake of the head. Madeleine pours herself another dollop.

Regretting her outburst, Kathleen continues on a milder note. "The archbishop's convinced I'm up to something nefarious. That I have designs on the immortal souls of sick children."

Madeleine lets out a low whistle. "Oh, Kathy, I'm sorry. That sounds like curtains for the hospital plan. What a waste!" She casts round for something to say by way of consolation. "Small minds are threatened by the unfamiliar. For a mind to grow, it must take a leap of faith. But it's extremely rare for archbishops to venture into the unknown. That's why Dr Byrne is dead set against you."

"It's the little ones from the tenements who'll suffer if the new children's hospital isn't built. The better-off will be taken care of, they always are." Kathleen lifts the poker and riddles the fire. "It's frustrating –"

"– that money isn't the issue for once," Madeleine finishes her sentence. Their thoughts often dovetail. "All the archbishop has to say is 'I do not consent' with an imperial wave of his hand and the hospital disappears in a puff of smoke."

Stony-faced, Kathleen nods. The Hospitals' Sweepstake has been generous and there are public funds available, in addition to donations. Without the archbishop's approval, however, they cannot proceed.

Madeleine chews on the inside of her cheek. "Couldn't you give him a written undertaking? *I, Kathleen Florence Lynn, do hereby solemnly swear not to give birth control advice to mothers attending the new children's hospital? Nor to instruct young people in matters relating to the other sex? Upon pain of eternal damnation, so help me God?*"

"I've already offered him all sorts of guarantees. He's impervious to reason. You'd never think it to look at him – he has charm, when he cares to use it, and his mind is razor-sharp – but scratch the surface and it's clear he sees us as the enemy. Because he can't tell us what to do." Kathleen pauses. "The odd thing is, I felt sorry for him. He's in physical agony, I suspect – muscular wasting – and suffers it with dignity."

"How about going directly to the Minister for Health?"

"The archbishop has the politicians and senior civil servants under his thumb. They daren't oppose him."

Madeleine scrubs her fingers through her scalp. "It's infuriating! The hospital could have been built by now."

"And Michael Scott went to such a lot of trouble, drawing up his beautiful plans. I can hardly look him in the eye when we meet."

Kathleen sits brooding. The babies she treats break her heart – she thinks of them as tiny human matchboxes because you could strike a match on their ribs. Dr Byrne seems to be convinced she's plotting to have the mothers sterilised, or brainwashed into practising artificial birth control, so that no more of these children will be born.

"Never mind, he'll get his comeuppance someday, Kathy. You'll have your revenge."

"Revenge is not civilised. It should be left to time and our

Creator. Eventually we all must stand before the Seat of Judgment."

Oh dear, thinks Madeleine. She's quoting her father, the canon. Things have reached a pretty pass.

"Though I must admit, Maddy, while he was mostly slippery as a fish, I did detect flashes of antagonism towards me. It feels as if there's something personal about it." Kathleen raises her thumb followed by two fingers. "I'm a woman. A doctor. And a Protestant. Three black marks."

Madeleine decides to fetch up their dinner on a tray. Kathy is hollow-cheeked with exhaustion. She's active and sturdy, especially for a woman in her sixties, but fighting battles takes a toll. Especially losing battles. There'll be no state-of-the-art children's hospital by the canal, after all – they'll have to carry on with their fifty-bed facility in Charlemont Street.

As for Kathleen, she stares into the flames, her mind a becalmed ship waiting for the wind to fill its sails. Since the age of seventeen, she has been brimful with certainty – a sense of destiny, you might call it. Now, for the first time, she has no idea how to proceed. She has a medical doctor's belief in logic. But the Most Reverend Dr Edward Byrne bats it away with the unshakeable certainty afforded to a Doctor of Divinity.

On the mantelpiece, a carriage clock belonging to her mother tinkles the hour. Kathleen took it from the rectory in Cong after her father died, when she and her sisters were clearing it out in preparation for a new incumbent. The clock's chime calls up her mother's patient face. How would she advise her to bell the cat? Something about being diplomatic, probably. Fardie would quote Ecclesiastes at her: *To every thing there is a season.*

"I thought we ought to eat off our knees in here. It's cosier." Madeleine is back from the kitchen with a feast of sorts. "Winnie's done us proud. There's game pie, and a hunk of Camembert and some celery for afters. I found a packet of Bath Olivers in a tin to go with the cheese. Tuck in, Kathy, you probably haven't eaten since breakfast."

"I don't remember."

"A sure sign."

"Maddy, I have to admit, I'm growing awfully disillusioned about joint projects with Roman Catholics. They do as their bishops tell them. Though there are some wonderful things about your religion. Like the serenity of the churches. And how you can go into one anywhere in the world and feel instantly at home. Of course, the art is dreadfully —"

"— gory," agrees Madeleine, buttering a bread roll.

"But the hierarchy seems to place no emphasis on the physical needs of human beings. It's all about the soul for them and the body doesn't figure."

"Never mind about winning support from archbishops. We'll just have to carry on doing good by stealth, Kathy."

Kathleen fingers her gold fibula charm on its chain. She disapproves of costly presents and considers them a waste of money — a jigsaw puzzle is extravagant enough, in her view. However, she makes an exception for her favourite piece of jewellery. It is inscribed *To Dr Kathleen Lynn from comrades, men and women, I.C.A.* and was given to mark her assistance with medical preparations in the Irish Citizen Army for the Easter Rising. She accepts that memory is inherently shifty. However, that period when she was immersed in the national cause — with Madeleine and their friend Helena Molony ending up as cellmates in Kilmainham Gaol — was a time rich in optimism, at least, compared with these grim 1930s.

"Didn't we all work together during the Rising? Irrespective of religion?"

"We did, Kathy."

"And before that, in the Lockout?"

"Certainly. I wouldn't idealise the Lockout, mind you — I don't miss those police baton charges. You're not eating, dear heart. Taste a few morsels or Winnie will scold me."

Kathleen chews a mouthful. "The foot charges were nastier

than the horseback ones."

"Certainly, they were. Horses try and avoid trampling you, unlike policemen. Remember how people opened ranks to let the animals through and closed up after them?"

"My family were convinced I was insane, quite literally." Kathleen speaks so quietly that Madeleine almost misses what she says. "If the British hadn't locked me up I think they might have had me put away. But I do believe I was never happier than in that cell with you and Helena."

Madeleine rests her head against the back of the armchair. "You, dear heart, are overworked and in need of a holiday in Glenmalure. Even a long weekend would help. How about St Patrick's weekend? Could we manage it?"

Kathleen closes her eyes, a Wicklow valley yellow with gorse filtering through her mind. She sees tendrils of smoke rising from a chimney pot, a brook rushing over stones in a tumble of spray, daffodils clumped in their green sheaths. "Yes, let's go in March." She pauses, debating something with herself. "But I can't let the archbishop have the final word. Even if he has a veto. I intend to write to him, Maddy. I know exactly what needs to be said."

"Which is?"

"He told me God is love, and nothing is more important than saving children's souls, so they can be gathered up by a loving Father."

"Preachy and predictable."

"I dare say he meant it in all sincerity. But here's what I'll tell him. That saving children's souls matters but it isn't the be-all and end-all where love is concerned. Curing sick babies is love, I'll say. Running a hospital well is love. Love comes in all shapes and sizes."

Madeleine sets down her plate and walks across to perch on the arm of Kathleen's chair. "He won't understand, you know. Especially not when he hears it from a splendid, uppity woman."

"I know." Kathleen reaches up to squeeze the hand resting on her shoulder. "But at least I'll have told him."

Kathleen Lynn and Madeleine ffrench-Mullen never saw a national children's hospital built in Dublin, although they continued to do important work at St Ultan's, which operated from 1919 to 1984. A Catholic children's hospital was being discussed in 1939, three years after it became clear the merger between the two children's hospitals wouldn't be allowed to proceed. Our Lady's Hospital for Sick Children in Crumlin, Dublin, didn't open until 1956.

DOROTHY MACARDLE

Born Dundalk, 1889: died Drogheda 1958
Novelist, playwright, historian, activist and journalist

Born into a wealthy brewing family, Dorothy Macardle taught at Alexandra College in Dublin. She was arrested and imprisoned during the War of Independence (1919-21), for which she lost her job. After the treaty leading to an Irish Free State, she worked as a journalist and activist on the Republican side and was jailed by the Free State authorities in 1922.

Later, her republicanism broadened into internationalism and she became a strong supporter of the League of Nations. In 1951 she became president of the Irish Association for Civil Liberties, forerunner to the Irish Council for Civil Liberties.

Dorothy's plays were produced at the Abbey and the Gate, and her novels included *Uneasy Freehold* – later retitled *The Uninvited* after being turned into a film by that name.

While imprisoned in Mountjoy she converted her Civil War experiences into a collection of ghost stories, *Earth-bound: Nine Stories of Ireland* (1924), dedicated to comrades including Alice Milligan. In the title story, two young Republicans on the run in Wicklow during the War of Independence are almost caught by a Black and Tans' patrol but are led to safety by the spirit of Red Hugh O'Donnell. It reprises the 1572 escape from Dublin Castle in the depths of winter by The O'Donnell, who took refuge in the Wicklow Mountains.

The tale below imagines how Dorothy may have heard about the timely intervention of a spectral guide, modifying it for her ghost story embedded with a political message.

Footprints in the Snow

There is nothing commonplace about a supernatural event. By its nature, such a happening is exceptional – few of us have direct experience. Those inclined to believe will require no proof. As for the disinclined, even the evidence of your own eyes may not convince you. So be it. My intention is not to convert anyone to belief in the spirit world – simply, I wish to share my tale. Make of it what you will.

It concerns the unfortunate history of a family named Reynolds who lived in a house called Bride's Peak. I heard about them from a fellow teacher at Alexandra College, Sarah Reynolds, a relative of theirs. She taught art, and we were friends when I worked at the school. I suppose she wouldn't want to know me now that I have a prison record. She had no political convictions, whereas I was possessed by them. But Sarah was kind to me because I lived on my own in Dublin, and now and again invited me home with her for a family supper.

It was Christmas Eve 1919 when we bumped into each other near the north end of Grafton Street, just as the light was fading. She was attending to some last-minute errands for her mother, while I was heading back to my flat in Ely Place. Since early morning, I had been engaged in Cumann na mBan activities. Now, I was weary and hungry, yet the festive atmosphere caused me to linger on the street. Tram bells pinged, feet hurried in all directions with a sense of purpose, seasonal greetings were exchanged at top volume – all serving to remind me that mine was a solitary life. I had no plans until St Stephen's Day. It was by choice but a tinge of dismay sheathed my mood.

I had told my parents that I intended to spend the holidays studying for some postgraduate exams, to keep me on my toes as the holder of the Pfeiffer Lectureship at Alexandra College. But the truth was that our Cumann na mBan president, Countess Markievicz, had appealed for helpers to deliver relief parcels to the dependants of political prisoners. For three days, I had been trudging about Dublin handing over food and blankets. Don't misunderstand me. The expression on faces was reward enough. However, I knew I was returning to a cold and empty set of rooms – housekeeping was never one of my strengths.

It was Sarah who spied me pondering the purchase of some flowers from a seller at the junction with Duke Street. We exchanged greetings and she expressed surprise that I wasn't at home in Dundalk for the holiday. I tried to brush it away but Sarah was an intuitive person – she guessed at my lack of plans.

"It would spoil my Christmas entirely to think of you spending the day alone!" she protested. "Besides, you're thin as a penny. You need feeding up." Impulsive, she proposed that I go home there and then to Ranelagh with her. I should spend the night and share their goose the following day. She could lend me a nightgown and any essentials I might need.

I agreed. Although with the proviso that I must make a halt en route for some gifts to add to the feast. After choosing a selection of nuts and candied fruit, I remembered that Sarah's mother was called Alice, and delayed at a bookshop to buy her Lewis Carroll's *Alice in Wonderland*. Even a mature woman must like to be reminded she shares her name with a fictional heroine.

"Ever the English teacher." Sarah softened her words with a laugh.

"Carroll's Alice is someone I admire," I protested. "She possesses what all children long for."

"Which is?"

"A sense of power."

Sarah glanced at me, a strange expression pinching her features, but made no comment.

The Reynolds' house was on Mount Pleasant, near the tram stop, and I knew Sarah's invitation for the happy impulse it was when we saw the glow of candles on their Christmas tree through a bow window as we hurried up. There was only Mr and Mrs Reynolds in our party that night. They came from decent stock and gave me a prodigal's welcome. There were grown-up children, I forget how many, married with families of their own – only Sarah was at home. I think she was glad to have a friend with her.

After supper, the weather took a turn for the worse with the wind howling fit to raise the dead. "Shakespearean weather," I suggested to Sarah. She gave me the same look I had noticed in town before proposing, for cosiness, that I share her room. Both of us were too keyed up to sleep, so we turned the paraffin lamp low and fell to telling stories.

"You've rescued my Christmas," I told Sarah at one point. "You're my good spirit."

She propped herself on one elbow, staring at me across the double bed. "Do you believe in good spirits?"

"I do and I don't." A typically Irish answer.

"I wouldn't be alive today if a good spirit hadn't intervened. Would you like to hear about it?"

Naturally, I nodded, and she began.

"It happened at Bride's Peak. That's my uncle and aunt's place in Wicklow, close to the Sally Gap. The wind tonight reminds me of it. It's a house that belongs in a fairy tale – a Gothic fantasy of turrets, battlements and arched windows. Only a moat and drawbridge are missing. It's just below Glenmacnass waterfall – a local landmark – and I used to think it a wonder the house didn't slide down the side of the mountain. To me, Bride's Peak seemed to defy gravity. It was always windy there. The wind moaned and shuddered and roared – but it was impish, too. I used to think the wind was playing hide and seek, teasing us, when it was in that humour. Whatever its mood, the wind was always there as a background noise.

When I was a child, I spent a week at Bride's Peak every now and again, loaned out by my parents. My aunt had a soft spot for me and my uncle liked her to have company. Once, he cajoled me into staying at the house over Christmas. I must have been about fourteen. That was the first and last time – wild horses wouldn't drag me there again overnight in wintertime."

"Why not?" I asked.

Sarah shivered. She busied herself tucking the covers around her neck before answering. "Bride's Peak is a remote place. There's always a risk of being snowed in. You have to remember, I'm from a big family. I'm used to a household with a steady stream of callers. My aunt and uncle were ..." A beat of hesitancy intruded. "They were childless."

She fell silent. Intrigued, I waited. Confidences can't be forced. When I had almost abandoned hope, she took up the threads of her story again.

"The trouble with Bride's Peak is it's a folly, in the middle of nowhere. It's furbished in the fashion of a medieval castle. The windows are set with tiny diamonds of glass that bar the light rather than admit it. Tapestries hang on the walls and the floors are flagstoned. Every bedroom has a four-poster bed. At first, I thought I'd suffocate when I slept in one, and used to leave the curtains open. But soon enough I recognised their value in keeping out draughts.

The house was built for a bride. She was my great-grandmother – I'm called after her. A hundred years ago, my great-grandfather chose the location and design, and when the house was finished he collected his bride from her French finishing school and installed her there. She was a neighbour's daughter, only nineteen years old. My great-grandfather thought it would be lucky to name the house for his bride. But not all brides are lucky. I know nothing as regards the fortunes of the first Mrs Reynolds of Bride's Peak, or the second. But the third mistress is my Aunt Delia. She's married to my father's brother, who inherited the house. And this I can say for certain: luck didn't smile on her.

Aunt Delia's from County Sligo and inclined to brood. She has a melancholy streak, I suppose. When I stayed with them, there were days when she hardly spoke. Misery would catch her by the throat and breathing was as much as she could manage."

The mattress springs creaked. Sarah walked to the window and opened the curtains. The wind had dropped and a line of watery moonlight slid in, edging as far as the brass bed. She followed its path back, climbed in, and returned to her story.

"I shouldn't have said what I did. About my aunt and uncle being childless. They weren't. They had two daughters. Both girls died of diphtheria within days of each other. They were only nine and ten. I was born around the same time as Lucy, my younger cousin. We looked alike – people mistook us for sisters. Claire was dark, like Aunt Delia, but Lucy was fair. I suppose her hair would have darkened, in time, the same as mine has, but it was pale gold when I knew her.

One December, the girls were left with their governess while my aunt and uncle travelled to France. My Uncle Justin is a wine merchant and persuaded Aunt Delia to keep him company on the trip through Paris and on to the Loire Valley. At first, she was reluctant to agree. But the girls had a Welsh governess, an extremely capable person called Miss Gurney in whose charge they could be left. Uncle Justin promised Aunt Delia on his word of honour they'd be home in time for Christmas with wonderful gifts in their luggage. He has always been hard to resist when he sets out to cajole.

While they were gone, the girls picked up an infection – Claire first, then Lucy caught it from her. Miss Gurney had taken them visiting in Laragh, to a household later discovered to have the diphtheria virus. When Claire fell ill, Miss Gurney sent word to my aunt and uncle. Naturally, they rushed home on the earliest possible crossing, but the tide was against them and there was a delay. By the time they reached Bride's Peak, Claire was dead two hours.

In her final minutes, she had cried out for her mother. It would have been kinder to withhold that piece of information from my aunt, who felt guilty about her absence. But Miss Gurney shared every detail. I suppose she was in distress herself and felt some responsibility for the tragedy.

Little Lucy fought against the sickness and initially it was hoped she might make a recovery. While Uncle Justin busied himself with Claire's funeral arrangements – I remember him saying there was no sadder duty than to choose a child's coffin – Aunt Delia kept vigil by Lucy's bedside. A trained nurse was employed but my aunt refused to spare herself and slept in her daughter's room at night. Once, Lucy asked for cherries, a favourite dish, but when they were carried in to her she was unable to eat them.

Aunt Delia was convinced she could save Lucy by the power of her love. She could not. The grave dug for Claire had to be reopened four days later, on Christmas Eve, to accept a second small body. The sisters were buried side by side.

Her double loss altered my aunt's personality. She became

withdrawn and would not consent to leave the house except to visit the graveyard at Laragh, where she became a familiar sight standing by the headstone. She had been a handsome woman, with that melancholy, Spanish-Irish look you find among people from Ireland's western seaboard. Now she grew haggard, except for her dark eyes which smouldered when they latched onto you. More frequently, however, she was glassy-eyed. What she saw, we didn't.

My aunt lived for my visits to Bride's Peak, or so I was assured, because I was the image of Lucy. My parents hadn't the heart to refuse her. Sometimes, one of my sisters would accompany me – I preferred having a companion. You see, I never said so to my mother and father but there were times when I was conscious of invisible eyes trained on me. The schoolroom in particular was a room I never felt comfortable in, although it had an elaborate dolls' house and at least a dozen sumptuously dressed dolls. I used to enjoy games of make-believe there with Claire and Lucy, before they were taken, but afterwards I hadn't the heart to play with their treasures. How could I? I was convinced they watched me while I dressed and undressed their dolls, or pretended to bathe them, or put one or other of them into a pram to wheel her about.

Sometimes, my father would go to Bride's Peak with me to spend a few days with his brother – they'd fish in the stream at the bottom of the garden or walk in the woods. After all, my father had grown up in Bride's Peak with Uncle Justin and it felt like home to him still. But following the two funerals, my mother refused to step foot in the house. She said she was susceptible to atmosphere and the place was like a morgue. Before my visits, I'd hear her and Father arguing. She didn't want me staying there but he always overruled her.

My mother used to quiz me after each visit. Was my aunt acting erratically? Was I afraid of her? What did she talk to me about? I stood up for Aunt Delia, insisting she was always gentle with me. It was the truth. She'd stroke my hair and tell me she could imagine how Lucy might have grown up when she looked at me.

I knew better than to tell my mother about the peculiar things I noticed in Bride's Peak. Like the smell of cherries which materialised out of nowhere where there wasn't a cherry in the house. Nor about the sensation of being watched. Nor about the dogs.

I missed the dogs the first time I stayed there after Claire and Lucy were gone. When I asked Uncle Justin about the three West Highland Terriers I used to play with, he fobbed me off. It was Mrs Conlon, the cook, who told me what happened. A week or so after the second funeral, the animals became agitated. Every chance, they made a beeline for the schoolroom. The door was kept shut but they'd paw at it, whining and barking. Before long, the bottom was covered in scratch marks. If they were allowed inside the room, they'd do a circuit of it, growling and running at shadows. They grew particularly noisy and troublesome after dark, until it reached a stage where none of the household could enjoy a wink of sleep.

Uncle Justin had the dogs banished to the stableyard but they continued their clamour through the night. Eventually, he was obliged to find another home for them. He was sorry to see them go, having reared them from puppies, but there was no help for it.

There were other differences at Bride's Peak. Aunt Delia hardly slept. The parlour maid, Agnes, told me my aunt used to flit about the house at all hours. Agnes was up early and worked late. She said there were times you'd turn a corner and find my aunt standing there, transfixed. "If I had to take a guess at what she was doing, I'd say she was listening," said Agnes.

One by one, the servants handed in their notice. Obviously, Miss Gurney wasn't expected to stay – on the day following Lucy's funeral, she was given an excellent reference and a month's wages in lieu of notice. But others dispensed with their own services in quick succession, from the housekeeper to the man who drove the pony and trap. Soon, just three staff remained: Mrs Conlon, the cook, who had been nursemaid to Uncle Justin and my father when they were boys, her husband Bernard who looked after the garden, and Agnes. She was an orphan and Bride's Peak was the closest she knew to a home – maybe that's why she made allowances. The Conlons had a home in a cottage on the grounds. Only Agnes lived in.

Time passed. Bride's Peak, for all its oddities, was stitched into the fabric of my childhood and I liked to visit there. I always packed a sketchpad and paintbox in my luggage and spent my visits rambling about with them. In time, I realised that art was more than a hobby to me and began to have hopes of earning my living as an artist. The Christmas after I turned fourteen, my school offered a prize for the best landscape. January the thirty-first was the deadline. Uncle Justin suggested the countryside around Sally Gap might prove inspirational, inviting me to stay after the New Year – I could scout for locations and make preparatory sketches. But Aunt Delia begged, instead, that I might be allowed to spend a few days before Christmas with them. The fifth anniversary of their daughters' deaths was approaching and I suppose she dreaded it, longing for some distraction. I was to go home on Christmas Eve.

My mother was reluctant to give permission but my uncle said he would regard it as a particular favour and my father hadn't the heart to refuse. Besides, Uncle Justin had taken my elder brother, Patrick, into the wine importation business, and was training him up to the trade. My father believed he owed him a good turn. As for me, I didn't realise how sorely I'd miss my family.

Mind you, I was ambitious for the art prize. That part of Wicklow has a wildness which speaks to me, city girl though I am. Whenever I stayed at Bride's Peak, I used to slip a sandwich and an apple in my pocket and roam the woods and mountain paths from morning till night. Often, the weather was misty, even in summer, because it was high up – you could miss your way and wander in circles. But I was never uneasy. I preferred to be outdoors than inside.

And there still were times when I was uneasy in Bride's Peak.
Not because I felt my cousins' presence, although I did. In itself,
that didn't distress me. After all, we were friends in life – how
could death change our feelings towards one another? But some
things happened that began to sow doubts in my mind. I sensed
one of the girls felt resentment towards me. Because I was living,
and she wasn't. I couldn't tell which of them it was but I knew it
didn't apply to both Claire and Lucy. Only one of them had a
grievance."

The lamp beside Sarah began to gutter and she paused to attend
to it. When it was put to rights, she slid a sideways glance at me.

"There's something I didn't tell you. I didn't want to say it, out
of loyalty to my aunt. She loved me, you know. As children, we
always recognise when we're loved. But something happened in
Lucy's bedroom the night she was taken. Agnes was there when
the commotion erupted. It shook her – she said she couldn't get
it out of her head. Mrs Conlon sent Agnes up to Lucy's bedroom
with a pot of tea and a plate of sandwiches for Aunt Delia, who
wouldn't leave Lucy, not even to eat. Uncle Justin must have raced
through his meal because he arrived in Lucy's room when Agnes
was still there, tidying up. He asked her to bank up the fire and she
was on her knees in front of the fender when it started up.

Something in my aunt went awry, according to Agnes.

'Lucy's frightened. She's scared stiff of Claire,' said Aunt Delia.

'Nonsense,' said Uncle Justin. 'Why should she fear her sister,
alive or dead?'

'Because Claire's come for Lucy. She wants a playmate. Help
me! We must keep her away from Lucy!'

Aunt Delia swerved into corners, flapping with her hands,
clawing at nothing but the air around her. The nurse was sitting by
the window and Aunt Delia launched herself at the woman,
tearing at her face. Uncle Justin had to overpower his wife before
he could drag her away. All the time, Aunt Delia was pleading
aloud to Claire to spare her sister.

'Don't take my baby, Claire!' she cried. 'You're doing it to punish me, aren't you, because I wasn't there when you called for me? Mama tried to come home for you. It's cruel to take Mama's baby away from her. Please, Claire. Please. Let her stay with me.'

Her wails reverberated about the house. The doctor was downstairs, having a bite of supper before his next call, and hurried upstairs to administer a sedative.

Aunt Delia was asleep when Lucy died. When she awoke, it was to news of her second loss.

'I took your place, Delia,' my uncle protested. 'I sat with Lucy right till the end. She wasn't alone.'

'I know she wasn't alone. Claire was there, ready to seize her chance. Waiting to take Lucy away from me.'

'You're upset, my dear. There was only me in the room when our little girl passed away – Nurse had just stepped out for a rest. Don't you think I'd have known if Claire was present? I'm her father, after all.'

'You wouldn't! It isn't in you to feel her presence. But I'd have known. And it would have made a difference. I'd have knelt down and pleaded with her, if she'd ever loved her mama, to stay away from Lucy. I'd have stopped her. She'd have listened to me. I know she would.'

It was the lament of a mother asked to bear too much sorrow. To bury one of your two children is hard but to bury both is beyond endurance.

At that second funeral service, something cracked inside Aunt Delia. As the small coffin was lowered into the grave beside her sister's, she tried to hurl herself into the hole after it. One moment, she was standing by the mound of earth with her head bent. The next, the priest, who was reciting the Rite of Committal, had his breviary knocked out of his hand. One of her feet was scrabbling against the wooden box. Uncle Justin managed to catch hold of her and grip tight, and he hustled her away. Both of them missed the rest of Lucy's burial."

Silence settled between us. The woman sounded unhinged by grief to me and I wondered at Mr and Mrs Reynolds for allowing Sarah to spend time in Bride's Peak after witnessing such a display. Something of what I was thinking must have communicated itself to Sarah.

She sighed. "My parents would have banned my visits to Bride's Peak if they were aware of how things stood with my aunt. Uncle Justin kept it from them – how damaged she was by the way their family life was up-ended – young as I was, I knew to hold my peace.

In time, I came to understand that Aunt Delia had developed a dislike of Claire. She held her responsible for Lucy's death. It was illogical but she couldn't be talked out of it. More than once, I heard Uncle Justin try to explain Claire had suffered and died, too. How could it be her fault?

'She was always inclined to jealousy,' said Aunt Delia. 'Remember how she said I paid more attention to Lucy than to her? She'd accuse me of loving Lucy more.'

'You were always inclined to pet Lucy,' said Uncle Justin

They had forgotten I was in the room.

'I always treated both my girls exactly the same!' Aunt Delia crumbled and folded in on herself, racked by hoarse sobs dragged from the pit of her stomach.

When Uncle Justin tried to comfort her, she shrugged him off.

'I can't bear the feel of your arms round me. It takes me back to that night when you frogmarched me out of Lucy's bedroom.'

'I didn't frogmarch you, Delia. The state you were in, you were going to do yourself an injury.'

I don't think Aunt Delia ever forgave Uncle Justin for persuading her to go to France that time the girls caught diphtheria. Poor man, he accepted his sentence with the resignation of someone who felt they deserved to be judged and found wanting.

He threw himself into his work, which gave him opportunities to take trips away from home. As for Aunt Delia, she shut herself up. My mother never allowed me to stay at the house when my aunt was alone apart from the staff. She put her foot down there.

'Let her own people send one of their children down from Sligo to keep her company,' she said.

That never happened.

My uncle would have let Bride's Peak and moved away but Aunt Delia refused to go. She would no more leave the vicinity of that small plot when her daughters were buried than she'd take a razor to her head and shave her scalp. Every day, without fail, she visited the graveyard.

It was the high point of her day. Four miles it was, down to Laragh, and four miles back again, uphill all the way. My uncle liked to maintain a pretence that the trip to the graveyard was a constitutional. Sometimes, he prevailed on her to take the pony and trap, which my aunt drove herself, but it was more usual for her to walk.

She'd dress herself with care for the outing, head to toe in black, but elegant, never dowdy, and a lace mantilla covering her hair. She used to stand straight-backed beside the white angel they raised over the girls' mound, pale and composed as if she was made of marble herself, and never so much as glanced at another grave. The rain could – and did – tumble down in sheets and still she wouldn't stir except to raise an umbrella.

I went with her when I stayed in Bride's Peak. My uncle told me he'd regard it as a favour if I kept my aunt company. She took it for granted I'd want to pay my respects to my cousins – it wouldn't have entered her head that a child might find a graveyard morbid. As it happened, I liked it well enough in that little country spot, with a sea of higgledy-piggledy headstones, some domed and others squared off, each containing a story you could decipher from the inscriptions on the markers.

I'd only spend a few minutes beside Claire and Lucy's before roaming off. Sometimes Bernard Conlon arrived to tidy the grave while we were there. Agnes told me he thought Aunt Delia should be discouraged from visiting it so frequently. 'She's pinned to that grave as though waiting for it to give up its dead,' according to Bernard. But my uncle could no more stop her from going than he could control the movements of the tide.

One night, we were disturbed by the scamper of mice. Uncle Justin consulted Bernard. While it was acknowledged that owls were excellent mousers, a cat was accepted to be the most convenient solution. The Conlons had several and could vouch for their effectiveness. A tortoiseshell puss was borrowed from them and all day long I fed titbits to Patch, alternating between stroking and sketching him while he dozed. I asked if he could sleep at the bottom of my bed, but my uncle said he must earn his keep. While the household slumbered, Patch would go to work.

Next morning, one of the kitchen windows gaped open and Patch was nowhere to be found. It was presumed he had bolted back to the Conlons but there was no sign of him at their cottage. Not a scrap of fur, not a whisker remained. It was as if he had never existed.

At the breakfast table, Aunt Delia was fidgety. 'I dare say it was Claire left the window open. She had strange ideas about not keeping animals inside. Said they belonged outdoors. Don't you remember how she poured Lucy's goldfish into the stream at the bottom of the garden?'

'You're very sore on our daughter, my dear. She had a child's natural high spirits, that's all.'

'High spirits? That's one term for it. Malice, more like.'

'Delia, really! There was no malice in Claire.'

A sniff erupted from my aunt. 'She was a wild animal, that's what she was. Couldn't sit still. Always up to mischief. How she hated wearing shoes! The struggle I had to get her into them! You'd think she was a child from the tenements, or a little animal from the woods, the way she ran about in her bare feet. Bernard found a new pair of her boots, once, buried in the rose garden. If it wasn't for the laces trailing through the earth they've never have been spotted. Bold as brass, was Miss Claire, when I tackled her about them. Said they pinched her. Another time she tried to give away a pair to one of the maids.'

I laughed aloud, remembering how Miss Gurney used to scold and bribe Claire into her boots in the morning. It had been a battle of wills between the two of them. Unfortunately, my reaction reminded my aunt and uncle of my presence.

'Sarah,' said my uncle, 'why don't you go and see what Mrs Conlon is serving for lunch?'

I walked slowly to the door and left it ajar, hovering outside. I admit it was wrong but curiosity overcame me.

'Do keep your voice down, my dear – it's not right to speak about our daughter like that.'

'But you know as well as I do, Justin, when there was tomfoolery afoot Claire was the instigator.'

'Whatever the right or wrong of it, that's all in the past now, Delia. They are our dear, departed ones.'

'Are they? I wouldn't be so sure.'

That night, perhaps influenced by the overheard conversation, I wakened to the sound of footfall. The movement did not belong to mice. Nor was it an adult's – my aunt or uncle, checking that the bed curtains were drawn. It was the rapid pitter-patter of a child's footsteps, darting about in play.

Was it one set or two? Just one, I thought. I sat up, rubbing my eyes, afraid to open the curtains and look out. Intent, I listened inside the cave of my four-poster, the blood roaring in my eardrums. Every nerve was strained from the effort. A gentle thud sounded, as if something was knocked over. You must look, I told myself. Yet still I wavered. Look out, I urged again. What if Patch had come back?

I could identify a dim glow outside the curtains. It came from the nightlight left burning on the bedside table, a candle inside a glass jar. With an effort of will, I prised open the curtains by an inch or two. Nothing to be seen. I pushed them aside a little more and hooked out my head.

It seemed to me as if there was a thickening of the air, suggesting a brooding quality in the room. A strong impression came upon me that someone was there. I can't tell why but my eyes were drawn to my shoes, lying half-underneath a chair. As I watched, one of them toppled onto its side. Above it, my nightdress-case which rested on the chair slowly drifted forward until its ribbons trailed on the floor, blowing back and forth. The sound of paper rustling caused me to turn my head towards a desk by the window. The pages of a book I had been reading fluttered as if someone was flicking through it.

Whoever was in the room was advancing closer to me. I felt as if a north wind had penetrated beneath my skin and was whistling among my bones. My breath began to enter and leave my body in panting gasps. *Stay where you are! Don't come any closer!* Yet I was incapable of crying aloud – the power to call for help was beyond me. Only my eyes were free to move and they panicked about, watching for what would happen next.

I did not have long to wait. The nightlight flickered. It wavered, righted itself, and was snuffed out. The bed curtains moved, the bedsprings groaned, and someone sat on the edge of my bed. My heart began hammering fit to tunnel through my chest.

'Which of you is it?' I managed to croak. 'Claire or Lucy?'

A giggle, quickly smothered. A whispered response. 'That's for me to know and you to guess.'

At that, every hair on my head stood up individually. I sank back into the bed, pulling the blankets over me. Through them, I could hear a voice – whose, I couldn't tell – saying, 'Come and play, Sarah.'

Terror lent me strength. '*No! Go away!*'

'Don't be a spoilsport.'

'I don't want you here!'

Just then, the door flew open.

'Sarah! I heard you calling. What's wrong?' It was my aunt's voice.

A hand yanked open the curtains and pulled back the blankets over my head.

'Sarah, dear girl, what ails you at all?'

I blinked up at her through the light from the lamp she held in one hand. Her face was blurry, except for her eyes, which glittered under straight black brows. On the wall behind, her shadow reared up to twice her height.

Incoherent with fright, I lay whimpering.

'Sarah, tell me what's wrong!'

'I want to go home,' I managed.

'Why? Did you see something? You did, didn't you! Tell me what you saw!'

'Nothing. But I heard her.'

'I knew it! What did she want?'

'Someone to play with her.'

Aunt Delia leaned over the bed, her breath falling hot on my face. 'Which of my girls was it?' When I didn't answer, she shook me. 'I need to know. Was it Lucy? Was it? Tell me!'

'I don't know! Leave me alone! You're scaring me!'

'Delia, do as Sarah says. Let her be.' It was Uncle Justin.

Teeth clenched, she glared at him. 'She saw my baby, Justin! She saw her when I can't. But I know she's here. I feel it!'

'I didn't see anything,' I protested.

Aunt Delia let out a howl and, as suddenly as it had erupted, her frenzy dissolved into tears. Uncle Justin took the lamp from her and set it on a table before leading her from the room. Over his shoulder, he called back to me, 'It's too bad Agnes hasn't stirred. I'll rouse her and send her down to keep you company. I'll be straight back to you as soon as I get your aunt settled. Stay where you are, out of harm's way.'

Rigid in bed, I made a nest for myself, propped up by pillows – and waited. By the glow of the lamp, my gaze patrolled the shadows. But the intruder did not return.

Agnes edged in, yawning, with a shawl over her nightgown, and curled up in the armchair. 'The master says you had a nightmare.'

'I suppose I must have.'

When my uncle returned, he was dressed and had a quilt over his arm. 'Off you slip to bed now, Agnes. I'll see you right for this.'

She shuffled out and my uncle took her place in the armchair.

'You're the best of girls, Sarah, but we're taking advantage having you to stay with us here. It's not fair. First thing tomorrow I'll arrange to take you home. Now, you settle down, and I'll stay with you for the rest of the night. Nothing will harm you, I guarantee it. And sure it'll be morning before we know ourselves. What do you say? Will we try and snatch a few hours' sleep before another day lands in on top of us?'

'I can go home tomorrow?'

'Immediately after breakfast. I'll take you myself, Sarah. That's a promise.'

Well, the night passed, and I must have slept for some part of it. As soon as I opened my eyes, I found myself squinting – the morning light was brighter than usual and the room felt colder. My uncle was gone but I could hear the clatter of a household making a start on the day. Scurrying to the window, I opened the shutters. Frost had etched lace patterns across the glass, clouding my line of vision, but I could make out enough to realise that snowfall had caught us unawares. A thick mantle covered the glen. Powdery snow was piled into drifts, not a footstep scarred its surface. Not a bird's print, or a woodland creature's, smudged its perfection.

I huddled into my clothes without taking the time to rinse my face and hands in the pitcher of water and basin on the washstand. Despite the previous night's visitor, the knowledge of that snowy world outside lightened my mood. Downstairs, I found my uncle alone at the breakfast table.

'Morning, Sarah. It's just the two of us. Your aunt is indisposed. Sit down and keep me company.' He lifted a silver lid off a platter. 'Poached eggs here. Bacon in the other one. Could you manage some? Good girl yourself. We need to keep our strength up, this weather.'

Usually, my uncle was silent at breakfast, attentive to his newspaper like a man duty-bound to absorb its contents. Today, however, he troubled himself to engage in small talk. He asked about school and whether I enjoyed other subjects apart from art, and did I know that his brother – my father – had been a gifted amateur cartoonist in his youth, and what a shame he'd put aside his sketchpad and never seemed to doodle any more.

I wondered if Uncle Justin was determined to pretend nothing untoward had happened. Once, I began to mention the previous night's events ... 'It wasn't a bad dream, you know, Uncle Justin ...' but a glint in his eye warned me off and I said no more.

After we were finished eating and a bleary Agnes arrived to clear the table, he said to me, 'I believe I might take a turn in the snow. Would you care to join me?'

I nodded.

'Excellent. Be sure and dress warmly. Double-wrap the extremities. Can't be too careful. Feet have to be kept dry – galoshes should do the trick. You're bound to find a pair that fit you in the boot cupboard. Nothing gets thrown out here. We have mufflers going back to my grandfather's time. Probably the odd hole in them from moths, or age, or both, mind you. Anyhow, off you go and get yourself ready. I'll meet you in the back hall in fifteen minutes.'

The boot cupboard was a treasure trove, just off the kitchen. In the past, I had played hide and seek there with Claire and Lucy, and we had chosen dressing-up costumes from its detritus. But I didn't feel like loitering there today. Mrs Conlon helped me to find some Wellington boots, along with warmer gloves to wear over the pair I had with me.

Clumping along the passageway to the back hall, I spotted a bulky shadow through the foggy glass of the half-door. Uncle Justin was on the doorstep outside, smoking a pipe. If he was anything like his brother, he only smoked when he needed to think.

I opened the door but was pulled up short by the smell of tobacco. Even diluted in the open air, its heavy sweetness conjured up my father. Homesickness swamped me. I took a deep breath and reminded myself I'd be going home that day. Uncle Justin had given me his promise.

My uncle was busy knocking out the contents of his pipe and didn't notice my reaction. Blindly, I rushed ahead, overbalanced and landed face down in the snow. He hauled me upright, mistaking my distress for wounded pride, and handed me the woollen tam o'shanter that had slipped off my head.

'Here's what we'll do, Sarah. You take my arm and I'll use this stout walking stick of mine to heave us along.'

'Where are we going?'

'To a viewing point. It's a mile away, above Glenmacnass waterfall. It'll give us a good outlook over the countryside. I want to see if the valley's under snow.'

Ungainly, ankles aching, I crunched along beside my uncle, chin tucked into my chest. The air was stinging but invigorating. It nibbled at the tip of my nose and scraped against my cheeks but the rest of me was warm from padding and exercise.

We trekked without meeting a soul. When we arrived at Glenmacnass, we rested against a stunted tree trunk. The waterfall, while not quite frozen, was sluggish. My uncle shaded his eyes against the blinding whiteness and took stock, while I followed his lead. I was accustomed to a patchwork quilt: purple heather showing up against the residual greens and browns, pepped up by splashes of yellow gorse depending on the time of year. But the landscape was naked. A snow blur, whiter than bone, stretched below us, every blade of grass and twig blanketed.

Standing out in stark relief were a few evergreens whose branches had shaken off their snowy load.

'Do you think it's snowing in Ranelagh, too?' I asked.

'If it is, it won't lie. Snow never lasts in cities. Too many feet, hooves and wheels churning it up. It's a different kettle of fish out here. Have you any idea why we came up to this viewing point, Sarah?'

'To give Aunt Delia peace so she can sleep?'

'I hope maybe she can catch up on her sleep. She's worn to threads, so she is. But no, I wanted to see what the chances were for taking you home today, like I promised. And now you can see for yourself the lie of the land.' He held my gaze, eyes steady.

Although I was only fourteen, I understood what he was doing. 'Can't the pony and trap cross through snow?'

He shook his head. "Not new snow like this. They'd get stuck.'

'We managed to walk this far. Couldn't we make it down to Laragh and hire someone to take us on to the railway station in Rathdrum?'

'We could probably reach Laragh but it's twelve miles further on to Rathdrum. It's too far in these conditions. Even supposing the railway lines have been shovelled and the trains are running.'

'But what do people do when this happens, Uncle Justin?'

'They wait for the thaw.'

'I can't wait! How about if we try your horse in the trap? He's stronger than the pony.'

'It's risky taking either horse or pony out – they could break a leg and maybe have to be shot. Never mind the possibility of the trap turning over and one or both of us coming to harm. Now, I gave you my word, Sarah, and I'm not a man to go back on it. So if you still want to go home, I'll give it a try. But those are the dangers. It's up to you. You must make the decision.'

As he was finishing his speech, a light flurry of snow began to fall, flakes speckling his whiskers. I bared a hand and watched them land on my palm. They melted when they touched it, their icy kiss puddling on my skin. I was playing for time. The truth is, I could have wept. I was too old not to recognise the dangers of attempting a journey through the snow, too young not to wish they could be ignored.

'I'll have to stay until the thaw, Uncle Justin.'

'Well said. I can see you're on the way to becoming a young lady. Let's head for home now. We don't want to get caught in a snowstorm and lose our sense of direction.'

'But don't you know every inch of the glen?'

He was walking at an angle to brace against slipping and I copied him.

'Makes no odds in a snowstorm. You can't tell north from south or east from west. You become snow-blind. But don't worry, this is only a passing squall – look, it's dwindling to nothing. And you can make out Bride's Peak from here. See?'

Bride's Peak was like a doll's house on the horizon. Gazing down at it, I felt a tug of belonging, and understood why my father was nostalgic for the place despite the home he'd made for us in Ranelagh.

Halfway back, I paused to admire a frozen puddle and was horrified when Uncle Justin's walking stick cracked it to smithereens.

'It was so pretty,' I protested.

'Pretty won't help the birds find a place to drink.'

At home, Aunt Delia was watching out for us and waved from the drawing-room window. "Mrs Conlon has soup simmering on the range for you," she said, chatting as though there had been no night-time disturbance. We ate lunch and afterwards my aunt played Christmas carols on the piano, the three of us singing along to 'I Saw Three Ships' and 'See Amid the Winter Snow'.

'Let's have one from my schooldays,' she suggested. 'I learned this in French. '*Les Anges dans Nos Campagnes*'. Can you guess which it is, Sarah?'

'One about angels? 'Hark the Herald Angels Sing'?'

'Not quite. 'Angels We Have Heard on High.' It was Lucy's favourite.' The opening bars were crashed out with vigour and she began to sing, gesturing to us to join in.

We were jolly that day, despite everything. Only once did the mood veer into darkness. It was over dinner, when my aunt toyed with the food on her plate and Uncle Justin urged her to eat.

She lifted eyes glistening with tears. 'It pains me, missing my daily visit to the girls.'

'The ground is treacherous underfoot, Delia. You could break your neck if you risked it.'

'But I keep thinking how lonely it must be for them.'

'They have each other, my dear.'

'There is that.'

A truckle bed was set up in my room for Agnes so I wouldn't be alone in the night. I woke up to the rustle of her undressing in the dark but soon drifted off again. Nothing happened to trouble me. The fresh air must have helped me to sleep.

Next morning was Christmas Eve, the day I should have gone home. I had woken earlier, when Agnes rose – she had to be up to set the fires – but after checking the snowscape through the window, I had tumbled back into sleep. Now, I rocketed downstairs, hungry for breakfast. As I approached the breakfast room, raised voices alerted me to an argument between Aunt Delia and Uncle Justin. I was tempted to slide into the kitchen and beg for a slice of bread and jam and some sugary tea from Mrs Conlon's teapot, which was never empty. Undecided, I hovered in the passageway.

'I will not miss a visit to the graveside two mornings in a row. That's an end to it, Justin. You do not have the right to forbid me.'

'Be reasonable, Delia. More snow fell in the night. It would be like walking on glass. You'll never make it in one piece. And it'll be no safer in the trap going downhill. The hooves could go from under the pony.'

I turned tail and had breakfast in the kitchen while Mrs Conlon and Agnes occupied themselves with various duties. They must have heard the ruckus because neither of them asked what I was doing at their table.

Afterwards, in search of a possible composition for my landscape, I thought about capturing the view from one of the windows. None of the sketches I had worked on since my arrival at Bride's Peak satisfied me. Fetching my drawing materials, I tried various vantage points before deciding the schoolroom offered the best view. I felt uneasy in the room but Agnes agreed to sit with me. She lit a fire and busied herself polishing the silver. By the time other chores demanded her presence elsewhere, I had pencilled out a sketch, was immersed in mixing paints and testing colours, and didn't mind being left alone.

The wall opposite the window had floor-to-ceiling presses. In one of them, old magazines were stacked. Claire and Lucy used to cut out the illustrations and paste them onto coloured paper to make cards or scrapbook fancies. When my cousins were alive, we had spent wet days in the schoolroom making collages.

A creak groaned behind me and one of the cupboard doors opened. I looked over my shoulder. Inside, the magazines were stacked in a haphazard tower. They're going to come crashing out, I thought, and crossed the room to close the door. The magazine on top caught my eye. Its cover illustration showed a girl gliding on skates across a frozen river. I began reading. The story concerned a girl who ventured onto thin ice despite warnings – with predictable consequences.

Before I had finished, my aunt walked into the schoolroom. 'There you are, Sarah. I have a special favour to ask, before the lunch gong. Will you oblige me? Say you will. Call it your Christmas gift to me.'

Everybody knows it's unfair to be pressurised into agreeing to something without knowing what the service is. But my aunt squeezed onto the bench alongside me, catching my hands in hers, and I said I would.

'I've struck a bargain with your uncle. After lunch, I'm to walk down to pay my usual visit to the girls, provided you come as well and make sure I don't stay out too late. He can't accompany us because a tree has fallen and is blocking the entrance to the kitchen garden. Your uncle and Mr Conlon have been trying to drag it away but it's too heavy. They've decided to cut it up and carry it off piecemeal.'

'Uncle Justin isn't worried we'll slip on the icy patches?'

'Uncle Justin's a fusspot and a goose. Of course we won't slip. Straight there and back – and we'll keep a close lookout for ice. We'll leave immediately after lunch and be home before dark. I have flowers for the girls' grave. Christmas roses. We always have Christmas roses in the house at this time of year. They'll feel the presence of the bouquet and know I'm thinking of them.'

Uncle Justin didn't join us for lunch, instead pressing on with the job he was engaged in with Bernard Conlon. My aunt and I ate quickly and wrapped up for our walk.

We paced slowly to Laragh, taking the hill at an angle, as my uncle had shown me the previous day. At the mouth of the graveyard, my aunt said something that caused me to stare.

'We'll have to look sharp about decorating the Christmas tree when we get home. Your uncle will wonder if it isn't ready when he lands in for dinner.'

A warning bell shrilled in my head. 'Is that how he thinks we're spending the afternoon, Aunt Delia?'

She nodded, her eyes fixed on the marble angel ahead of us.

Shock that my aunt had lied to me was followed by a flood of alarm. It meant nobody knew where we were if anything happened.

'We should go home at once, Aunt Delia.'

She paid no attention, absorbed in picking her way along the path. Maybe once she puts the flowers in the holder at the angel's ankles she'll be ready to turn back, I thought. She took care arranging them, while I hopped from one foot to the next. Finally, she straightened but didn't move away. I tapped her arm, again suggesting we should start for home. She didn't acknowledge me. When I pulled at her sleeve, she shook me off.

I looked up at the sky. There were clouds, low and pale grey, heavy with snow. Flakes began to corkscrew down. Desperate now, I put my arm round my aunt's waist and tugged her towards the gate. This time, despite her trance, she allowed me to steer her.

But the night was sinking in fast and the snowflakes obscured what daylight remained. Taking my aunt's hand so that we wouldn't be separated, I began to walk uphill. But we could make hardly any progress with the snow spinning in all directions, blinding us. We plodded on but must have wandered off the road because we found ourselves near Glenmalure Wood.

'Should we rest here?' suggested my aunt.

I knew if we slept there we would never wake up. 'No, we have to keep going.'

'I'm too tired.' Aunt Delia's eyes were glazed, a whine entering her voice.

'We can rest back at Bride's Peak.' I pushed us onwards.

Night was thick about us now, the moon covered by drifting cloudbanks. But a scattering of stars glimmered through the heavens and by their light I noticed a series of small grooves in the snow. I leaned down for a closer look. They were footsteps pointing uphill.

I placed a foot alongside the nearest one. It was smaller than mine. Cautious, I examined the prints, wondering if it was safe to follow where they led. What if they were a ruse intended to lead us to harm? What if they guided us to a drop? As soon as our absence was noticed my uncle would surely put together a search party. But what if we were found with our necks broken at the bottom of a ravine?

My aunt took a step towards the woods and plunged chest-deep in a snowdrift. That decided me. I hauled her out, jammed my arm through hers, and forced her to follow the trail that had been laid.

I can't tell how long we shuffled through a world muted by twirling snowflakes. I tried not to focus on their hypnotic dance — afraid I'd stand watching and forget to keep moving. Lumbering along, my feet like icicles, I tagged behind the footprints. Somehow, despite my aunt's weight dragging at me, we made progress through the whited-out landscape.

'*Hallo! Delia! Sarah! Hallo!*'

A moving speck of yellow light appeared ahead. It came closer, swinging in an arc. It was a lantern. The hand holding it belonged to Uncle Justin. He and Mr Conlon were searching for us. Without realising it, we were in the field in front of Bride's Peak.

At that, my strength caved in. I let go of Aunt Delia and sank to my knees.

The men carried us home. Agnes and Mrs Conlon bathed us, fed us hot milk laced with brandy, and put us to bed. I slept heavily but towards morning dreamed of being chased by a hunter with a rifle who thought I was a deer.

On Christmas morning, I started awake with a racing heartbeat.

Agnes popped her head round the door. 'Morning, sleepyhead. I'll fetch you a nice boiled egg and let your uncle know you're awake.'

Soon, I was dipping toast soldiers into egg yolk while my uncle interrogated me on what had happened. He looked at me quizzically when I explained about the tracks guiding us home.

'Your aunt mentioned no footprints. But she's adamant that Lucy was with you. She says she felt her presence.'

'Didn't you see the trail, Uncle Justin?'

He shook his head. 'The snow will have covered any marks by now. What matters is you're both safe and sound. I can't bear to think how this might have turned out.'

By mid-morning, I was judged well enough to visit my aunt's

bedside. Her dark hair streamed over the pillows. Her face was austere, pouches beneath the eyes. Reluctant to waken her, I was about to tip-toe away when she stirred.

'You dear girl, come closer. Yesterday I thought I was on the brink of joining my Lucy. My heart was full, knowing she was waiting for me. But today I realise how selfish I was. It would have meant sacrificing you and depriving another mother of her child. You stopped me from making a mistake that could never be righted. You led us home. Thank you, Sarah.'

'It was Claire who showed us the way home, Aunt Delia. She saved us. Not me.'

'I don't understand.'

'She left a trail. We followed where the tracks led. Don't you remember?'

'There may have been some traces. An animal's markings, I imagine.'

'But they were barefoot.'

'What's that you say?'

'They were made by someone who was barefoot – a child. I could make out the dent left by the heel, and the hollows from the toes. I counted five on each foot. It was a human foot. No animal makes a print like that.'

'But what kind of child goes shoeless in a snowstorm?'

'Don't you know?'

As she gazed at me, moisture began to coat those black eyes of hers. She tried to speak but was defeated. Instead, she laid her hand on top of mine.

By and by, she managed to whisper a few words. 'I have been ungenerous.'

And she wept."

At that, church bells began to peal, jolting Sarah and me back to Ranelagh. The wind was moaning still and the bells could not drown out the rattle of glass in the window frame. A shiver juddered through my body, not because I was glad to be indoors on such a night but from a sense of the uncanny which gripped me.

"And there's my ghost story," said Sarah. "I don't expect you can make much sense of it. And she wept."

"What an extraordinary adventure," I said. "How brave you were!"

She shook her head, rejecting the praise. "Earlier, when you told me you believed all children long for a sense of power, I remembered that journey uphill through a snowstorm. I knew my survival and my aunt's depended on me. I suppose there was power in that realisation. But what I mostly remember is the fear. I was terrified we wouldn't see the morning. I don't ever want to find myself in that position again."

"But you had a good spirit to guide you," I reminded her.

"Ah, you can't expect a good spirit to intervene every time you land in bother."

"Do you still visit the house?"

"It's been a decade since I set foot in it. The place is locked up – my aunt and uncle make their home in Paris these days. The shutters are closed day and night, dustsheets cover the furniture. Agnes has the Conlons' cottage and looks in on the house every once in a while. But nobody lives there."

"Nobody?" I queried.

She rolled on her side towards the paraffin lamp and extinguished it with a twist of the wrist. Across the sudden darkness, her voice came floating. "Bride's Peak is vacant now. But not for one minute do I believe it's empty."

During the Civil War, Dorothy Macardle took the anti-Treaty side and served six months in prison until she was released on health grounds. While there, she asked for some books to be sent in, including The Republic *by Plato. It arrived with the word Republic scored out by the censor.*

HANNA SHEEHY SKEFFINGTON

Born Johanna Sheehy in Kanturk, County Cork, 1877;
died Dublin 1946
Feminist, activist, journalist, politician

Hanna straddles the feminist, nationalist and labour movements, and fought a range of battles from suffrage to anti-partition to women's access to education.

In 1908 she was a co-founder (with Margaret Cousins) of the Irish Women's Franchise League, which embraced militant tactics in campaigning for the vote for women. For her the vote was the cornerstone of democracy and a vital part of citizenship. She served two prison terms in Dublin after being convicted in relation to suffragette activities and went on hunger strike on both occasions, in 1912 and 1913.

Hanna's feminist and pacifist husband, Francis Sheehy Skeffington, was seized, imprisoned and summarily executed by an out-of-control army officer during Easter 1916, despite being a civilian. She refused officialdom's attempts to gloss over the circumstances of his death and forced a Commission of Inquiry to be held.

In 1918 she was jailed again, this time without charge, following her return from a US speaking tour, 'British Militarism as I Have Known It'. She was sent to Holloway Prison in London and promptly went on hunger strike. After two days she was released under the 'Cat and Mouse Act' – where hunger strikers were allowed out on licence because it would embarrass the government if they died in prison, with the threat of re-arrest once they regained their health suspended over them. No effort was made to take her back into custody.

In 1933 she was again imprisoned, this time in Armagh, for breaching an order banning her from entering Northern Ireland.

Night Sky in London

H.M. Prison Holloway, London

1918

Lights out. Meals shimmer before her eyes. A mushroom omelette, chives sprinkled on top. Cauliflower cheese tangy with mustard. Potato-and-leek casserole, cream swirled through it. Slices of wheaten bread crumbling under the weight of country butter. *Kaffe und Kuchen*, an afternoon tradition acquired after trips to Germany.

Stop thinking about food! It would be easier if she could nod off. But dread prevents Hanna from sleeping. Tomorrow they may start force-feeding her. She shrinks from the knowledge. Yet she has to accept it's a possibility – they do it to impose their will on an uncooperative prisoner. They can't allow her to flout their authority. It stirs up dissent.

Perhaps that's why she was spirited away to England after being arrested in Dublin – to break her will. In Ireland, force-feeding Skeffy's widow would spark protests. Here in Britain, preoccupied with the Great War, it could pass without notice.

Hanna cannot settle. She knows she should stay in one place to conserve her energy, which will soon dwindle without food, but nervous irritability leaves her restless. Cabinet ministers will arrive at a decision about whether or not to force-feed her. Maybe they have made up their minds already. As they sit down now to supper, swapping news of their day with family members, her fate may be determined. The governor of Holloway isn't a bad sort but if the order arrives from the government he will act on it instantly.

She has no power to change what they do to her. She can only control her reaction to it. She must be resilient. Her stomach churns, an acid reflux rushes into her mouth, and she takes a sip of water. Drinking fluid is critical or she'll collapse after a few days.

If she imagines the steps methodically in her mind it will help her to conquer fear. So, in the morning she may be sent to the governor's office. Hunger strike is self-murder, he will tell her. He may mention her child, left orphaned if she dies. On balance, she thinks the governor will not refer to the murder of Owen's father. The circumstances are too murky for any Crown official to raise them, even obliquely. Nevertheless, he will 'invite' her to eat.

She pauses, visions of food filling her mind. A baked potato with melted cheese oozing from its slit, pickles on the side. The sweet explosion of Italian tomatoes ripened by sunshine. Honey from the comb crunching against tongue and teeth.

She will refuse to eat. Skirmishing over, the governor will proceed to coercion. Pinpricks of perspiration erupt along her hairline. She must find the courage to resist. It will not happen in the governor's office. She will be taken elsewhere. To her cell? Maybe. She is in an empty wing, apart from three other Irish women prisoners. Countess Markievicz, Maud Gonne and Kathleen Clarke are being held on trumped-up charges involving an imaginary plot with Germany to ferment insurrection in Ireland.

The force-feeders will disregard her protests — she might as well be a dog refusing its bath. Anyhow, her struggles will be pitiful. Overpowering her will not be troublesome. They will tie her to a chair and produce their paraphernalia. A tube will be pushed against her teeth and rammed down her throat. She will bite it, twisting her head from side to side, and thrash her body against the leather restraints. Her throat will be torn raw, the inside of her mouth cut and leaking blood, her teeth loosened — maybe one or two broken. But she will not be able to prevent the tube from funnelling an avalanche of pulp into her stomach.

This will happen irrespective of the physical damage it may cause her. The mental damage is of less relevance again to them. They are concerned, not with treating her gently, but thwarting her resistance. Regardless, she must brace herself. She cannot submit tamely to physical force.

At least the Irish prisoners will be alert to sounds of a struggle. The authorities have taken the precaution of leaving three empty cells between each of them but, even so, they're bound to hear something. She's relying on them to raise a ruckus. Perhaps they'll shout and find some object to make noise with. Their chamber pots? They could clatter them against the floor. She hopes they make an almighty racket — she'll need their support.

A wave of misery crashes over her and she plops down on the camp bed. It has no springs, just iron slats, and a mattress that feels as if it's stuffed with straw. She rummages under the pillow for Owen's drawing. Her son is nine, being cared for by one of her sisters. In a worst-case scenario, her sisters will raise him, but she cannot bear the idea of her boy losing both parents. Maybe she's being selfish, using a hunger strike to challenge the state. But how else can she protest at being held? With any luck, starvation tactics will open the gaol gates sooner. The authorities can't keep her locked up indefinitely. Can they?

Hanna is unable to see Owen's artwork clearly but a trickle of starlight meanders through the tiny window, allowing her to pick out some blurred outlines. Besides, she knows what the drawing represents. There are three figures. Owen in the middle, holding hands between Hanna in a swashbuckling hat with a buckle, like a particularly stylish pirate, and Frank in his graduation gown. He copied the image of his father from their wedding photograph, when they wore their University College Dublin robes rather than bridal regalia.

The feel of the paper beneath her fingers reminds her of Frank's love letters, tied together with a blue ribbon. A raiding party stole them after his death, when soldiers broke into their home searching for evidence to blacken his name. As though a man's endearments to his beloved, his "*You are 'such stuff that dreams are made on', my thrice-sweet Hanna*," could count as sedition. She folds Owen's picture back into eight squares and returns it to its place.

It's quiet here, the most silent gaol she's ever been housed in. The usual whispers and whistles of communal life are absent because of all the vacant cells in the 'Hard Nails Wing' – the other inmates were cleared out when the Irish prisoners were moved in. There are four tiers of cells and she's on the top floor, in a room measuring about seven feet by thirteen feet. Outside are exercise yards, to be used daily for the regulation one hour. She has already walked in dreary rings about one set aside for the Irish, following a circle marked in the asphalt – the four women forbidden to talk to each another but glad to inhale the air and watch the pigeons congregating there. Expectant, the birds fluttered towards Maud Gonne, and were not disappointed. She managed to produce some crumbs and scatter them while the warders looked the other way.

Prison hadn't interfered totally with Maud's habit of doing as she liked. Hanna stared to see her carrying a scarlet geranium in a pot to the yard, setting it in a sunny patch. Hanna thought of geraniums as flowers that smouldered at people, and it seemed appropriate to see Maud Gonne with one. Between whispers and mime, Maud managed to convey that the air in her cell suffocated plants – nothing sent in by friends lasted more than three days. Her solution was to leave them outdoors on alternate nights.

Just then, a pop of saliva explodes in Hanna's mouth. The smell of food sitting on her table is drifting across. The warders leave every meal there, removing breakfast when they replace it with lunch, while supper keeps her company overnight. Her stomach gurgles. Even the cold tea in a tin mug smells fragrant right now. An image of *al fresco* dining slips in uninvited. A slice of Roquefort, a bunch of blue-black grapes and a glass of rosé – no, perhaps something bolder, a pinot noir. The colours are tantalisingly bright. She licks her lips before banishing the fantasy.

That's the odd thing about hunger strike, she reflects. You don't stop being hungry. The pangs are less acute after three days but they never vanish. Tomorrow will be tough. She brings her palm close to her mouth and breathes on it to see if her breath is rancid already. Nothing yet. But it will happen, it's a common side-effect.

She learned a lot on her first fast, back in Dublin in 1912, when she was given two months for a spate of window-smashing to register her dissatisfaction at the vote being withheld from women. Dublin Castle received the attentions of her cherry-wood stick. Before that hunger strike, Hanna imagined food would start to repel her by and by. In fact, she discovered she would never stop fantasising about it. Visions of French onion soup, a cheesy slice of baguette floating on top, tormented her.

Enough about food! She intends to keep on refusing it. But what if she falters when they hold up the tubes? What if she chokes on them and dies? They killed Tom Ashe when they botched his force-feeding and punctured his lung.

Senses sharpened, she hears the jangle of keys and the clang of a metal gate. Footsteps slap against concrete, approaching from the far end of the landing. They halt outside her cell. The glitter of an eye at the spyhole. She stares back at it. Challenging its right to look at her.

All at once, a thought paralyses her. What if they decide to force-feed her now, in the night? While others are sleeping? No witnesses that way. There's nothing to stop them – they can do whatever they like to her body.

The eyeball disappears. A click. The warder moves on.

Convulsively, her teeth chatter – her body's response to danger averted. For now. Drained, she slumps back on her bed, wrapping the coarse, prison-issue blanket about her shoulders, like one of the shawlies on the Dublin quays. Is she coming down with a chill? The August heat barely penetrates these prison bars. A few words exchanged with another human being would be a comfort right now. Kathleen Clarke is in the nearest cell but it's too far away to whisper to her. Kathleen suffers from sleeplessness – chances are she's wide awake, too. She's riddled with anxiety about her three sons, convinced they'll be targeted and killed in her absence. Further along the landing, Maud has been fretting about her boy, Seán. It occurs to Hanna that all four of the Irish prisoners might be lying awake. On second thoughts, maybe not Con Markievicz, who appears to take captivity in her stride. Except you never know what's inside someone else's head – she might be putting on a brave front.

They've been here longer than her. Hanna tries to feel sympathy for her fellow inmates but the image of a tube snaking along her insides, pumping its cargo into her belly, overshadows everything. She shudders, covering her face with her hands. Is resistance worth it?

A headache beats a tattoo at her temples – oh, for the mercy of rest from a wheeling imagination! She believes that by opposing the authorities she can expose their bullying certainty. But at what price to her health? Her head sinks onto her arms. She knows that after two weeks she will experience difficulty in standing, will be dizzy, sluggish and lose coordination. Four weeks on, it may become difficult to swallow water. Breathing becomes laboured. Hearing and vision loss will maybe occur. Organ failure is a risk.

Beyond forty-five days lies the danger of death — not least because infection might set in.

The longer the fast continues, the more strain is placed on the systems that keep the body alive. There is a chance she could injure herself permanently, including the harm she recoils from — brain damage. But it's a battle of wills between her and the authorities.

"Hallo, Hanna, how are you managing?"

That sounded like Frank. Is she hallucinating? It's early days to start hearing voices but not impossible. Her research indicates starvation can affect the mind as well as the body. She's finding this hunger strike, her third in six years, the hardest of all. And it's only the close of the second day.

"I know you can hear me."

She lets her hands drop from her face. "Frank? Where are you?"

"Right beside you on the bed."

Hanna turns her head. As she stares, her husband's frame takes shape and solidifies. It happens from the bottom up. Boots, woollen stockings, knee breeches, jacket with leather patches, beard covering the lower half of his face. Why, he's even wearing his Votes for Women badge, although a soldier at Portobello Barracks robbed it from his body.

She stretches out to touch him, thinks better of it, and drops her hand. If this is a figment of her imagination, she doesn't want to end it just yet. Instead, she studies him. He looks exactly the same. Not a day older. His tweedy smell rushes into her nostrils. Even if she can't believe the evidence of her eyes and ears, surely her nose isn't capable of lying?

"Where have you been, Frank? In — heaven?"

"You know perfectly well I'm an atheist, Hanna. I don't believe in an afterlife. Nor should you."

"But how is it you're here if there's nothing after death?"

"I'm here because you need me to be."

"I've needed you plenty of times over the past two years and four months, Frank. What's different about tonight?"

He scratches his bushy red beard. "Don't know. But if I had to take a guess, I'd say going on hunger strike's knocked a few things loose, myself included. Is that your supper over by the door?"

"Yes, they think I'll weaken if they leave it."

"Tempted, me darlin'?"

"Too right I am."

"Fasting is medicinal, it's good for the body. Like vegetarianism."

And being teetotal and not using tobacco, thinks Hannah. Frank had a frugal nature. Personally, she likes the odd glass of wine. Fasting is beneficial for a day or two but she might have to spend weeks on this hunger strike. She must trust to her friends to alert the public and drum up support. Con Markievicz claims publicity will embarrass the government. 'They'll be in a fearful funk over your stand, Hanna,' she says. Which is gratifying. Except, what if they decide to weather the backlash and teach her a lesson?

She catches Frank's eye. "I suppose I could do with whittling back on the weight. I'm heavier since, well, since what happened to you happened."

He gives her the sweet smile which transforms his serious face. "I love your curves, Hanna. Go easy on losing them."

She smiles back. From Frank, that counts as a compliment. They're as rare as hen's teeth.

"Are you the only one striking? Or do you have others to keep you company – like that time in Mountjoy?"

"I'm the only hunger striker this time round. But I'm not on my own. I share a landing with Con, Maud and Kathleen Clarke, Tom Clarke's widow. She's had a tough couple of years. Con, too, of course. Con and Kathleen can't go on hunger strike because they're Sinn Féiners, and it's contrary to party policy since Tom Ashe died. Maud Gonne says she doesn't feel able for one right now. Maybe further down the road. Incidentally, she's taken to calling herself Madame MacBride, which is a bit of a liberty since she couldn't stand her husband while he was alive. She wouldn't be Madame MacBride if he'd been run over by an omnibus. Executed revolutionary? That'll do nicely. But that's Maud for you, always spinning myths." Hanna's stomach rumbles and Frank politely pretends not to hear. "Actually, Con tried to talk me out of striking. Not from lack of courage – she doesn't have a cowardly bone in her body. But she says they'll probably do forcible-feeding."

Hanna flicks a glance at him to test how he responds to her *bête noire*. Rather infuriatingly, he radiates detachment. Probably because he was force-fed himself. If I can weather it so can you, he'd think.

"Cross that bridge when and if you come to it. You can't change your course because of what-ifs."

"Frank, I'm only telling you this because I know you won't think any less of me. Each time, it gets harder to see the thing though. That first time wasn't so bad, considering. Apart from the nausea. And losing my teaching job."

"Petty people, Hanna. We managed without their money."

Barely, she thinks. The 1913 hunger strike was harder. She couldn't sleep, had vomiting attacks when she drank water and was released in a state of extreme exhaustion. And now, here she is, back at the coal face.

"To tell you the truth, I'm dreading the effect of this strike. I'm five years older than last time. At forty-one I'm no spring chicken." She gives him an opportunity to contradict her but he doesn't take it. "I'm not one to complain. But life's been difficult, Frank, since that Easter. When I lost you."

His polished pebble eyes blink at her behind their spectacles. "Willpower is the most potent weapon of all. You have that in cartloads, Hanna. Besides, you'd be a disgrace to your own sense of self if you colluded in their denial of your right to refuse food. You have every right. And more than that, a duty, to go on hunger strike. The Votes for Women cause is a just one."

Resentment courses through Hanna. She loves every inch of her husband but he's always had a capacity to infuriate her. Frank has never understood that moral indignation is all very well but there's a time and a place for crusading. "You probably don't realise it, Frank, but women have the vote now. At least, some of us do. It's been extended to the over-thirties just this year. With conditions attached. But we can work to have them removed. The fact of the matter is I'm behind bars this time because" – she can't help a note of pride entering her tone – "the government regards me as a dangerous subversive."

"That's my girl." He slaps a hand against his thigh, the Downpatrick accent lengthening his vowels. "Not much point in being a subversive if you aren't dangerous. So, women have the vote. How's it being used?"

"Nothing done with it, yet. There hasn't been a general election. The world's still at war."

"Pity. But if the people who control the state are forcible-feeding, they've learned nothing about an individual's conscience. The state can't do wrong and pretend it's right because it has the law – which it makes – on its side. And the state can't compound its wrong by expecting citizens to fall into step and agree that what's wrong is really right."

"Oh, stop addressing me as if you're at a public meeting, Frank!"

Taken aback, he looks crestfallen.

Before guilt about her temper spike trips her up, she charges on. "We haven't seen one another in more than two years! You might at least ask after Owen."

"How is our dearest of boys?"

"As well as can be expected, considering he has one parent in the grave and the other in gaol."

He moves beside her, not a hair's breadth between them. "I'd be with you both if I could, my love."

She sighs, laying her head on his shoulder. Except there's

nothing beneath her cheek. She's tipping into thin air. He isn't flesh and blood, as she knows perfectly well.

"Frank, I'm a rational person so I know you're not a ghost. I don't believe in them. But at the same time, you can't be a physical presence. Your father had you buried in Glasnevin. Yet here you are. Does that mean I can't tell what's real and what's not any more? It's a risk, on hunger strike. My mind might be deceiving me."

"I'm as real as you want me to be."

"Not real enough to hug me."

They gaze at one another. His tender concern soothes her.

"You're looking a wee bit frayed, Hanna. Aren't you sleeping?"

"How could anyone get a decent night's rest in prison with warders peering at you through spyholes? It gives me the shivers being watched while I sleep."

"Rise above it, Hanna. Focus your mind on higher things."

"You and your higher things. You don't seem particularly grieved to see me here."

"Sure you've been in and out of bridewells and barracks for years. With the world the way it is, prison's the only place for a self-respecting woman or man to be. You just keep in mind, they can lock up your body but not your conscience. It's as free as if you were strolling along Bray seafront, taking the air."

"And you by my side."

"I'm always by your side. You know that."

She closes her eyes for a few moments but flicks them open again quickly in case he's gone. Still there. He appears rested, she notices. Death agrees with him. The thought sours her mood. An accumulation of cares has aged her. But life's stresses are gone from him now – money worries, primarily, resulting from his struggle to keep the *Irish Citizen* newspaper afloat. Look at him, brimming with life. Except he's not.

Thirteen years wasn't much of a lifetime with Frank. The Sheehy Skeffingtons were meant to be in the vanguard of a war on inequality, using their tongues and pens as weapons. But she has to carry on without him by her side. Life interrupted.

"You're looking stern, Hanna. We can't have that. Tell me, are you allowed to read? Do books help you pass the time?"

"Yes, but I avoid Dickens and Sir Walter Scott – too many passages glorying in meals. The Brontës and Austen are safe enough. They have an abstemious approach to food."

"And how do you feel? Apart from hungry?"

She takes a tally. She supposes she must be foggy mentally – talking to Frank is a sign. Her hair and nails haven't started to break yet. Again, that's to be expected. Her skin will become brittle, with red sores appearing. She checks her hands. Is that pouch between thumb and forefinger becoming cracked already? It feels itchy. Chronic diarrhoea hasn't set in although she has that to look forward to. She suffered dreadfully with her bowel on hunger strike number two, back in Dublin.

"There's something I need you to tell me, Frank. About your last minutes. Did you have any inkling of what was coming? I know you didn't get a chance to speak before they shot you. I know you weren't blindfolded. But did it hurt? Did your life flash before your eyes? What did you think about?"

Tell me, "I thought of you, Hanna. Between the moments when the order rang out – load, present, fire – and I fell to the ground, yours was the last face I saw. Only you. It was always only you." It would be a comfort if you'd say that. Could you, Frank? Please?

"Ach, it didn't hurt at all, Hanna. Don't be fretting yourself. Put it out of your mind."

He doesn't have it in him to flatter. Never did. Still, she feels the goodness flowing from him. Decency is better than blarney.

It would be easier to let him bat away her questions. But she can't do it. "Frank, there must have been pain. You didn't die immediately. I've made it my business to find out what happens with firing squads. I know the officer in charge usually performs the *coup de grace*, putting a bullet from his handgun into the executed man's head afterwards. But Captain Bowen-Colthurst didn't do you that service. Why would he behave humanely then, when he did nothing legal let alone civilised in the days before your murder? I was allowed to attend the captain's court martial. Two other men, journalists, were executed along with you. I heard a young lieutenant say he examined you after the first volley, and noticed your leg was still twitching. He sent someone after the captain to the orderly room. A message came back: fire another round of shots. Then someone put a bowler hat over your face, and you were carted off to the mortuary. Why aren't you saying anything, Frank? Am I cruel, to make you relive it?"

He stands up and strides about the cell, bouncing as briskly as in life. She watches him, wondering – not for the first time – how five feet four and a half inches can encase such an energetic mind.

"You could never be cruel, Hanna. I'm silent because what is there to say? That violence solves nothing? Of course it doesn't. That it was unjust? One injustice among many."

"Always so forbearing, my love. I try to be stoical, too, but it doesn't come naturally to me. I declined their blood money, you know. It was a trade, to shut me up. I refused to be silenced and forced them to hold an inquiry."

"Aye, when you're on the warpath, you're a force of nature." He produces a spotted handkerchief, removes his spectacles, and rubs at some smears. As he polishes, he says quietly, "I know gaol's no picnic. I've done time myself. Chin up, girl. There are brighter days ahead. Remember our plans for Owen. I'm trusting you to follow through on the things we talked about for his future."

"I'll do my best, Frank."

"You always do, me darlin'. Sure, I love you for it."

"About the firing squad –"

"You're like a dog with a bone!"

"But they butchered you, Frank! No trial, no defence, no due process."

"It was panic on their part. Their killing instinct was let loose.

But don't be too hard on them. The Irish side was hypnotised by war, too."

"I can't believe how saintly death has made you!"

"Look, here's the thing. There were three parties to my story. The poor wretch in front of the rifles – that was me. The poor wretches told to take aim and fire. And the poor wretch who shouted the order. Now, if I had to be one of them, I wouldn't choose to be the officer giving the command to kill another human being. And I wouldn't choose to be a Tommy pulling the trigger. That only leaves me. I wouldn't swap with any of them, even to avoid a hail of bullets. I choose to be me."

"Yes, dearest. I see that."

"I knew you'd understand."

"I do. But still, I'd have liked a widow's privilege. To close your eyes, wash away the blood, sit with you and hold you against me before they buried you – to keep you warm with my body heat. Just for a little while."

He hunkers down beside her, the sheen of love in his eyes.

"I never saw you afterwards, Frank. They rolled you in a sheet and dumped you in a hole in the barracks yard at Portobello. I've been there, you know. I wanted to see for myself where it happened."

Frank sighs. "Hanna, what good is this doing? Tell me about Owen."

"No, I want to talk about the cloak-and-dagger agreement between the military authorities and your father. They refused to return your body to me. But your killing couldn't be hushed up. Your doctor-daddy gave them a way out. He caved in to their dodge: they'd hand over your remains provided the burial took place discreetly at night and I was kept out of it. They were afraid of me making a public spectacle, your father said. I'm your wife, your next of kin, the mother of your only child. But they settled it without me. Man to man."

He springs to his feet again, her Jack-in-the-box of a husband.

How he managed in that cell in Portobello Barracks she'll never know. His arms windmill through the air before settling in his pockets.

"My father was hurting, too, Hanna. You must make allowances. For my sake."

"I can never forgive him. He should have given the army their marching orders over that squalid proposal. He didn't have your best interests at heart. You were a problem to them, Frank, after they doubled your body weight with bullets. Other prisoners heard what happened. There were witnesses. Not even the pretext of martial law could justify it."

She presses the heel of each palm into her eye sockets, holding back tears. The air in the cell has shifted: taut with strain now. Hanna knows her behaviour is the reason for it.

"You've had two burials, dearest, and I wasn't allowed to be present at either. How many widows can lay claim to that? Anyhow, you're lying beside your mother now. That's something, I suppose."

"I'm not lying anywhere, Hanna. I'm alive inside you. I'm always with you. Death makes no difference."

Hanna traps her lower lip between her teeth and bites down. "I wish that was true. But you're not beside me when I'm trying to find the money to pay the grocer's bill or worrying about schools for Owen. I keep losing teaching work because one board of governors or another objects to my political views, or fears some parents might. I'm doing hackwork for shillings. A competent cook would be insulted by the wages I'm forced to accept."

"We knew the life we chose would never make us rich, Hanna. But we believed it would enrich us."

She is silenced, caught fast by memories from their courtship days, when they'd eke out two cups of coffee in the privacy of a Bewley's booth, talking, talking, talking. About the way society was organised, whether God existed, how to cook nourishing vegetarian meals, the woman question, whether they ought to hyphenate their new surname after marriage, was he being fair in proposing to ban visitors from smoking in their house after they set up home together. Early on, perhaps even by the end of their first conversation, she recognised Frank's uniqueness. Some scoffed at him, calling him a crank – but he turned the tables in style: a crank, he said, was a small instrument that made revolutions.

They were engaged informally for a year before he applied to her father for her hand in marriage – yes, the iconoclastic Frank Skeffington solicited David Sheehy's permission, two men sorting out a woman's future between them. How she used to tease Frank about that salute to traditional values when he was on his high horse about something.

"I worry about Owen, Frank. He needs a man's hand as well as a woman's to guide him."

"I have complete faith in you, girl. I always did. You're a tower of strength."

"A leaning tower, I'm afraid. I wish …"

"If wishes were horses then beggars would ride. That's a thing my mother often said. What do you wish?"

"I wish you'd come home with me that Easter Tuesday."

"But there was looting. And Dublin's civilian population was being tyrannised. I needed to rally decent people into forming a guard. I had to do what I thought was right."

"How can it be right, Frank, that I'm in prison, and a process to free John Bowen-Colthurst is under way? He was found guilty but insane over your killing. Eighteen months in Broadmoor and he's miraculously cured. No longer mad. They must think me greener than cabbage if they imagine I'm fooled by that charade. A campaign's under way now to have him released – Carson and Craig are championing his case. Already, he's been moved to a private hospital in Surrey. I know he'll get out. It's only a matter of time."

Frank clears his throat. "Hanna, I wouldn't be too hard on

Captain Bowen-Colthurst. His reason snapped. As for the boys he commanded, some of them swapped their school uniforms for khaki. Others were war wrecks from the trenches."

"Don't make excuses. The captain broke the rules of war and should be held accountable."

"Rules of war? What nonsense! Rules suggest a code of conduct. But war is never noble, it always degrades. I told the captain that to his face." Frank allows himself a snuffle. "He wasn't impressed. Here's something I learned when they held me in Portobello Barracks. Brutality is contagious, like the measles. As for collective hatred, it's indefensible. From them towards us and us towards them. We have to resist it."

"Even so. It infuriates me that Captain Bowen-Colthust will live to see his child grow up, while your son's had his dadda stolen from him."

"Answer me this, Hanna. Would you prefer our boy to have the captain for a father? Or me, blind though I was to the danger for our family?"

She nods. Her shoulders slump. "I get so lonely. I keep busy, of course. But I miss your foot-rubs. Waking up with you burrowed against my back. Those early cups of tea you'd bring me in bed. Sometimes, I feel overwhelmed by everything that's lost."

"You must listen to the voice inside you."

"Are you the voice, Frank?"

"Silly, you don't need me. Your own voice is enough."

Footsteps advance along the landing and halt outside her door. Instantly, Frank vanishes. There is no fading away. One moment he is present, the next he is no longer there. Hanna twists her head to the wall, ignoring the intrusive eye at the spyhole. A rattle at the lock and the door opens. That's ominous. Flinching, she looks up and sees a uniformed shape enter her cell. Instantly, her mind flies to force-feeding. They can do anything they like with her here — she's entirely in their power. Adrenalin floods her nervous system, she hears the blood roar in her ears.

"I see you're still awake. I've brought you a nice, fresh mug of tea and a slice of toast."

"No, thank you."

"I'll leave it here in case you change your mind."

"I'd rather you didn't."

"The governor thought you might welcome a hot drop in the night."

"Please take it away."

"I'll just set it on the table. I put a dab of jam on the toast."

The door clatters shut, the key is turned. She can smell the food – it percolates through the cubicle, more intoxicating as each second passes. Is it blackberry jam? She daren't look.

"Come back to me, Frank!" Hanna cries aloud.

But the link is broken. Resigned, she lets her mind go blank and tries to curl into sleep.

Hunger pangs, intensified by hot tea and toast an arm's stretch away, prevent her from drifting off. She slept like an infant in Mountjoy, that first time. The other suffragette hunger strikers were envious. But that ability's gone, like so much else from her life.

Hanna pricks her ears for sounds from the outside world. London is teeming beyond these walls. It's a city she has always liked – there is more to England than the machinery of the state and its tyrannies, large and small. She hears wheels bowling along. Soon, Londoners will waken and proceed about their business.

How far is it from Holloway Prison to the House of Commons? It seems a lifetime ago since she took tea on Westminster's terraces with the honourable member David Sheehy and other MPs belonging to the Irish Parliamentary Party. Bite-sized cucumber sandwiches spread with some piquant paste. Bowls of strawberries and cream. Scones, crumbly from the oven. Chocolate cake as light as air. Stem ginger biscuits that melted on the tongue. Pot after pot of Earl Grey tea.

Enough!

That was back when she was lobbying for women to have the vote. Most MPs were never persuaded, her father included. He was in a perpetual state of fury with her after she turned militant. So long as she belonged to a law-abiding group presenting petitions to Parliament, he was prepared to be tolerant. After all, equality was never going to happen by passing resolutions – the status quo was safe. But he dropped the mask of amused indulgence when she decided genteel protest was a waste of time. When she smashed government glass, heckled senior politicians, marched with placards, spoke at public meetings. For an old Land Leaguer, with six prison stints under his belt, David Sheehy is remarkably intolerant of anything smacking of lawlessness.

"Why play fair by a state that won't play fair by us?" she demanded. Her father needn't think he was the only political animal in the family. "You know as well as I do, politicians operate by *realpolitik* – they don't listen to polite arguments. Pressure is what they yield to."

"Women should trust their men to think and act for them," said her father.

That set Hanna hopping from one foot to the other, blue eyes blazing, while her mother made signals intended to dissuade her from contradicting him.

It was the last real conversation she had with her father. Subsequently, when she entered a room, he left it. Her mother beseeched her to apologise, for the sake of peace, but her father's wounded pride did not interest Hanna. It incensed her that he belonged to a select band with power to change the law – his party's combined votes could have forced through legislation for women's suffrage. Instead, the Irish Parliamentary Party – Irishmen who ought to understand how discrimination felt – tried to deny the tidal wave of history. Still, she shouldn't dwell on her failures. She ought to remember how many loyal friends there were in England's capital, and in other English cities.

Hannah yawns and fidgets in her prison bed. She needn't

expect her father to use his influence to have her released. Maybe he's relieved to think of her behind bars. At large, there's no telling what she might get up to. Little does he guess that what she'd really like to do is buy a newspaper twist of chips and wolf them in front of the stall, burning the roof of her mouth but too greedy to wait for them to cool. She's never had tastier chips than in London: crisp on the outside, soft on the inside, drenched in salt and vinegar. Her mouth waters. She must distract herself. Food never entered her mind when Frank was in the cell with her. Would he return tomorrow night? There are things she wants to talk over with him.

She'll say: Why won't you let me be frivolous, Frank?

But frivolity doesn't become you, Hanna.

Even a serious person enjoys some giddiness now and again, Frank. It can't be all about principles and righting wrongs.

He'll look bewildered.

Picturing his bafflement, she can't help laughing.

Whenever she bought a new hat – and hats were a pleasure she couldn't sacrifice, no matter what fell by the wayside – she'd invite a compliment.

"What do you think, dear? Is it *a la mode?*" she used to ask. Not that he'd recognise style if it was his next-door neighbour.

His face would pucker, at a loss, before offering the view that it did what it was designed to because it kept her head covered. As though warmth or being rainproof mattered in a hat.

Another man might play along. 'Aren't you the fashion plate?' he'd tease. It wasn't in Frank. Words were reserved for important business.

Unable to relax, Hanna pushes back the blanket, pulls on her slippers, and stands on the floor in her nightdress. How still the night is. A sound is carried in from the outer world – a clock striking the half hour. Her eyes seek the upper corner of the room, where an exterior window has been cut through the stone. It is a barred window, one pane of its dusty glass lying open for ventilation. On an impulse, she removes the tea and toast and pushes the table towards the window wall. She climbs onto her stool, and from there to the table top, the wood and her bones creaking in unison. By dint of holding on to the wall and stretching on tiptoe, she can just manage to see a patch of sky.

A whisper of air touches her face. It's too early for birdsong but blush-pink ribbons streaking the darkness are putting night-time to flight. Stars flicker here and there in lone positions. Like guardians, it occurs to her. Not intervening. But bearing witness. How gallant the starlight is – it's keeping faith. Soon, the stars will fade, but when twilight gathers they will return.

As she yearns upwards towards the night sky, her restlessness evaporates and hunger's pinch recedes. A sense of kinship engulfs and saturates her, stirred by the portholes of light in the heavens. She knows herself to be at one with the stars, the world they glimmer down upon, and the vast ocean of universe through which their beam travels.

She feels replenished – exalted. The starlight drenches her parched soul. A sense of trust swells inside Hanna, more substantial to her than the table underfoot and the damp stone against her hands. Tears of joy well up in her eyes and trickle down her cheeks.

She has every reason to hope.

Hanna wrote to her son Owen in 1930, as she was making arrangements for a group trip to Russia, about having to fill out forms which asked how often and for what she'd been gaoled. She admitted to feeling "chippy" until she realised it only applied to time behind bars in Russia.

One more prison term lay ahead of her: in Armagh, for crossing the border into Northern Ireland contrary to an order. At her 1933 trial, feisty as ever, she said, "I recognise it as no crime to be in my own country."

ACKNOWLEDGEMENTS

Thanks are due to a great many people.

To Lia Mills, Evelyn Conlon and Justin Blanchard for reading all of these stories while I continued to work on them – your reflections were invaluable. And Lia, we've chatted about these women for a number of years now over coffee: your insights have always kept me motivated. I know you love them as much as I do.

To Ciara Ferguson for the *Truth & Dare* title and for reading 'Nano's Ark'.

To Sinéad Gleeson for inviting me to contribute a story to *The Glass Shore* collection – I wrote about Alice Milligan, who became the trailblazer for the *Truth & Dare* women. Sinéad, this collection originates with you.

To Josephine Kerr of Mountfield, County Tyrone, for handing over her garden for an event as part of the Benedict Kiely Weekend (now the Omagh Literary Festival) to honour the 150th anniversary of Alice Milligan's birth in 2016. I set 'No Other Place', the short story written in Alice's memory, in Josephine's house and garden where Alice once lived. Also thanks to an ever-supportive Frank Sweeney for helping to make that commemoration happen.

To Lucy Keaveney for her passionate lobbying on behalf of Anna Parnell, which has led to her grave being repaired by the Irish State and a formal event held in her honour in Ilfracombe, Devon.

To Kathleen Barrington and Women for Election for inviting me to write a piece which grew into an early version of the Countess Markievicz story.

To Mary Mitchell O'Connor T.D. for later giving me another public platform to read it in Dún Laoghaire – and also for caring about Anna Parnell.

To Pat Marshall for checking my Dublin dialogue in the Countess Markievicz story.

To the Linen Hall Library in Belfast for allowing me to read Mary Ann McCracken's letters, and to the people – staff and volunteers alike, especially Gerry Devaney – who spoke about her as though she had only just stepped out of the room.

To locals near Clifton Street Cemetery in Belfast for unlocking the gate and letting me in to pay my respects at Mary Ann McCracken's grave.

To Dr Paul Delaney and Dr Carlo Gébler at Trinity College Dublin for allowing me to talk Somerville and Ross with them incessantly and for their insights. And to TCD's ever-welcoming library staff for allowing me to read the Somerville and Ross letters in their collections.

Also to the McClay Library at Queen's University Belfast for sharing its Somerville and Ross papers. And to Tom and Jane Somerville of Drishane House, Castletownshend, for giving me access to their family archive.

To Nano Nagle Place in Cork for keeping her story alive and for welcoming me there.

To the Royal College of Physicians of Ireland (RCPI) in Dublin where I read Dr Kathleen Lynn's diaries.

To Dr Margaret Ward for her wise comments on the Hanna Sheehy Skeffington story, for pointing me towards the Russia and caviar references, and for answering any obscure Maud Gonne query I pitched at her.

To Michael Farrell for sharing his recollections of being on hunger strike as a civil rights activist, which contributed to the Hanna Sheehy Skeffington story.

To Maria O'Sullivan and the ever-helpful staff at Dalkey Library for sourcing so many of the books I needed to read. Libraries are among my favourite places.

To all at Poolbeg Press, including publisher Paula Campbell and editor Gaye Shortland, for taking a chance on me yet again.

And to Sarah Webb for telling me – repeatedly – there was a short story collection inside me.

A FINAL NOTE

If you're interested in learning more about these extraordinary women – and all of them reward further reading – some of the books I found useful are listed below.

'A Biographical Note: Nano Nagle, 1718-1784' by Dolores de Bhál ('Studies: An Irish Quarterly Review' Autumn 2000)

Ariadne's Thread by Margaret MacCurtain (Arlen House Galway 2008)

A Servant of the Queen: Reminiscences by Maud Gonne (Victor Gollancz London 1938)

Angel in the Studio: Women in the Art and Crafts Movement 1870-1914 by Anthea Callen (Astragal Books London 1979)

Dorothy Macardle, A Life by Nadia Clare Smith (The Woodfield Press Dublin 2007)

Earth-Bound and Other Supernatural Tales by Dorothy Macardle (The Swan River Press Dublin MMXVI)

Easter Widows by Sinéad McCoole (Doubleday Ireland Dublin 2014)

Edward J. Byrne 1872-1941: The Forgotten Archbishop of Dublin by Thomas J. Morrissey SJ (The Columba Press Dublin 2010)

Fanny and Anna Parnell by Jane McL. Cote (Gill and MacMillan Dublin 1991)

Genteel Revolutionaries: Anna and Thomas Haslam and the Irish Women's Movement by Carmel Quinlan (Cork University Press 2002)

Guns and Chiffon edited by Sinéad McCoole (Stationery Office Books Dublin 1997)

Hanna Sheehy Skeffington, A Life by Margaret Ward (Attic Press Cork 1997)

Hanna Sheehy Skeffington Suffragette and Sinn Féiner by Margaret Ward (UCD Press Dublin 2017)

Inglorious Soldier by Monk Gibbon (Hutchinson and Co London 1968)

Irish Feminism and the Vote: An Anthology of the Irish Citizen Newspaper 1912-20 by Louise Ryan (Folens Dublin 1996)

Irish Women's Letters compiled by Laurence Flanagan (Sutton Publishing Gloucestershire 1999)

Kathleen Lynn: Irishwoman, Patriot, Doctor by Margaret Ó hOgartaigh (Irish Academic Press Dublin 2006)

Maud Gonne: A Life by Margaret Ward (HarperCollins London 1993)

Maud Gonne: Ireland's Joan of Arc by Margaret Ward (Pandora London 1990)

'Nano Nagle (1718-1784): Educator' by Caitriona Clear ('Studies: An Irish Quarterly Review' Summer 2009)

No Ordinary Women by Sinéad McCoole (O'Brien Press Dublin 2015)

Petticoat Rebellion: The Anna Parnell Story by Patricia Groves (Mercier Press Cork 2009)

Revolutionary Woman: Kathleen Clarke 1878-1972 An Autobiography edited by Helen Litton (The O'Brien Press Dublin 1991)

Smashing Times by Rosemary Owen Cullens (Attic Press Dublin 1984)

The Adulterous Muse: Maud Gonne, Lucien Millevoye and W.B. Yeats by Adrian Frazier (The Lilliput Press Dublin 2016)

The Collected Letters of Nano Nagle, held by Union of Sisters of the Presentation of the Blessed Virgin Mary © Public domain. Digital content by various copyright holders – see individual records published by UCD Library : <http://digital.ucd.ie/view/ucdlib:153347>

The Diary of Mary Travers, A Novel by Eibhear Walshe (Somerville Press Bantry Co Cork

The Laughter of Mothers by Paul Durcan (see his poem The MacBride Dynasty) (Harvill Secker London 2007)

The Life and Times of Mary Ann McCracken 1770-1866: A Belfast Panorama by Mary McNeill (Blackstaff Press Belfast 1988)

'The Life of Miss Nano Nagle as sketched by the Right Rev. Dr. Coppinger in a funeral sermon preached by him in Cork on the anniversary of her death' (Published by James Haly, Cork, 1794)

The Politics and Relationships of Kathleen Lynn by Marie Mulholland (The Woodfield Press Dublin 2002)

The Tale of a Great Sham by Anna Parnell, edited with an introduction by Dana Hearne (Arlen House Dublin 1986)

The Years Flew By: Recollections of Madame Sidney Gifford Czira (Arlen House Galway and Dublin 2000)

The Uninvited by Dorothy Macardle (Tramp Press Dublin 2016)

The Unforeseen by Dorothy Macadle (Tramp Press Dublin 2017)

Wilde's Women by Eleanor Fitzsimons (Duckworth Overlook 2015)

Women, Power and Consciousness in 19th Century Ireland by Mary Cullen and Maria Luddy (Attic Press Dublin 1995)

Also:

Witness Statements, Bureau of Military History

Also published by Poolbeg

THE HOUSE WHERE IT HAPPENDED

It is 1711, and the Ulster-Scots community in a remote corner of
Ireland is in turmoil. A pretty young newcomer is accusing one
woman after another of witchcraft. But Ellen, the serving girl in the
house where the visitor is staying, is loyal to the family –
and over-fond of her master. Yet she knows that Knowehead is a house
like no other.

And so she watches and ponders, as a seemingly normal girl claims she
is bewitched – as a community turns against eight respectable women
– and as malevolent forces unleashed more than half a century earlier
threaten a superstitious people beyond their understanding.

Martina Devlin has fictionalised a compelling episode from history,
transforming it into a spine-chilling tale.

MARTINA DEVLIN

ISBN 978178199-9301

Also published by Poolbeg

ABOUT SISTERLAND

Welcome to Sisterland. A world ruled by women.
A world designed to be perfect.

Here, women and men are kept separate. Women lead highly
controlled and suffocating lives, while men are subordinate – used for
labour and breeding.

Sisterland's leaders have been watching Constance and recognise that
she's special. Selected to reproduce, she finds herself alone with a man
for the first time. But the mate chosen for her isn't what she expected
– and she begins to see a darker side to Sisterland.

Constance's misgivings about the regime mount. Is she the only one
who questions this unequal society, or are there other doubters?

Set in the near future, About Sisterland *is a searing, original novel which
explores the devastating effects of extremism.*

MARTINA DEVLIN

ISBN 978178199-9196

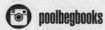